SPIRITED SITUATION

A Ghostly Guardians Novel

LOUISA MASTERS

Spirited Situation

Copyright © 2022 by Louisa Masters

Cover: Booksmith Design

Editor: Hot Tree Editing

All rights reserved.

No part of this book may be reproduced in any form or by any means without the prior written consent of the author, excepting brief quotes used in reviews.

This is a work of fiction. Names, characters, places, events and incidents either are the product of the author's imagination or are used fictitiously, and any resemblance to persons, living or dead, business establishments, events or locales is entirely coincidental.

To the extent that the image or images on the cover of this book depict a person or persons, such person or persons are merely models and are not intended to portray any character or characters featured in the book.

Spirited Situation

When you can talk to ghosts, things are bound to get spirited.

The ghosts have been there since before I can remember. When I was a kid, they doted on me, but as I got older, they got more demanding. I've spent my whole life seeing and talking to dead people and trying to pretend I'm not, because the living just don't understand. Nobody wants to be around the freak who claims to see ghosts.

Until I go to Mannix Estate.

Once a private country home, then a posh hotel, it was closed after a suspicious incident but is now an immersive historic experience. It's also haunted AF, and everyone knows it. Finally, I've found a place to work and live where I can be useful. Where I'm actually wanted.

There are only two problems: I spent a hot, sweaty, satisfying night with Ewan the blacksmith before I knew we'd have to work together. Everyone knows sex with colleagues is a bad idea, right? Even if he's the world's most ripped cinnamon roll.

Plus, the ghosts are keeping secrets. There's something going on that's not normal, even for a haunted estate. And I suspect that when the truth comes out, I'm the one who'll have to deal with it… and it won't be good.

Chapter One

EWAN

I prop my elbows on the bar, ignoring the way they stick to the surface, and bask in the knowledge that I don't have to get up at five tomorrow. I love my job, even with all its quirks, but a night—and more importantly, the next morning—off sometimes is essential. Instead of an early night and a dawn awakening, I get a burger, a few drinks, and hopefully someone to spend the evening with. The complicated living situation at home means it's been a while since I last got off with anything other than my hand and internet porn, and I'd really like to have sex with another person.

Hookup potential is limited in this town, but I didn't want to make the drive into Chicago. That would have meant getting up early tomorrow anyway to get back at a decent hour. So… I'll just have to hope for the best.

Wanting to hook up is part of the reason I came here, to Rusty's Bar. It's basically a dump, but the drinks are good and the food is amazing. Since I'm not having dinner with my grandmother, who cares if the floor is sticky and the vinyl on the barstools is ripped? Or that the bikers at the pool tables are so noisy it's hard to hear myself think? The bartender brings me a beer right away and a burger in less than ten minutes, and the mirror behind the bar might be cloudy, but it's good enough for me to check out the other patrons. Or at least, it will be, after I finish my dinner.

I'm on my second beer and mopping up ketchup with fries when the bartender brings me a shot. Could it be that the hard work has been taken care of?

I raise a brow at him. "Who?" Please let it be a man. I'm really not in the mood to tell a perfectly nice woman that she's not my type.

The bartender nods toward the other end of the bar, already turning away to help another customer, and I swivel my head to look.

It's a man. And he's just my type. Slender. Messy dark hair. Big eyes. His small smile is tentative as he lifts his glass in my direction, and I pick up the shot and salute him with it before knocking it back. By the time I put the empty glass back on the bar, he's on the stool beside me. I'm surprised to see how much shorter he is —I mean, most people are shorter than me, but he must be only around five-six or -seven.

"Looking for company?" he asks, still with that tentative smile.

"Yep. You?"

"Yes. I'm only in town one night, though."

I push aside the wistful pang that this isn't a meet-cute and embrace the possibility of a fun night instead.

"I'm Ewan," I say, just as the bikers erupt into raucous cheers. He shakes his head.

"Didn't hear that, don't care," he shouts over the noise, although there's something in his expression that makes me think the words are bravado. "You about done here?"

I glance longingly at the remainder of my fries. I'll sacrifice them for sex, but I'd rather not if I don't have to.

Luckily, he snorts a laugh. "Finish them. Want another shot?"

"Sure," I say happily. "Want some fries?"

He doesn't bother answering, just waves down the bartender with one hand while swiping a couple of my fries with the other. I like a man who can multitask. "Same again?" he asks with a sideways glance. I nod, and he tells the bartender, "Two, please."

The bartender grunts—he's not known for his charm, but Arissa, who works with me, tells me he's a wizard with margaritas—and a few moments later, we have shots.

My new friend clinks his glass against mine, then knocks back the contents. I follow suit, enjoying the way the warmth of the liquor spreads through my chest. When I put the glass down, I catch him eyeing my biceps.

So I flex. It's not the first time someone's been attracted to my physique. I've always been a big guy, but when you add that blacksmithing is hard work and builds muscle… well, I'm ripped, and a lot of people like that.

He sucks in a deep breath, meets my gaze, and huffs a laugh. "Sorry. You're just… impressive."

I smile, flattered by his word choice, and grab another fry. "It's fine. If it bothered me, I'd wear a sweatshirt." It's not an accident that the T-shirt I chose tonight fits me very well. While I'd love to have a steady boyfriend who enjoys my company and wants more from me than just my body, I'm not against using said body in order to meet prospective candidates… and not-so-prospective candidates. There's nothing wrong with spending time with Mr. Right Now while I'm searching for Mr. Right.

"Are you visiting someone in town or just passing through?"

He shrugs. "Visiting, I guess. I have a meeting tomorrow morning." He doesn't say anything more, the vinyl beneath him creaking as he shifts on the stool, and I don't press. Maybe he doesn't want to share personal information with the stranger he just picked up. That's fair enough, I guess.

Ten minutes later, we stroll out onto the street. Rusty's used to be outside the city limits, but the town's grown a lot over the past decade, and now the bar's in what's called the "new area"—despite having been here for over thirty years. That means the new motel is just a couple blocks away, and we head in that direction. It's a nice enough night, a bit cool, but not out of the ordinary for spring, and the breeze on my face is refreshing.

As we walk past a convenience store, my hookup hesitates. "Do we need to stop here? I'm on PrEP."

So am I. "Only if you don't have lube." I have a couple of packets in my wallet, but more never hurt anyone.

He scoffs and resumes walking. "Please. I didn't know if I was going to be stuck in my room by myself with bad cable all night. Of course I brought lube."

Gotta admire a man with a plan.

I follow him into his room and let the door close behind me. The only sign of his habitation is a duffel bag on the generic armchair in the corner. He glances around, then hurries into the bathroom, emerging with a bottle of lube. "So, uh…" He holds it up. "I got it. I guess we should get naked?"

I laugh and pull my T-shirt over my head, kicking off my shoes. "How do you want to do this?"

He watches, smiling, as I open my jeans and shove them to the floor. "I want that in me. I don't care about the rest."

I close the distance between us, bend my head to kiss his pouty mouth, and reach around to pinch his ass. "Then you'd better get your pants off." I leave him to it and climb onto the bed, stacking the pillows behind me and settling in to watch him strip. The bed is surprisingly comfortable.

"Expecting a show, are you?" he asks, yanking off his shirt and sitting on the edge of the bed to take off his shoes. I admire the smooth, slender line of his back, the muscles toned but not defined, as I slowly stroke myself. I want to leave a mark there.

"It's not my fault you're slow to get naked."

He laughs as he stands again and shucks his pants and underwear, then gets onto the bed and crawls over me, straddling my lap and lowering himself to drape over my body. The first skin-on-skin contact sends electric shocks through every inch of me.

Then he's gone.

"What—"

"Lube," he informs me, dumping some into his palm before handing me the bottle. I hold it and watch, mesmerized, as he preps himself. He sees me watching and grins. "See something you like?"

I settle back against the pillows and skim my gaze

over him. "Oh yeah." My cock has never been harder in my life. I squeeze just under the head, and a drop of precum seeps out. With barely a hitch, he leans over and licks it off, and breath catches in my throat.

Turnabout is fair play.

Releasing my dick, I reach instead for his. It's long and slim, as hard as mine, the head flushed red, and as I stroke up the length of it with a firm grip, he closes his eyes and moans.

"Fuck, that's so good," he pants. "It's been too long."

"I know what you mean."

Opening his eyes, he meets my gaze. "If we make this round quick, can you go again after?"

Yesssss.

I scan slowly over his body, the toned, pale skin, dark nipples, and the happy trail leading down to his cock in my fist. "Fuck yeah. It'll be no trouble at all."

He leans forward and licks one of my nipples, his hot, wet tongue wrapping around it, and goose bumps break out over my whole body. My head falls back, thunking against the wall behind me, but I don't care. All I can feel is his mouth on me.

Suddenly, it's gone, cool air rushing over the wet skin, but before I can protest, he's back, sinking his teeth into my pec. I whimper at the rush of pleasure/pain, my balls drawing up. I don't usually need to come so quickly; it's obviously been way too long since the last time I had someone's hands on me.

And then he's moving again, gently unwrapping my hand from around him, shifting forward, rising onto his knees. I open my eyes to watch as he takes hold of my cock and positions himself.

"Unghhh." The guttural sound he makes as he lowers onto my dick vibrates through my whole body, overtaken only by the sensation of his tight hole giving way to let me slide into the hot clasp of his ass.

Until finally I'm fully seated inside him.

We're both breathing hard. The muscles in my thighs tremble with the need to thrust up into him. "Okay?" I gasp, shifting slightly, and his breath catches.

"Oh god *yes*."

He starts to move, slow but steady, riding me, and I keep my eyes on him as the tension builds inside me. His head is thrown back, lips parted as he pants, and he's so fucking sexy I could come just from watching his pleasure.

Opening his eyes, he meets my gaze and whispers, "Take me."

I need no other encouragement.

Surging up, I wrap my arms around him and flip us so his back is in the mattress. He draws his legs up, and I hook my forearms under them, bracing myself on my knees. I take just a second to check he's into this, then drive into him.

"Yes, harder!" he yells, arching against me, and the world falls away into a medley of sensations and sounds, thrusting and panting and *needing* until I feel as though I can't bear it for a second longer.

"Are you close?" I croak, and in answer, he snakes a hand between us to grab his cock. One stroke, two, and he comes, jizz striping our torsos as he shouts wordlessly, his ass clamping around me.

I explode, my vision blurring with the intensity of it.

When I can think again, I find myself sprawled over him, crushing him into the bed. "Sorry," I mutter, easing out of his body and flopping down beside him. We're both still breathing hard—he doesn't need the added difficulty of my weight on him.

"You don't need to apologize for anything that's happened here. You're insanely talented."

I huff a laugh. "Thanks. You're no slouch either."

For a few minutes, we just lie there, catching our breath, bodies cooling and cum beginning to crust on our skin.

"So," he says at last, rolling onto his side. "How long until you're ready to go again?"

I look at his flushed cheeks and big eyes and remember the way they glazed over when I was inside him. "Not as long as I thought."

Chapter Two

JOSH

Squinting blearily in the sunlight streaming through the window of my motel room—why the fuck did I leave the curtains open?—I try to work out what time it is and why I feel like I ran a marathon yesterday.

The answer to the latter rolls over behind me and puts a thick, muscular arm around my waist, and memories rise of our all-night fuckfest. I can't help the smug little smile. I might be sore all over this morning, thanks to our exertions, but it's a price I'm willing to pay. It's been so long since I had sex with someone, I was starting to wonder if I'd forget how to do it.

I'm happy to say that's not the case. And the agonizing nerves that were choking me when I sent over that shot were totally worth it. I guess it's not that hard to pick up a stranger after all.

Though it helps that nobody ever died in that bar.

Letting my eyes drift shut, I snuggle into my pillow. I'll have a doze, then maybe whatshisname will wake up and want another round before I have to go to my—

Fuck!

My eyes snap open, and I lurch upright as my bed companion groans in complaint. The sun is *up*. Like, *up* up. It's not early, which means I might be late.

I knock my phone off the nightstand in my haste to grab it, then end up leaning off the mattress to scrabble on the floor for it. Of course it's just out of my reach. I stretch a tiny bit further…

…and tumble face-first out of bed.

I don't have time to nurse my bruised face, though. I grab my phone and check the time.

"Shit!" My interview is in fifteen minutes. Fortunately, the coffee shop we're meeting at is only a block away, but I'm covered in cum—including some in my hair. There's no way I can get away with not showering, not if I want to make a good impression.

And I need to make a good impression. I need this job.

My sore muscles protest as I leap to my feet and head toward the bathroom, calling over my shoulder, "Hey, uh… guy! It's time to go." Guilt stabs me, but I don't have time for diplomacy right now. Although next time I pick up a stranger, I should make an effort to get his name. It's kind of rude to kick him out without saying his name. Right? Especially when he was so nice.

He makes sounds that might be words, but I'm already in the bathroom and closing the door. I don't bother to wait for the water to warm up, hissing under the cold spray of the shower as I begin scrubbing crusty, dried cum off me as fast as I can while mentally preparing myself for the interview.

It would be a great job, and it would get me out of the city. I long for that. My soul aches with the longing. I want to live somewhere like this: a town that's mostly new and doesn't have a dense population. Somewhere I could let down my guard and finally just be me.

Somewhere like Mannix Estate. An old country home, converted to a hotel and retreat for the wealthy about a hundred years ago. It was closed in the seventies due to something Google couldn't give me any information about, empty and abandoned for thirty years, and then renovated and reopened at the turn of the century as a museum and immersive historic experience. Schools visit on field trips, and historical societies descend for weekend retreats. There's the small museum, interactive workshops (learn how to churn butter!), extensive grounds for lazing around or playing croquet, a small farm, and accommodation. Including on-site quarters for an admin-slash-overnight guest liaison.

The best part? The absolute best part? The whole place is reportedly haunted as fuck. It says so right there on the website. They advertise based on it. So if a staff member should happen to be caught talking to "nobody," he could claim to have been chatting with a ghost, wink wink, and the guests would probably think it was part of the whole "immersive" experience.

Because that happens to me. A lot. I see ghosts, hear them speak, and often get dragged into whole fucking conversations with them. It's exhausting, but worse than that, it's ruined my life. I can't hold down a damn job because stupid ghosts are *everywhere* in a big city. Especially a city as old as Chicago. And after your workmates and customers catch you talking to ghosts—or, as they see it, no one—a few times, or you fuck things up because the dumbass ghosts startled you, it doesn't take long until you're no longer "the right fit" for the job. Let's not even talk about living situations. I can't have roommates because they freak about the whole ghost thing—see above comments about talking to no one and being startled. That, or they're creepily into it and I wake up to find them chanting over my bed in the middle of the night.

That's happened twice.

And my landlords haven't been much better. They hate the salt. I use a lot of salt, because it's one of the few ways I can get any peace and privacy. I try to keep it contained, but it's hard to vacuum up every grain, and for some reason, landlords and management companies hate that I line rooms with salt. I even tried doing only the bedroom and bathroom—because come on, surely I deserve to be able to take a dump on my own—but my lease has been mysteriously not renewed at five different places. I tried fighting it once, but strangely enough, it's hard to get character witnesses when you talk to ghosts on the regular.

So… I'm in search of a job in a place my eccentricities will blend in, need a living arrangement and a town with low ghost population so I can experience a somewhat normal life. Is that too much to ask?

Turns out… yes. Which is why this interview really has to go well.

I finish rinsing off, dry myself on the rough motel towel, and wrap it around my waist before leaving the bathroom in a cloud of steam. My bedmate is gone, thank fuck. I don't have time for drawn-out goodbyes. Although if I do end up getting the job and moving out here, I might try to track him down—that was one hell of a night.

Dressing quickly, I glance at my phone and see I'm down to five minutes. Fuck. I spare a hasty glance at the mirror to make sure my hair's not a disaster, then shove my feet into shoes, grab my wallet and key, and hightail it out of there… carefully stepping over the salt line at the door. I haven't seen any ghosts at the motel, probably because it's only a few years old and located in what used to be a field, but it's easier to lock them out than to try and get them out after they've settled in. I'm just lucky my hookup didn't smudge the line when he left, or I might've been greeted by a curious ghost when I came out of the shower.

I hotfoot it in the direction of the coffee shop, trying to maintain that weird pace between a walk and a jog. I don't want to turn up to this interview all breathless and sweaty, but I also don't want to turn up late. So… balance. Thank god it's not far.

Pausing outside the coffee shop to smooth myself down and take a deep breath, I glance through the plate-glass window to try and spot Kieran, who'll be interviewing me. I guess this is actually my second interview? We had a Zoom meeting last week. I did the whole thing in a salt circle, praying the evangelical ghost that lives on the downstairs landing hadn't somehow managed to get into my apartment and was about to pop up to ask me if I'd heard about Christ our savior. It's a miracle Kieran called me back for this interview.

I can't see Kieran, but the shop is bigger than I expected, and there are some tables I can't quite see from here, so I summon all my cool and push open the door.

Inside, I glance around again, making my way toward the counter, and finally spot Kieran sitting at a four-top table in the back corner. There's someone sitting with him, and I wonder if they're here to help with the interview. He didn't mention that, though. Maybe this is someone else he's interviewing? I don't want to interrupt if that's the case; talk about unprofessional.

But… he's not looking at the other person. In fact, he's scrolling on his phone, sipping a coffee, acting as though he's alone.

Sigh.

I look more closely, and yep, that's a fucking ghost. Sitting at the table with my (hopefully) future boss. Where she can fuck up all my chances for this job.

Bracing myself, I start toward them. There's no help for it. If I want this job, I need to get through the interview. I just need to be careful not to react in any way to the ghost. If she realizes I can see and hear her, she'll want to chat, and that's when things start to go bad. Hopefully she'll just sit quietly for the next half hour, absorbed in her own thoughts.

Kieran looks up when I'm a few feet away and smiles, putting his phone down and standing to shake my hand.

"I hope I'm not late," I start, but he shakes his head.

"Nah, you're bang on time. I just couldn't wait another few minutes for a coffee, you know?" He rolls his eyes self-deprecatingly. They're a startling green, a shade that makes me wonder if he wears contacts. But his hair is vivid red, and he has the kind of porcelain-pale skin—covered with freckles—that often goes with it, so they might be natural. "Do you want a coffee?"

I hesitate, because I really, really do, but I also don't want to spill hot coffee all over my lap and possibly Kieran in the middle of this interview if the ghost—who seems to be watching us with avid fascination—startles me.

"C'mon," he coaxes. "I can tell you do. What'll it be? It's on me." He gazes at me with earnest sympathy.

Oh fuck, he thinks I'm hesitating because I can't afford it. Sure, money's tight, but I can swing a few bucks for a fancy coffee every now and then.

But there's no way to explain that without making the whole situation worse and having to explain why I didn't just go order myself a drink already, so I smile weakly and say, "Thank you. That's really kind. Um, a cappuccino would be great." Milky breakfast-y goodness.

"No worries, have a seat." He waves a hand toward the free chairs at the table, then turns in the direction of the counter and calls, "Hey, Mindy!"

Mindy—and half the patrons in the place—looks over. "What?"

"Can I have a cappuccino for Josh, please? Just add it to my tab."

Mindy gives him a thumbs-up, and Kieran joins me at the table.

"So, you come here often, huh?" I say, then want to kick myself, because it almost sounds like a come-on.

Fortunately for me, Kieran seems to get my humor, because he laughs. "Every day, pretty much. Sometimes twice. I might be slightly addicted to coffee."

"That's me with nail polish," I joke, and immediately wish I could take it back when his gaze drops to my hands. My polish-free hands. "I wanted to make a good impression today, so I took it off." Fuck. That sounds like I think he'd be closed-minded about it. Which, after our Zoom call, I don't, but still, I wanted to hedge my bets.

This interview is not going well, and it hasn't even properly started. I'm too nervous. I need to chill.

"We're not all that strict about the dress code," he says, seemingly not offended. "Neat and clean and no profanity. If we're having a themed event, you'll be asked to dress in appropriate costume—which we'll provide—and the guides and instructors wear period clothing, but the rest of us just try to dress presentably. What you're wearing now is fine. And so is nail polish or any other cosmetics you might want to wear."

"That's good to know." And surely he wouldn't be telling me about the dress code if I'd blown my chances. "Uh, I also wanted to thank you for meeting me here instead of at the estate."

He smiles. "That's no problem. I live here in town, so it was just as easy to delay going in and meet you. When you said you'd be catching the bus to town, it seemed like the best solution. There's no easy way to get out to the estate without a car."

I've never had a car because I've never been able to get a license. You try learning to drive with a ghost yammering in the back seat... or another one strolling nonchalantly in front of the car and nearly giving you a heart attack. But I could have gotten an Uber or Lyft out to the estate if I had to. The town's not *that* small. Like I said before, though, the estate is haunted as fuck. No way did I want to try to have this interview surrounded by ghosts. It's bad enough there's one staring fixedly at the side of my head right now.

Kieran's still talking. "...so you'll probably be able to get by without one if you only leave the estate when you can grab a lift from someone, but I'd be happy to ask around town and try to find you a cheap car if you want. Just let me know."

"That's so nice, thank you, but I don't have a driver's license. Never needed one, living in Chicago. The L and buses took me wherever I needed to go. It could be fun to learn to drive," I announce perkily as Mindy brings over my coffee.

"Here you go. And go you, learning new things at your age."

At… my age?

"Thanks?" I blink at her retreating back, then glance over at Kieran, who's hiding a smile behind the rim of his coffee cup. "Um, did I age fifty years in the last two minutes?"

"No. Mindy's eighteen. Everyone over twenty-five is old to her."

"So I must seem ancient at… twenty-eight."

He lifts his cup in salute. "How do you think I feel, at thirty-five? Plus, I used to babysit her when I was home from college. She literally thinks of me as being her dad's age. Which isn't far off."

We laugh, and I mentally thank Mindy for breaking the tension.

Kieran begins by reiterating what he told me about the job during our Zoom call, then asks a few questions about my past work experience. I answer this bit carefully, aware that most employers don't like to see such a… er, *varied* job history. To be honest, I think the only reason I'm even in the running for this job is because it's basically a twenty-four-hours-on-call general dogsbody position, nearly two hours from the city and a ten-minute drive from the outskirts of the nearest town.

There wouldn't have been thousands of applicants. And sure enough, he's more interested in the types of duties I'm used to performing, especially the customer-facing ones, than in how long I was in any previous role. I slowly start to relax.

This is going pretty well. I even manage to get another laugh out of him. I think he genuinely likes me, which bodes well if I'm going to work for him.

Meanwhile, the ghost is still sitting there, staring at me. It's gone beyond unnerving and is taking every ounce of willpower to ignore her. At least she's silent. It's easier to block out staring than words, especially since I can barely see her in my periphery.

Kieran sits back in his chair and pushes his empty coffee cup away. "Do you have any questions for me?"

Ah, my chance to sound insightful and intelligent. "Actually, yes. You mentioned last time we spoke that I'd be required to pitch in and help with other duties when I'm not busy, and that's fine, but are you able to give me any insight on what those duties might be?"

His smile is wry. "They could be anything. For example, yesterday morning I was standing ankle-deep in what I really hope was just mud helping Daniel pick broccoli. Daniel's in charge of our farm," he adds. "Have I told you about the farm?"

"No, but I knew the estate had one. It's used to showcase old-fashioned and organic farming methods, right?"

He nods, beaming, clearly pleased I've done my research. "Yes. It's not big, only about ten acres, but Daniel makes the most of every inch. And the crops make a wonderful supplement to the restaurant menu for our overnight guests. In fact—"

His phone rings, cutting him off, and he glances at the screen, then frowns. "I'm so sorry, Josh, I'm going to take this."

"No problem," I assure him, picking up the cup with the dregs of my cappuccino. As he answers and heads toward the door, I lean back in my chair and let my gaze drift toward the artwork on the wall behind the ghost. Now's my chance to check her out.

Sipping from my cup and nonchalantly studying what might be the ugliest painting I've ever seen, I get a better look at the silent-but-intrusive ghost.

She looks like my grandmother. White hair cut in a sleek cap, twin set, pearl earrings, and glasses hanging from a chain around her neck. I wish that told me more about her, but here's a hard-learned fact about ghosts: they don't spend eternity in the clothes they died in. Their visual forms, even the ones most people can't see, are basically pure energy, so they can make themselves look however they want to. It can be a real mindfuck when a ghost who looks like an extra from a punk music video speaks like an old-school British duke, three-hundred-year-old idioms included.

So, I have no idea if this ghost was actually born during the twentieth century, the nineteenth, or even this one. Though usually, young ghosts don't like to age themselves until they're thoroughly bored of being young.

I let my gaze slide away from the ugly painting and finish the last of my cappuccino. I don't know what the ghost is doing here, but she seems harmless. Maybe she just likes this table and we're intruding on her space.

Kieran returns, dropping into his chair with a sigh. "Sorry about that. We're shorthanded at the moment—

clearly, or I wouldn't be here, right? But it means I can't ignore a call, just in case they need me."

"That's fine." I smile brightly.

"So, let me just make sure there's nothing else I wanted to ask," he says, tapping his phone.

From the corner of my eye, I see the ghost lean toward him. "YOU SHOULD HIRE THIS ONE! HE HAS A GOOD AURA!" she yells.

I flinch, bumping the table and making the cups rattle.

Both Kieran and the ghost look at me.

I try not to sweat.

"You okay?" Kieran asks.

"Yeah. Sorry. I, uh, my leg twitched." God, please let my face not look guilty right now.

He scrunches up his face. "I hate when that happens."

"HIRE HIM! HIRE HIM! STOP CHATTING AND HIRE HIM SO WE CAN GO HOME!"

I can't help it; my eyes flick toward her.

She notices, straightening in the chair and turning the full force of her attention back to me even as I glance away, trying to recover.

Worse… Kieran notices. He studies my face, then flicks a glance toward the ghost, almost as if he knows she's there, then looks back to me.

Fuck. What's even happening here?

"CAN YOU HEAR ME?" the ghost, who is still shouting for reasons I don't understand, demands. I swallow the giant lump in my throat, determined not to screw this chance up. I'm ignoring her no matter what.

Kieran leans forward. "Uh, this might sound weird, but can you hear her?"

Oh my god.

Oh my god.

Did he…?

Does he…?

He said "her," right? A specific reference to a woman. He wasn't just asking if I'd heard *something*.

Maybe… can he hear her too?

I clasp my hands together to hide how much they're shaking. "Uh, h-hear… who?"

Disappointment flashes across his face, and he shakes his head. "Never mi—"

"DON'T BELIEVE HIM. HE CAN HEAR ME! DIDN'T YOUR MOTHER TEACH YOU LYING IS A SIN?"

My whole body jerks in reaction. Why can't I fake anything like a normal person?

Kieran's eyes narrow.

We sit there in awkward silence. I can feel the ghost glaring at me, but there's no way in hell I'm turning to look at her.

"You've done some research on the estate," Kieran says, seemingly casual.

I clear my throat. "Yes. N-Not anything special, but I've checked out the website and some of the review sites."

"Then you know we're haunted. That deters a lot of prospective employees."

"Really?" I squeak, then clear my throat again. "I mean, that's surprising. Don't people love a good ghost story, ha ha." My fake laugh game is so weak.

"Are you deterred by ghosts? Since you'd be living on site, you'd be dealing with them a lot."

"Nope!" That sounds a bit too enthusiastic. "Uh,

that is, I've never had much experience with ghosts. Do they, like… moan and rattle chains?" I try to pick the biggest ghost cliché there is, and Kieran seems to buy it.

The ghost, on the other hand, harrumphs loudly. I'm not making a friend there.

"No, there's no moaning. Not the sense you mean, anyway. They're very good at moaning in the whiny sense, though."

What?

"You mean… they talk to you?" A tiny kernel of hope begins to unfurl inside me.

He nods. "Sometimes. We don't fully understand how it works, but there's something about the estate that gives them… power? Energy? Whatever it is, it allows them to sometimes manifest to most of us."

"R-Really?" Ohmygodohmygodohmygodohmygod.

"Yes. So part of your job will also be calming down guests and… well, ghost wrangling, for want of a better word."

Okay, I wasn't expecting that. "Sorry?"

He sighs and flicks another glance toward the ghost… or, actually, toward her chair? His gaze isn't quite focused on the right area. Maybe he can't see her? Is he pulling my chain here?

But he knew to call her "her." This is too complicated.

"I'm going to cop all sorts of trouble for saying this, but ghosts can be… enthusiastic. Our ghosts are all so happy to see the estate restored and full of visitors. Well, most of them are. And they try to help. A lot. But… uh, have you ever been around little kids?"

Not really. "I had a neighbor with twin toddlers a

few years ago. I watched them once while she went to a job interview." And boy, wasn't that a disaster.

But it seems to be what Kieran wants to hear. "Great! So, think of the ghosts as those toddlers. They're enthusiastic and want to do all the things, but sometimes they're not successful."

"EXCUSE YOU, YOUNG MAN! HOW DARE YOU MALIGN OUR ABILITIES?"

This time, I manage to restrain my reaction to only a tiny twitch. Kieran studies me.

"So yeah, cleaning up the ghosts' messes is something you'd have to deal with. Incidentally, we've found that while some of the stronger ghosts are able to leave the estate, our ability to perceive them fades the further we go. Here in town, I can't hear or see any of them, but if they express themselves strongly enough, I can get a sense of what they're feeling." He winces slightly and tips his head toward the ghost. "For example, I can tell right now that Hattie's very displeased with me."

I can't help it; my eyes slide over to the ghost. Hattie? She looks very displeased, but she's nodding reluctantly.

"IT'S TRUE. I HAVE TO SHOUT HERE SO HE CAN HEAR ME. IT'S MUCH EASIER AT HOME."

Wow. Okay. Wow. This… I blink back tears. This could change my life.

I suck in a deep breath. "You can really see ghosts and talk to them when you're on the estate?"

He huffs out a laugh. "Yeah, you want to run from the crazy man, don't you? I swear, I'm not nuts. I really thought you might be able to hear her, just from how you reacted before. It would be awesome if someone could."

"IT WOULD CERTAINLY MAKE THIS PROCESS EASIER," Hattie agrees, and I can't take it anymore.

"Ma'am—Hattie—do you mind not yelling, please?" I ask as courteously as I can manage.

They both stare at me in shock. "You can really hear her?" Kieran whispers.

"You can hear me?" Hattie echoes, thankfully at a normal decibel level.

I swallow hard and nod.

"You're hired," Kieran declares. "Wanna start right now?"

The laugh bursts from me, sharp and hysterical, and I bury my face in my hands, eyes stinging with tears. It's been so hard for such a long time.

A hand tentatively touches my forearm. "Can I get you anything?" Kieran asks quietly, and I shake my head, rubbing my hands over my face and then lowering them. I meet his gaze as I let out a sigh.

"Sorry. I guess it's my turn to worry that you're going to run from the crazy man."

"Don't be foolish, dear," Hattie says, and for the first time in years, I allow myself to react openly to a ghost in a public place, turning my head to look at her. She smiles kindly. "I'm sure it's been very difficult for you, having to pretend all the time."

"It has," I admit.

"What has?" Kieran asks, his gaze tracking from me to where Hattie's sitting. "Sorry, do you mind, uh, interpreting?"

My smile is so wide, my cheeks hurt. God, finally a way I can be useful! "That's fine. Hattie was just saying it must have been hard for me to pretend not to notice ghosts."

"Hell, yeah," he agrees. "Not to be pushy, but what do I need to do to get you to take the job? I wanted to offer it to you before I knew this, especially since Hattie liked you, but now it's essential."

I clear the sudden roughness from my throat, still unable to believe my luck. "I'll take it. Thank you." Then I chuckle. "Wait, so when Hattie was shouting that you should hire me, you could sense that?"

He nods. "Yep. It was a sense of approval, along with mild consternation that I'm such an idiot." He glances toward her. "Right, Hattie?"

"He tries," she tells me. "And mostly he's a good boy. But his job is to look after the living, and it's not like he can always hear us. Manifesting is *hard work*, even at the estate. Thank goodness we've got you now. It's going to be so good to have a representative."

Whoa… was that part of the job description?

"Hattie thinks you're a nice boy," I parrot, "and, um, apparently I'm now the ghosts' representative?"

"Hattie," he says in exasperation. "Don't scare him away!"

She sniffs. "You look like you've got too much fortitude to be scared off by the likes of me."

"Thank you," I say automatically, then when Kieran raises a brow, "She thinks I have fortitude. So… should I be asking questions?"

"The ghosts will likely be talking your ear off most of the time," he confesses. "They do that to us, every second they can. The only time we get peace is when they're too tired to manifest."

"Excuse me," Hattie says indignantly. "Peace? We're very peaceful!"

Kieran, unable to hear her—or sense her, since she's not yelling—blithely continues, "So when they know you can hear them all the time, they'll probably bring their complaints to you."

"Complaints?" Hattie's voice rises shrilly.

"He's not saying you complain nonstop." My hasty attempt at mediation earns me a look of doubting disapproval from Hattie and a cringe from Kieran.

"Whoops," he says. "Sorry, Hattie. I'm not calling you a complainer. I just meant that there are things you and the other ghosts need, which are sometimes genuine complaints about guest behavior, and someone who can speak to you even when you're tired is a good thing."

She purses her lips but nods. "Apology accepted."

I relay that to Kieran, then add, "I guess that sounds fine. But Hattie, if I'm going to live on-site, you and the other ghosts need to respect my privacy. If you don't, I'll salt my room and keep you out by force."

Hattie's eyes widen. "Goodness, you're a feisty one." She leans closer. "Are you a proper medium?"

I shake my head. "No. I met one once who wanted to train me, but then she left town, and I didn't have the money to go with her."

"Um," Kieran begins apologetically, and I repeat Hattie's question. "Oh. We've had a few mediums come through the estate over the years. They like it there because our ghosts are all friendly and nobody treats them oddly. If you want some training, maybe I can reach out and see if someone's interested?"

My head spins dizzyingly. Is this Josh-wins-at-life day?

"That would be… great," I manage, then pull myself together. "Maybe not right away, though? I'd like to get settled in first."

"The offer's open whenever you're ready," he assures me. "I'm sure one of them will pop back through for a weekend or something over the next few months, if you want to meet them before you decide."

I nod. "Let's do that." Wow, medium training? I wouldn't have to rely on salt to keep nasty ghosts away. I could force them to move on.

Mind you, if I'm living at the estate, where, so Kieran says, all the ghosts are friendly, that's not going to be an issue anyway.

"Do you want to come out to the estate and have a tour?" he offers now. "What time's your bus back to the city?"

"Not until five. I wanted to allow plenty of time for this interview." And, in the event it went badly, give myself time to look around town for other jobs and somewhere to live. Because a mostly new town like this has few ghosts, and that's somewhere I want to be. Wanted to be. Somewhere I can openly be myself is even better.

"Great! Someone will bring you back in plenty of time, and we can get the paperwork started. When can you start, by the way? And do you need to stop at the motel to pick up your stuff and check out?"

"Uh, yes, please. And… Monday? If that works for you." It'll give me a few days to tie up loose ends in the city and pack my meager collection of stuff.

"Monday's perfect. I'll show you your rooms today. They're clean and ready for you, so if you want to come down early, that's no hassle, but we'll set your start date for Monday." He looks toward Hattie. "How's that sound?"

"Wonderful," she approves. "That will give me plenty of time to ensure everyone's aware of the rules. But maybe lay in a supply of salt, just in case," she suggests. "Some of the younger ghosts are still somewhat rowdy and like to push boundaries." She rolls her eyes. "Children."

"Thanks for the tip," I say solemnly.

Kieran and I carry our cups back to the counter, where Mindy takes them with a smile and a wave, then we step out onto the street.

"I'm parked just there," he says, pointing to a late-model blue sedan at the curb about twenty feet down. I'm reaching for the passenger door handle when I realize Hattie is hovering at my elbow.

"Um… would you like to sit in the front seat?" I offer after a quick glance to make sure there are no strangers nearby, feeling wholly stupid. I mean, she's a ghost.

She smiles at me. "What lovely manners you have, dear. Thank you, but no." She fades through the side of the car and reforms in the back seat, leaving me blinking like a fool. Did she just want me to ask?

Deciding it's safest to let it go, I get into the car and close the door. Here we go. I can't wait to see the place where the next stage of my life begins.

Chapter Three

JOSH

When Kieran turns in the front gate, I can't deny the sensation of peace that washes over me. I'm not even sure exactly why or how it happens. There's the faint tingling of energy against my skin, the way it sometimes feels when a ghost is really close to me. But it doesn't feel bad or scary. It's... welcoming?

"So... before you said you don't know why the ghosts can manifest here on the estate?" There's got to be a reason.

"That's right," Kieran confirms. "Hattie?"

"We never used to be able to," she agrees. "It started around the time the house was closed. How long's that now, dear?"

"About fifty years," Kieran tells her, and yep, he can hear her now. That's so trippy. Five minutes ago, out on the road, I needed to interpret for them, but now that we're on the estate, bam!

I look out at the house as we approach. After all the time I've spent on the website and looking at people's vacation pics online, it's familiar to me, but there's a sense of coming home that I've never had before.

Kieran pulls the car around the side of the house to an area marked Staff Parking Only and parks. "Let's go in the front entrance your first time," he suggests. "I'll show you the staff door later."

"Fine by me." Excitement is fizzing in my veins now.

"Today's a good day for a tour," he says as we walk around the front and I admire the manicured gardens. "There aren't any school groups due and no events until tomorrow night. We've got a few guests, but mostly it's quiet. That's why I scheduled your interview today."

"And there was a big to-do with the school group yesterday," Hattie adds, "so most of the ghosts are resting. It's the perfect time for you to look around without being mobbed."

Ahh… yay?

"Great," I manage, although I can't deny that part of me is excited about being able to openly interact with ghosts, and even help human-ghost relations. Maybe I should ask Kieran to make my official title Ghost Ambassador.

I could wear a cape.

Or not.

But that reminds me… "Hattie," I begin as we walk up the front steps, "are any of the ghosts likely to feel uncomfortable if I wear nail polish?" It's my one vice. I've never really been into cosmetics, but I like having colorful, sometimes sparkly nails.

"Pfft." She waves a hand. "Not likely. Maybe Grumpy Joe, but he's got a problem with everything. Don't you worry about that, dear. Wear what makes you happy, and I'll deal with the malcontents." There's a somewhat militant gleam in her eye on that last bit, and I resolve to stay on Hattie's good side as much as possible.

Stepping into the house, I find myself in a charming entrance hall dominated by a reception desk. To the left, there's an opening into a cloakroom, lined with lockers and hooks for coats. Through the opening to the right is a gorgeous living room area, furnished to look like we've stepped back to the eighteenth century. I recognize it from the pictures on the website. If I remember the map on the website right, down the hallway is a series of rooms opening into each other that have been turned into a museum of local history.

There's a peppy-looking guy who might still be in high school sitting behind the reception desk, wearing period costume. His gray plaid coat is double-breasted, with wide lapels, and the front ends sharply at the waist though it looks like it's longer at the back. There's a white shirt under it with a very high collar and a thin scarf wrapped around a few times and knotted. I can't see his pants behind the desk, but his shoulder-length hair is a complete contrast to his outfit, beautifully done in unicorn colors. It's not a look I'd go for myself, but he rocks it.

The jacket looks uncomfortable, though, and I'm glad I'm not going to be required to wear one every day.

"Hi!" he calls. "Kieran, I've got messages for you." He smiles brightly at me while waving a fistful of message slips at Kieran. "I'm Skye."

"Josh," I reply, distracted by the ghost wandering in from the hallway. She appears to be in her early twenties and has seemingly embraced style from every decade of the twentieth century, from bell-bottomed jeans to a tailored jacket with massive shoulder pads, white wrist-length gloves, saddle shoes, a flapper headband complete with feather, and masses of jewelry. I can't even count the number of necklaces, rings, and bracelets she's wearing. It's an interesting effect.

"Josh is going to be our admin assistant and after-hours guest liaison," Kieran says, taking the messages while I try to focus on Skye and not the new ghost. Hattie's gone to talk to her, but neither of the other two living humans have noticed her, so I assume she's not manifesting to them.

"Great!" Skye exclaims. "I run reception and handle whatever admin Kieran doesn't have time for, so we'll be working together a lot."

That kernel of hope from before? It begins to unfurl. Maybe I can actually make some friends here. Maybe my workmates won't all think I'm looney tunes and hate me.

I smile back. "That sounds great. I love your hair." It really does look amazing, and I feel like a compliment can only help this situation.

"Thank you!" He seems about to say something more, but Hattie and the other ghost drift our way, grabbing my attention.

"Josh," Hattie begins, "I'd like you to meet Maisie."

Skye and Kieran look over, surprised. "Maisie's here?" Skye asks. "Where?"

"Josh can see ghosts," Kieran begins, then launches into an explanation, but I'm not listening.

"Aren't you handsome?" Maisie says coyly, fluttering her eyelashes. "How do you feel about inter-corporeal relationships?"

Inter-corporeal…

Oh my god.

"Uh, I bat for the other team," I blurt. "So… sorry."

She pouts. "Oh, boo. It's been so long since I've felt the touch of a man."

I clamp my teeth down on my lip to keep from smiling. "Same." Not really—still sore from last night, after all—but it seems mean to boast when she's unwillingly celibate.

Her stupidly long lashes—can ghosts have fake eyelashes? It's not something I've ever come across before—blink in surprise, and then she laughs. "I like you! You can be my gay best friend." She looks over at Hattie. "That's the right way to say it, isn't it?"

"I believe it should be 'gay BFF.'"

Maisie nods solemnly. "I should spend more time watching television with you. I'm just so hopeful that one of the guests will want to sweep me off my feet."

"Aren't we all, dear." Hattie pats her arm sympathetically. I don't know what to say, so I keep my mouth shut. "Now, you can run along and tell everyone about Josh, but be sure to remind them that his personal space must be respected. And nobody's to come and bother him today. We're just giving him a tour. He doesn't start work until Monday."

"I'm on it," Maisie declares. "Welcome to the family, Josh!" She rises up to the ceiling and disappears through it, a sight I should've gotten used to by now but still find unsettling.

Hattie watches her go, then leans in close and says, "Maisie's a dear, but she was somewhat, er, *loose* in life, and she has a habit of cuddling up to the male guests. Most don't realize she's a ghost until they've taken her back to their room."

Well, that's going to make my job fun.

"I imagine that startles quite a few of them," I reply blandly.

"Oh yes. There's a lot of shouting when she reaches completion and can't maintain a corporeal form anymore. And not the good kind of shouting."

My jaw drops. Does she mean…?

Ick.

"And I bet Maisie gets upset when she realizes they're not interested in a… how did she put it? Inter-corporeal relationship?"

Hattie nods, her lips pressed together in sympathy. "Terribly upset. We've been trying to tell her she doesn't need a man to be happy, but old habits are hard to break." She sighs. "Well, I'll be off. It's been a big morning, and I think a rest will do me good."

"It was great to meet you. Thank you for your help today." The words sound so trite, but there's nothing I can say that would truly convey how I feel right now. Hattie's presence at the interview changed my life.

She pats my arm. "You're most welcome, dear. I'm glad to have you here." Then she looks past me to where Kieran and Skye are still talking in low voices. "Bye, boys!"

"Bye, Hattie! Rest up so we can watch *Drag Race* tomorrow!" Skye calls back.

Hattie follows Maisie, and I ask Skye, "Aren't we between seasons?"

"Yep, but we're still on season five. I made the mistake of watching a YouTube clip on my lunch break one day, and now I spend three lunch breaks a week watching old episodes with them so they can catch up." He shrugs. "There are worse things in life. Want a tour?

Kieran can watch things while he's returning those calls."

I meet Kieran's gaze, and he nods. "Go for it. Skye knows everything there is to know, anyway. I'll take over when it's time to go outside."

"Let's do it," I tell Skye, and he claps his hands, reinforcing my first impression that he might be a teenager. "Do you, uh, work here full-time?" I fish as I follow him into the living room.

"I'm twenty-six, if that's what you're asking," he answers wryly. "Baby face gets me carded everywhere."

"I didn't mean—"

"It's fine." He flips a hand in dismissal. "I'm not offended. I get asked that all the time. So… this is the main communal space for the guests and day-trippers. As you can see, Arissa, our catering manager, keeps it stocked with snacks." He gestures to a sideboard where there's a basket of muffins covered with one of those dome-fly-screen thingies, a bowl of whole fruit, and two manual drink dispensers on little stands, one filled with water and the other with some kind of juice. "The snacks are complimentary, and most people are respectful of that, but I do occasionally need to shoot a nasty look at someone filling a bag. We used to have coffee and hot tea out here, but day-trippers would deliberately tip it on themselves and then ask us how we could recompense them for their suffering, even after we showed them the security camera footage. The last time, it was such a busy day that nobody had gotten around to refreshing the pot for hours and the liquid was barely lukewarm, but that didn't stop them from trying. So now we only offer hot drinks to overnight guests."

"People suck," I commiserate.

"There's always someone who ruins it for everyone else," he agrees, leading me toward double doors at the back of the room. There's a discreet card reader to the side of them, and he pulls a set of keys from his jacket pocket and swipes a small blue disc over it. The light changes from red to green, and he opens one of the doors.

"This part of the house is for overnight guests and staff only. You may have noticed that there's no staircase in the front entry. That's deliberate to keep day-trippers out of the private accommodation, and required some redesign when the house was renovated twenty years ago. The front entrance was originally a central hall that extended almost the length of the house, with the receiving and entertaining rooms on either side and the main staircase in the middle." He pauses. "Sorry, I'm using my tour guide voice, aren't I?"

"Yep, but I like it. And I probably need to know all this anyway, don't I?"

"It would help, in case we're shorthanded and need you to give guests a tour. Um… so when the new owners renovated, they put up the walls to divide the front entrance from the rest of the main hall and to create a narrower corridor into the museum space."

"Got it. That's a better solution than a velvet rope and a sign saying Do Not Enter."

Skye laughs. "Right? Anyway, this is the private parlor. As you can see, it's smaller than the living room but has a better array of snacks. It's the place you're most likely to find guests who want to be social with each other or need a pick-me-up after Ewan and Daniel have put them to work."

"We put guests to work? I mean, I knew it was an

immersive experience, but I didn't realize it was quite that interactive." Maybe I'm lazy, but I can't imagine wanting to spend all that money to stay here—and it's not cheap—just so the owners can get some free labor.

"It's optional, but a lot of guests like to see how it feels to use a forge or a scythe. Especially if they have experience with modern farming or blacksmithing. The guys are accredited instructors and keep a very close eye on things. And nearly everyone likes to take a turn feeding or grooming the animals, because Ewan has a policy that you only get to pet them if you earn it."

The sound that bursts from me is half scoff, half laugh. "Say what? And the guests go for that?"

Skye shrugs. "The only times I've known him to make exceptions are when people are physically unable to do those chores. Even little kids have to pass him the curry comb or whatever. Ewan's a big guy, and few people are willing to argue over it. Some have complained to Kieran, and he just tells them Ewan and Daniel are responsible for the care of the animals and get to set the rules."

We head toward another set of double doors to our left. If my mental map is right, they should lead into the space behind reception, where the main staircase is.

Skye throws the doors open. "Ta-dah!"

"Wow." Even seeing it from the side instead of the front, the staircase is impressive, wide and sweeping. I look up, and the two floors above both have wide galleries overlooking this "main" hallway. "This is special," I admit, just as a dapper-looking middle-aged ghost in a 1930s-style three-piece suit complete with watch chain, cane, and hat comes down the stairs.

"Special," he scoffs. "These modern folk have no

appreciation for fine architecture. This staircase is *spectacular*."

I'm pretty sure he's talking to himself, but Maisie was going to tell all the other ghosts about me, so maybe he's talking to me? I don't want to accidentally be rude. Pissed-off or offended ghosts can be a real drainer.

"I beg your pardon, sir," I say as respectfully as I can manage. "I was, um, swept away by the moment and couldn't think of the right word."

Skye shoots me a startled glance before comprehension dawns, but the ghost is so surprised by me speaking to him that he screeches and drops *through* the stairs. I shudder at the sight of him suspended in the middle of a solid object.

"Who is it?" Skye whispers. "Pompous-looking man dressed like a banker?"

I nod.

"Frederick Walton III," he murmurs. "He'll try to get you to call him Mr. Walton, but he goes by Freddie to most of us."

"Thanks," I whisper back as Freddie extracts himself from the stairs, brushes off imaginary dust, then gathers his dignity and descends the remaining steps to the ground floor. Skye and I move forward a little.

"Is he manifesting?" I mutter, and Skye shakes his head. "Good morning," I say louder, smiling at Freddie. "I'm sorry I startled you. My name's Josh, and I'm going to be working here starting Monday. Maisie was supposed to tell you."

He sniffs. "I try not to associate with that woman too frequently. Her reputation leaves much to be desired."

Yeouch. Poor Maisie. "Uh, well, as you've no doubt guessed, I can see and speak to you even when you're not manifesting. And off the estate. Hattie can tell you all about it."

He studies me with a pinched expression, then nods. "Well, this will be convenient. It's been *such* a hardship having to manifest every time I need to pass along instructions."

Instructions? Oh man, this is going to be interesting.

"If you'll excuse us, Skye here was just showing me around. I look forward to speaking with you next week."

"And you, young man. I shall take myself off and make a list." He turns before I can say anything else and heads back toward the stairs. I dread to think what he's going to put on that list. And how much energy it's going to take him to write it.

"Excuse me, sir?" I call, winking at Skye, who's only heard my side of things and is mostly clueless. "What was your name?"

"Mr. Walton," he throws back over his shoulder. I stifle my grin until he's three steps up, clearly decides haste is more important than dignity, and shoots off at a diagonal.

Then I laugh.

"Okay, you gotta fill me in," Skye demands, smiling, then laughs like a loon when I do. "It's going to be so much fun with you here."

It's kinda dumb, but that makes me feel warm all over. Nobody's ever said it to me before.

Skye shows me through the rest of the rooms on the ground floor, which include a small library, a dining room, a glass-walled conservatory, Kieran's—and now my—office, the staff break room, the utility room, and the kitchen, where I meet Arissa the catering manager, two cooks, and three kitchenhands. They're having a planning meeting ahead of the weekend rush, but I get a warm welcome when Skye introduces me, which warms up even further after he tells them about my abilities. Turns out, some of the ghosts like to play pranks in the kitchen, which has almost led to accidents a few times. They tried salting to keep the ghosts out, but it's not a practical option with the heavy foot traffic, high heat, and the fear of a surprise health and safety inspection. I promise to do what I can and make a mental reminder to revisit the notes I took when I was training with Lisa, the medium.

The storeroom is next. "This is boring, but believe me, you'll spend a lot of time in here," Skye warns me. "Sheets and towels are in the hall linen press, but everything else is kept here." He explains the shelving system, which is pretty simple but makes it easy to find things quickly. As we get toward the far end of the room, the hair on my arms stands on end, and I shiver.

"Cold?" he asks. "It's always cool in here."

"Uh, I guess." I didn't think I was, but... Glancing around, I spot a door. "What's that?"

"Basement," Skye says. "It's unfinished, and we don't keep anything down there."

I nod and follow as he heads back toward the hallway. But I can't help looking back over my shoulder. That basement might be empty, but it gives me the creeps.

Skye takes me upstairs via a cute little elevator tucked in a back corner. "This floor and the one above are all guest rooms," he says. "We have nine double rooms in total, each with a private bathroom, so the maximum number of guests you'd ever have to worry about is eighteen. There are six here at the moment, three couples who all know each other and have stayed with us before. We're expecting a full house this weekend, though." He shows me a couple of the unoccupied rooms. They're furnished to look old-fashioned, with all signs of modern life neatly hidden away in cabinets and drawers, even the phone. The bathroom fittings look "old," and the outlets are tucked behind a hinged panel, but everything is fully up-to-date. It's newer than the bathrooms in my last three apartments.

We approach a door at the end of the hall, and Skye pulls out his little fob once more. "The elevator doesn't go all the way up to your room," he says apologetically, but I wave him off. When you've lived in as many walk-ups as I have, one flight of stairs is nothing.

The light on the panel changes, and Skye opens the door. There's a small clear space, then a flight of stairs. Light is flooding down them, but I can't see the source.

"Light switch here," Skye says, flipping it on and off, "for after dark. There's another at the top of the stairs." He starts up, and I follow him. The source of the light becomes apparent halfway—it's a big-ass skylight.

We reach the landing, and Skye opens the door on our right. It's a neat little room with twin beds. There's a shirt strewn over the end of one bed and an overnight bag on the floor. An open door in one wall shows a small bathroom. "Temporary accommodation for any staff who have to work late or stay over because you're having a night off or get sick or something. Kieran and I have been trading off nights recently."

"Not for much longer," I promise. I can't believe how excited I am about babysitting a bunch of hotel guests and shuffling paperwork. If my room is as nice as the one he just showed me, this will officially be the best job I've ever had.

"That's storage," he says, pointing to the door straight ahead and then turns to the door on the left. "You'll have a key for this, but we haven't been locking it since Adele left." He opens it, then gestures me forward.

I'm expecting another bedroom, maybe a bit bigger than the one he just showed me, since it will be my full-time home, after all. Instead, I walk into a full-size studio apartment. And when I say full-size, I mean I've seen actual two-bedroom places smaller than this. It must take up most of the attic space. There's a king-size bed, two nightstands, a six-drawer dresser, and a double closet. At the foot of the bed is a chest with a padded top, doubling as a seat and more storage. Along one wall is a kitchenette, including a four-burner hotplate, small oven, microwave, and fridge. Not just a dorm fridge, either—it's not huge, but it's full-sized. The only luxury missing is a dishwasher, and I've never had one before anyway. There are cupboards above and below the wall of appliances, and also a small island with a sink and about two feet of counter space.

An overstuffed, squashy-looking three-seater couch faces a wall with a flat-screen TV on it, the coffee table between them holding a remote control. Over by the dormer windows are a plush armchair and ottoman. The floors are a warm-toned wood, with soft-looking rugs under the couch and bed, and there's just so much *space*. Nothing's crammed together.

To top it off, a massive skylight overhead floods the whole space with bright sunlight.

I'm speechless.

Skye's not, though. "So, the instruction manuals for

all the appliances are in the top drawer of the island, but they're pretty user-friendly. This panel here," he points to an electronics panel beside the door, "is for the air-conditioning and the blinds for the skylight."

"It has blinds?" I manage, tipping my head back to squint up at the pitched roof. Sure enough, it looks like there's someth—

With a quiet whirr, the blinds begin to descend, slowly dimming the light in the room. They get to halfway before reversing direction, and I glance over at Skye.

"I'll show you how it all works," he promises, "but I swear, it's easy. Adele told me she usually only closed them on really hot days and really cold nights, but you'll work out what you prefer."

"Sure," I agree, because what else is there to say?

"If there's any furniture you want to bring with you, we can move this stuff into storage."

"That's fine. Easier to just sell mine. None of it's worth much." Definitely not the cost of moving it. This is all much nicer.

"Great, that's easy! Let me show you the bathroom."

Obediently, I follow him to the door in the wall next to the kitchen and through into a bright, airy bathroom —thanks to another skylight. There's a walk-in shower stall, a big soaker tub, a vanity with plenty of storage, a sleek white toilet, and—

"Is that a washing machine?"

"Washer-dryer combo. The owners figure it isn't fair to make the guest liaison schlep all the way to the laundromat in town, and since we send the estate's laundry out to be done, it's not like there's another washer in the house."

I start to laugh. I can't help it; the chuckles bubble up out of me. Skye must get it, because he just grins at me.

Then he says, "Trust me, dude, you're going to earn this. We get some pretty demanding guests. And the ghosts are like toddlers sometimes."

"Worth it," I tell him, turning in a circle to admire the fresh, clean bathroom.

"We'll see. Now, before I forget, you may have noticed there's no bedding. That's on you. So are towels and kitchen stuff. You're also responsible for keeping the place clean, and the employment contract you're going to sign says it has to be in good condition when you move out, or you'll forfeit your last two weeks' pay, so if I were you, I'd take pics of any scuff you see before you officially move in."

I've dealt with dodgy landlords who wanted to keep my security deposit before, so I know what to do. I doubt Kieran and the owners will be that bad.

"Got it."

"If you can't be bothered with the cleaning, Keisha will do it for you for thirty a week. She's one of the housekeepers, and she can always use the cash."

I'm hesitant to pay someone else to do what I'm capable of managing. Maybe when I've settled in and my bank account has some padding. "I'm good for now, but I'll talk to her if I need to."

"Any questions?"

I step past him into the main room again and look around. "Can you pinch me, please?"

Laughing, he walks toward the door. "Come on. Let's see if Kieran's ready to show you around the grounds."

Chapter Four

EWAN

I whistle as I clean bridles, enjoying the sunshine and fresh air. The birds are whistling with me, and I've got an affectionate cat rubbing up against my leg. What more can a man ask for?

A good job I love? Got it.

Great place to live? Yep, got that too.

Hot, sweaty, athletic sex with a stranger? Had some last night.

See? My life's perfect. How many people get to sit in a courtyard on a gorgeous spring day, cleaning tack after showing off their blacksmithing skills to a bunch of tourists… *and* get paid to do it?

I reach out for another bridle, feel the pull of overtaxed muscles, and grin. My bedmate last night was certainly energetic. I should have gotten his name and number, but he said he was only in town for one night.

There's a bang from inside the stables behind me, but I ignore it. Daniel put the horses out in the pasture to graze this morning, so they can't get startled by it, and I'm not going to feed attention-seeking behavior. If

Johnny wants to waste his energy throwing a shit fit, he can go right ahead.

A laugh carries through the warm morning air, and I glance up toward the house. Kieran, his bright hair aflame in the sun, is walking down toward me with some guy. A tourist? Usually the drop-in crowd comes on the weekends, but occasionally we get someone during the week. Or… wait, Kier was interviewing for Adele's replacement this morning. Maybe he decided to hire the guy and this is him. That'd be great—he and Skye have been run ragged lately.

They come a bit closer, and I squint. The guy seems kinda familiar? Could he be a local? But I thought Kieran said he'd exhausted the possib—

Oh no.

I squeeze my eyes closed, just in case they're playing tricks on me, then open them to look again. It was a mistake, because now the sun seems blindingly bright and I have purple blobs dancing before my eyes.

"…can meet Ewan first," I hear Kieran say, and I blink rapidly to clear my vision. "Ewan!"

I get to my feet as they step into the three-sided courtyard, and yep, the guy with Kieran is none other than the man I fucked into oblivion last night, three… no, was it four times? Are we counting the time I ate him out and then made him come with my fingers? I didn't get off that time, but it's still sex even if you don't come.

"Josh, this is Ewan," Kieran's saying, and wow, talk about awkward. First because I had no idea what his name was before this moment, and second, what am I supposed to say right now? Do I admit that we've met? Does it count as meeting if we didn't know each other's names? If it doesn't, and therefore we never really met, does that mean everything that happened last night never really happened?

Did I just turn a "hi, nice to meet you" moment into a philosophical debate about existence?

"Hey," Josh says, his face a bit pale. "Good to see you again." Having solved that dilemma for me, he turns to Kieran. "I actually ran into Ewan last night after I got into town. But I never caught his name."

Ooh, smooth. That was one hundred percent truth, and yet never mentioned the fact that we met over tequila shots and then competed to see who could generate the most cum in the course of one night.

"If I'd known what you were here for, I could've given you some pointers," I say genially. And, you know, then walked away as fast as possible. Because working with someone you hooked up with? *Awkward.*

Though it does present an opportunity. It could be nice to have someone so close to have sex with.

"That's great." Kier grins, genuinely happy that we seem to be getting along. He's the best boss I could ask for, but sometimes he can be kind of oblivious. That works in my favor right now. If Skye was doing the intros, you can bet your ass he'd have picked up on the weird vibe. "So, Josh, Ewan's our blacksmith. All the metalwork you saw in the gift shop comes from his forge, and we can barely keep it stocked."

Josh looks over at me with an expression of respect. "Wow, you made that stuff? You're insanely talented." As soon as the words are out, his cheeks go pink. Possibly because he's remembering the last time he said that to me.

"Thank you," I say politely, restraining the urge to laugh.

"And Ewan and Daniel are responsible for looking after our animals," Kier continues. "Is Dan around this morning?" he asks me.

"He's got the guests picking lettuce and sowing seeds," I say, jerking my thumb in the direction of the kitchen garden. "Then he said something about taking them out to plow the back field." The guests got really excited about that. That won't last once they realize what hard work it is, even when you have a horse to help.

"We'll catch up with him later, then. You won't get to talk properly with guests there."

There's another loud bang from inside the stables, and Kieran and Josh jump.

"Sorry about that," I say. "Johnny's in a mood."

Josh looks inquiringly at Kieran, who rolls his eyes. "Johnny is another of our ghosts. He was a stable boy here in the middle of the nineteenth century and died at the age of nineteen when the stables burned down. Unfortunately, he still seems to be in possession of teenage drama."

"He's sulking today because he missed the drama with the school group yesterday," I add. "He'll get over it, but I'm ignoring him until then."

"Good call," Josh says dryly. "Uh, Kieran, did you want to tell Ewan...?"

I look between them, suddenly intrigued. Tell me what?

"Yes, definitely. Ewan, Josh here is able to see and talk to ghosts even when they're not manifesting."

I blink. Then blink again. "Really?" Man, that

would suck. It's bad enough when they have the energy to get in my face. Imagine having to deal with that all the time.

Josh nods, eyeing me warily, and I hold up my hands to show I'm no danger.

"Are you a medium? Can you make them stop 'helping' me? I can never find anything in the smithy when Hattie and Maisie get it in their heads to come and 'tidy up.' And Johnny's convinced the stables were perfect back in 1856 and keeps trying to reorganize them. It's driving Daniel nuts."

Johnny must hear me, because he comes flying out of the stables before Josh can reply. "They *were* perfect, you steel-hearted bastard! Everyone knows there's only one right way to store tack, and you're doing it wrong!"

"He calls me steel-hearted because of the forge," I explain calmly to Josh, who's taking Johnny in with only a little bit of surprise. I'm impressed. Most people are shocked to see a stable hand ghost in nineteenth-century clothing with a neon green mohawk and multitudes of piercings. Sometimes he likes to add tattoos too, and because they're always changing, we never know what we're going to get. "Johnny, this is Josh. He's going to be working at the house."

Josh gives a little wave. "It's nice to meet you, Johnny. If you have a chance to talk to Hattie, you should. I'm going to be the new ghost liaison, and she can explain it all."

Johnny loses the sulky pout. "Are you gonna fix it so we can have our own TV? Sharing with the guests is the worst."

"No," Kieran says.

"Ah…" Josh bites his lip. "Nobody mentioned that yet. Definitely you should talk to Hattie."

"Tell her there's no chance of your own TV," Kieran adds, and Johnny glowers at him.

"You can't treat us this way," he blusters. "I've watched them movies. I know we got rights. How'd you like to have a union in here?"

I cough to cover my laugh.

"Most of the staff are already union members," Kieran says. "You can remind Hattie of that, if you like."

"It ain't fair that we ghosts got no union." Johnny crosses his arms and pouts. From the way Kieran pinches the bridge of his nose, I can tell this is an argument he's had with the ghosts many times.

"Elect a representative from among you, and we'll negotiate in good faith," he promises. "I've told Hattie and the others this. But your demands have to be reasonable. A TV playing twenty-four seven in a room just for ghosts isn't something I can give you."

"That would be terrible for the environment," I say solemnly. Johnny watched one of Greta Thunberg's speeches on YouTube over Daniel's shoulder a few months back, and since then, he's been obsessed with "preserving the planet for our future." Never mind that he's a ghost and won't be impacted by environmental issues.

Sure enough, he perks right up. "Don't worry, I'll set them others straight. Twenty-four-seven TV! What were they thinking?" He starts off in the direction of the house, getting as far as the edge of the courtyard before he decides to flash the rest of the way.

Leaving the three of us staring after him.

"So… that was Johnny," I say finally. "He's a good kid, mostly. Loves the horses. Sometimes he's even helpful." I'm babbling.

"I might need to set office hours for the ghosts," Josh mutters. Then he laughs. "That way their union rep can only bug me between nine and five."

"Those negotiations are going to be fun," Kieran agrees, sounding less than thrilled. "That reminds me, Josh, if you run into big problems during the night, you can call Ewan and Daniel for backup. They live in the old farm manager's house."

Shock sweeps across Josh's face and is gone a second later. "Really? Where? Skye didn't mention it."

"It's over near the dorm cabins for school camps," Kieran says, pointing in the right direction. The barn's in the way, so Josh won't be able to see anything, but at least he'll know which way it is if he needs to find us.

"If you dial star six on the landline, you'll get us," I advise. "But we'll make sure you have our cell numbers too. The guests are usually easy to settle down, but don't hesitate to call if someone's getting aggressive." It's more likely he'll need to call us to soothe the guests while he deals with ghostly mischief, but I don't want him thinking he has to take on any of it alone.

"Thank you," he says, but his voice is different. Colder. Like I've offended him somehow. And if looks could kill, the one he's just shot at me should knock me dead. Maybe he thinks I'm implying he's not capable of dealing with an aggressive guest?

Kieran's cell rings, and he fishes it out of his pocket. "Sorry, guys. It's Skye." He answers, half turning away, and I pick up the bridle I was cleaning.

"Want a tour of the stable?" I offer. "I need to put these away."

He shrugs, then seems to realize how fucking rude that is and adds, "Sure. Thanks."

I gather up the other bridles, and he grabs the sponge and saddle soap without me having to ask. Our first stop is the little tack room just inside the main door. The stable isn't big, so it's really not more than a stall itself. I hang the bridles in their spots and put the cleaning equipment away.

"Do they just go anywhere, or…?" Josh asks hesitantly. "Kieran said I might need to fill in when you're busy, so the more I know now…"

"Yeah, we all help each other out," I confirm. "And no, the tack doesn't just go anywhere. Each piece belongs to a specific horse, and we don't mix them up. They're labeled—see?" I grab the nearest piece and show him the little tag with the horse's name, then point to the tape on the wall above the hook, where the matching name is. "If we do need you, you'll probably get stuck with grunt work, but we label pretty much everything to make it easier. Unless you've worked with horses before?"

He shakes his head. "Nope."

It seems like he wants to say more, so I wait, but he just presses his lips together and puts his nose in the air. I don't know what's crawled up his ass in the last five minutes, but he'll need to get over himself.

I show him the stalls, the feed bins, and the hayloft, which still has an old cot for Johnny to sleep on. "He won't give it up and sleep in the house," I explain. "Says his job is to watch out for the horses overnight."

"That's very dedicated of him. You know he doesn't really sleep, right?"

"Sometimes he pretends to," I say. "Fake snores and all. And we know he's pretending because if he were really asleep, he wouldn't be manifesting to us, right? It took me and Daniel way too long to figure that out."

His jaw tightens again. Am I not supposed to say I've figured things out about ghosts? Is he supposed to be the ghost expert? I don't have time for shit like that.

Pushing down the disappointment that my fun bedmate from last night is less fun in the light of day and a repeat doesn't look to be on the horizon, I'm about to suggest we go out to see the horses when we hear Kier calling from the front doors.

"Coming!" I yell, leading the way back to the courtyard.

"There you are. I have to head back to the house and help Skye with something. Ewan, why don't you show Josh the smithy? And then see if Daniel's free."

"I can come back with you," Josh says quickly.

Well, fuck you too. Whoops, did that already. I smirk, making sure Josh can see it. Petty? Maybe.

Kieran shakes his head. "This is going to take a while, and you'd be bored brainless. Besides, I'd really like for you to meet Daniel and get an idea of how things work out here, because for all of next week and probably most of the week after, you're going to be stuck in the house, helping us catch up on paperwork."

"Okay," he concedes with clear reluctance, and Kieran frowns slightly, glancing between us. "I mean, if you're sure I can't be of any help," Josh adds quickly.

"Thanks, but not right now. If that changes, I'll call

Ewan and get him to send you up." Kieran leaves, and I point across the courtyard to the smithy.

"This way." I don't bother adding any pleasantries. For whatever reason, Josh has decided to dislike me. I'm not going to waste energy trying to change his mind.

Inside the smithy, he seems to perk up a bit, so I give him the history spiel I use for the guests and then explain what I normally do during a demonstration.

"It's not likely you'd need my help in here, though, is it?" he asks, looking apprehensively at the forge. I'm not expecting to have to use it again today, so the fire's been banked, but it's still hot.

"Sometimes, yes. Not for any of the blacksmithing," I assure him hastily. "But if we've got a big crowd, it can be hard for me to keep an eye on everyone and work. Usually the guides are all over it, but if it's a day when we're shorthanded, they leave a group here and go to orient the next one, and it's helpful to have someone give handsy tourists the evil eye. Plus, cleaning up after a busy weekend can be a big job. We get some local teens in to help out during peak summer season, but they need supervising… which is also something you'll be able to do."

He snorts. "So when Kieran said this job involved a lot of general dogsbody duties, he was serious."

I shrug, not sure if he's okay with that or not, but before I can speak, we hear voices.

"Sounds like Daniel's done with the guests." I walk over to the door and stick my head out. Sure enough, the three couples currently staying with us have just crossed the courtyard and are making their way toward the house. They're walking slowly, probably tired, but their chatter is animated enough. Daniel comes out of the barn, whistling. "Come on," I tell Josh. "Let's introduce you two." And then Dan can deal with him for a while.

Josh reluctantly follows me out of the smithy—what's with the guy? Does he think Daniel and I aren't worthy of his time because we don't work in the house? Or maybe it's because we get a whole house to ourselves and he has the studio apartment? Because he seemed fine before Kieran mentioned that we live here too.

"Dan!" I call, and he glances over, then changes course. We meet in the middle of the courtyard. "Josh, this is Daniel, our historic farming expert. Dan, Kieran just hired Josh for Adele's old job."

Daniel's face lights up with a grin, and he grabs Josh's hand and shakes it. "Great to meet you. They really need the help up at the house. If we weren't heading into the busy season, they probably would have tried to drag me and Ewan in there." He pulls a face to show what a disaster that would be, and I shudder. It's bad enough dealing with the tourists in the smithy. I'm not going anywhere near the museum.

"Josh is also a medium," I add.

"I'm not," he says quickly. "I mean, I haven't had any real training. But I can interact with the ghosts even if they're not manifesting." His gaze skitters over Daniel's shoulder, and I frown. A lot of people don't like me—I have limited patience, and my size can be intimidating—but Daniel's the friendly sort. Plus, they've barely said hello. How can Josh possibly have a problem with Daniel already?

"That's amazing!" Daniel enthuses. "Although you're definitely going to want to put up some kind of ghost repellent. I don't know what ghosts are like in other places, but the ones here like to talk."

A reluctant smile tugs at Josh's lips. "They're mostly the same everywhere. I think they get lonely. The ones who don't like to talk are usually aggressive." He wraps his arms around himself, the smile slipping away. Daniel and I exchange glances.

"None of our ghosts here are mean," Daniel promises. "I think there was a nasty one when the renovations first started, but the way I understand it, the others kicked him out?" He squints. "I never quite got that whole story."

"Me either. But Kieran or Skye will know," I suggest. Probably, anyway. They seem to know everything else about this place. "Dan, are you good to show Josh around the farm and explain what you do here?"

Daniel smiles. "Sure! Nothing I like more than talking about farming. You got any other shoes, Josh?"

We all look down at Josh's Chucks.

"No?" His answer is full of uncertainty.

"Don't worry," Daniel assures him. "There are spare boots you can borrow. We keep them for guests. Come on."

"Nice to meet you, Josh," I say. He barely spares me a glance over his shoulder.

"You too," he mumbles.

I watch them go and sigh. So much for a convenient workplace hookup.

It's my turn to get the animals settled that night, since Daniel did them last night *and* this morning, allowing me to go out and get laid. We like to do each other favors like that. It's easier all round than bringing hookups back here and having to deal with Carter.

By the time I get to the house, Daniel's got dinner heating in the oven, and it smells amazing. Neither of us likes cooking, and fuck knows we hate cleaning, so we chip in to get Keisha, one of the housekeepers, to keep the place in decent condition and Jorge, one of the cooks, to stock our freezer with easy-to-heat food. We can manage salad in a bag to go with it.

"Let me wash up, and I'll set the table," I call from the tiny mudroom-slash-laundry room as I yank off my boots.

"You've got ten minutes," he yells back.

When I join him in the kitchen, he's leaning against the counter, reading a paperback. I don't know why he's chosen to do it there; Daniel's got his own ways of doing things, and I've learned not to question them. I leave him to it and work around him to put out cutlery, plates, and beer. Then I change my mind and switch mine for a soda. I had a couple of beers and two shots last night, and I like to have some alcohol-free days every week just to prove I can. I've got two uncles who are drunks, and it's not a path I want to go down.

The oven timer dings, and Daniel puts down his book and comes to the table while I dish up. It's only after we've both shoveled in several mouthfuls that we talk.

"Was that Josh guy weird with you?" he asks.

I finish chewing and swallow. "Yeah, but I met him last night, so he kinda had a reason. Was he weird with you too?"

"You met him last night? Wait, he's the guy who had

you all smiles when you got back this morning?" He puts his fork down. Daniel's a sucker for gossip.

"Yeah. But that stays between us, right?"

"Of course."

"Won't breathe a word," another voice says, and we both jump.

"Jesus Christ," Daniel hisses, clutching his chest. "What have we said about warning us?" He scowls at Carter, who's suddenly materialized in one of the other two chairs at the table.

"This is *my* house, young man," Carter snarks. "You're lucky I choose to let you live here." Carter was a farm manager when the estate was still a private home. There was a lot more land then, and apparently the estate was self-sufficient and even profitable. The house Daniel and I live in was originally the manager's cottage, making it almost as historic as the main house, and Carter lived here back when he was alive... and died here of a heart attack. Or maybe a stroke. There wasn't a doctor nearby at the time, and obviously no requirement for an autopsy or anything like that, so nobody's really sure how he died, only that he was found the next morning by a farmhand who came looking.

And he's been here ever since.

In case you're wondering, yes, it's odd having a ghost for a roommate. Although he likes to hang out with the other ghosts at the house a lot, which gives us a break. Apparently Daniel and I are too boring for him, now that we've stopped bringing dates home.

"We've talked about this, Carter," I remind him. "We all need to show respect for each other. Or we'll hire an exorcist." Not that we'd have any idea where to find an exorcist, but the threat of it is usually enough to pull him back in line.

Carter heaves a sigh. "Very well. I'll try to ring a bell or something. Oh, I know, a ghostly wind! If you feel the air stirring, know I am near."

Because that doesn't sound disturbing at all.

"Now, tell us everything, Ewan." He plants his elbows on the table and props his chin in his hands. It's eerie sometimes how solid and real ghosts can look.

I shrug. "I've basically told it all. I met Josh—you know who Josh is?"

He nods. "Hattie called a meeting. I'm quite looking forward to meeting him. It will be good to talk to a human without having to expend so much energy on manifesting." Somehow, he manages to make it sound like our fault we can't see dead people.

"We can't wait for you to do that either," I say with a straight face. "Anyway, I met Josh last night, then this morning Kieran hired him, and we realized we knew each other. That's it."

Carter narrows his eyes. "Did you just meet, or did you *meet*?"

"Carter, that's an intrusive question about Ewan's personal life," Daniel says solemnly. "I think it might even constitute sexual harassment."

"So report me to HR," Carter retorts. "You're not tricking me this time. I watch TV. I know how these things work. Kieran can't fire me, because I don't officially work here anymore. Even if I *do* try to help out." He sniffs, and Daniel rolls his eyes.

"We appreciate your help, Carter," I say, trying really hard not to laugh. Carter *loves* modern farming methods and drives Daniel to distraction insisting that we upgrade the farm. Last year he spent an entire afternoon trying to convince Kieran that demonstrating nineteenth-century farming practices was stupid and that if we'd just let him buy all the latest equipment, he could make the farm profitable.

Which... no. Even if the estate wasn't an immersive historic experience, there's no way the little bit of land remaining could be made profitable by farming alone. But Carter won't be dissuaded.

"But I'd really rather not discuss such personal details," I finish, crossing my toes that he'll accept it.

He sighs. "I don't know why you won't talk to me about your sexual exploits," he complains. "It's downright odd that you never bring anyone here to sodomize anymore. You always stay in town."

"It's just more convenient. Also, after what happened the last time..." Carter manifested in my bedroom while my date and I were *busy* and asked—loudly—if that position was comfortable, and wouldn't we get more pleasure if our limbs weren't at such odd angles?

Needless to say, my date *freaked out*. Ghosts can look astoundingly real, so first he thought I'd invited another guy in to watch. I finally convinced him—with a lot of unhelpful commentary from Carter—that our visitor was a ghost, and then he freaked out about that too. Nobody came that night.

Of course, that's nothing compared to the *first* time I brought someone back here. Carter had never seen two guys fucking before. Fortunately, he was already a big fan of *Ellen* and *Queer Eye*, so I didn't have to deal with any hate, but he was very interested in the mechanics of it all and had questions.

It's Carter's turn to roll his eyes. "Will you never forgive me for that? I've said I'm sorry. But how am I supposed to learn if I don't ask questions?"

Daniel snorts. "There's a time and a place for questions, Carter. That was not it."

Pouting, Carter turns puppy eyes on me. I used to have this image of nineteenth-century farmers being stoic and taciturn, but boy, have I learned different. Or maybe most of them were, and Carter's just adapted over the centuries. He does watch a lot of sitcoms and shitty reality TV. "But you'll tell me about your *meeting* with Josh, right?"

"No. You'll blab to all the other ghosts, and then someone will say something to Josh and make him feel uncomfortable. Which will make me the asshole for telling you in the first place."

He frowns. "You were the asshole? I thought it was called the bottom? And don't you prefer to—"

"Holy crap, Carter, stop talking now," Daniel shouts, laughing so hard I think he's going to fall off his chair. I bite my lip to hold in my own guffaws.

"I'm not talking to you about Josh," I tell Carter. "And you're not talking to the other ghosts about what you heard here. Okay?"

He grumbles but finally agrees.

"Good. Now, I'm going to finish my dinner before it gets completely cold."

"That's not interesting at all. I'm going up to the house to watch *Kardashian* reruns."

"Enjoy," Daniel says, sounding somewhat strangled.

We wait until we're fairly sure he's actually gone, killing time by talking about the weather and the upcoming hockey playoffs. Carter hates hockey, so it's not likely he'll stick around to hear about that.

"So…," Daniel begins. "You hooked up with the guy Kieran hired?"

"Complete accident." I shake my head. "We didn't even exchange names. Then he kicked me out this morning on his way into the bathroom."

"Yikes. Poor guy. Can't have been fun for him to turn up here and see you. Is he out, at least?"

Oh, wow. I hadn't even thought of that. "I think so? He wasn't trying to be discreet or anything when we met." Fuck, did I just out him to Daniel? "Dan—"

"Relax. I won't say a word. It's up to him if he wants to come out to me." He purses his lips. "He might think I already know? Maybe that's why he was being so weird today. He could barely look me in the eye."

"Really?" That is weird. People generally get along well with Daniel.

"Yeah. And conversation was a nonstarter. I was lucky to get short sentences instead of monosyllables. I'm not used to working so hard."

I shrug. "It wasn't like he was chatty last night, but he seemed okay this morning… until he wasn't. I dunno. I guess we'll have to wait and see."

"And hope Carter keeps his mouth shut in the meantime. Hey, do you think Josh could do something to keep Carter out of our bedrooms? It would be nice not to wake up to find a ghost watching me sleep."

"We can ask." That would be a luxury. And that's only the times we *see* him. Who knows when else he's watching us? I've gotten some creepy feelings while in the shower.

Daniel lifts his beer bottle and clinks it against my soda. "I've got a feeling things are going to change around here."

Chapter Five

JOSH

It doesn't take as long as I thought to pack up my life in Chicago, and isn't that sad. But it means I can move into my gorgeous new apartment so much sooner, so Saturday morning, I catch the first bus out of Chicago and arrive in town just before noon. Because buses are shit and take nearly five hours to cover what would have taken a third of that in a car.

But I'm here! I breathe in the glorious air of my new hometown, choke on the fumes of the departing bus, and swipe at my watering eyes. A couple of teenagers hanging out nearby snigger at me, but I'm okay with that. You know why? Because this wonderfully "new" bus station has not a single ghost. And even though my next stop is somewhere with a *lot* of ghosts, nobody will blink twice when I talk to them. My life is all sunshine and roses.

I yank out my phone and open the rideshare app. There's a car two minutes away, and I gleefully claim it, then gather my things together. When it pulls up, I'm surprised to see someone in the passenger seat. Are they being dropped—

Oh. Nope. Here's my first encounter with a town ghost. I open the back door and poke my head in. "Hey! Could you pop the trunk? I've got a few bags."

My driver, a guy in his early twenties whose profile says his name is Tom, says, "Sure," and hits the release. "Do you need a hand?"

"Nah, I got it." There's not *that* much, just a duffel and my backpack. The laptop bag with my million-year-old laptop can come in the back seat with me. And I have to sit in the back seat, because there's no way I'm sitting on the grandma ghost in the front passenger seat.

When I'm settled, Tom pulls smoothly out of the bus station parking lot and onto the road. "Are you having a weekend break at the estate?" he asks politely.

"It is bad enough you pick up strangers, Tommaso," the ghost says in a gloomy, accented voice. Spanish or Italian, maybe. I'm not sure which. "Try not to be memorable to them."

Oh man. This is not going to be fun. "Ah, actually, no. I've just been hired to work there."

"At the haunted house? Santa Maria," Grandma says, crossing herself. Which… does she realize she's a ghost herself?

"Oh wow, that's cool," Tom says. "Adele's old job, right? I'm friends with Skye."

"He is a nice boy, Skye, but his hair…" She clicks her tongue. "This is what happens when there is only one parent."

Oh my god. Digging the fingernails of my left hand into my right wrist to keep from laughing, I reply to

Tom. "I met Skye. He seems really cool. I'm looking forward to working with him."

"Tommaso, you drive too fast. You're just like your no-good uncle."

"You should join us for drinks one night," Tom continues blithely. "I know you're scheduled to work weekend nights, but we could do a weeknight."

"*Dio mio*, partying on a worknight," Grandma mutters. "What did I do to be punished like this?"

"That sounds great, thanks. Ah—"

"Tommaso, slow down! Why do you never listen? You didn't listen when I lived, and you don't listen now."

I cough to cover my hesitation. "Tom, has Skye told you about the ghosts at the estate?"

Tom shrugs and glances in the rearview. "Sure. But it's pretty much general knowledge around here. I was just a toddler when it was renovated, but my mom says high school kids used to go out there to hang out with the ghosts."

"Such a bad place. All those ghosts, and *not one* stopped the kids from making the babies," Grandma mourns.

"Hang out with them? That's a new one." My voice sounds a bit choked, and I make a show of coughing again. Oh my god, did Hattie and Maisie and the rest really just stand around watching while teenagers got it on? That's so gross.

Tom chuckles. "Yeah, but the way I heard it, the ghosts were so lonely, they welcomed the company of teens drinking beer."

Grandma just moans, burying her face in her hands.

"I'll bet. So you believe that ghosts exist?"

The look I get in the rearview this time is wary. "Yeah…"

"Great. Because there's one in your passenger seat who'd like you to slow down a bit, please."

The car swerves, and Grandma's head snaps up. She twists around. "You see me?"

"What the fuck?" Tom gasps, and she instantly turns her attention to him, smacking the back of his head… or at least she would have, if her hand hadn't gone right through him.

"Watch your mouth, Tommaso!"

"Is your name Tommaso?" I ask.

"Oh my *god*," he croaks. "Nonna? Is it my grandmother?" He eases up on the gas, and the car slows immediately.

I look at the ghost, who's turned around to look at me again. "Are you his grandmother, ma'am?" I ask. She's studying me like I'm something particularly nasty she scraped off her shoe.

"I am. Who are you? Do you have the devil in you?"

Heard that one before. Always makes me feel real good. "No, ma'am, there's no devil in me. My name's Josh, and I've always been able to talk to ghosts." Then I say to Tom, who's casting anxious glances at the passenger seat, "She says she's your grandmother."

"Holy—" He cuts himself off, possibly because he knows his grandmother won't like him swearing. "Nonna, what are you doing here? Have you been here since… um, all along? Why didn't you go to heaven or wherever?"

She sniffs. "How could I leave? Your mother is my greatest failure, and your no-good uncle is running the business into the ground. I had to stay and *try* to make them do better."

Wow, this is going to be a fun conversation. "Uh, she wanted to keep looking out for the family," I prevaricate, earning myself a glare from Grandma. Nonna? I don't know what to call her.

Tom laughs. "She just crapped on my mom and uncle, didn't she?"

Okay, that's a relief. "Pretty much."

"But, Nonna, why are you in the car right now instead of yelling at Zio that he's making the gnocchi the wrong way?"

"I needed a break. And someone needs to remind you not to drive like an idiot."

I relay that. Tom grins and rolls his eyes, then glances back at me. "Is this okay, you translating? I don't want to take advantage."

"It's fine," I assure him. "Usually it's just me and some lonely ghosts, so being able to facilitate a family reunion is nice." I wonder whether whatever mojo is going on at the estate will affect Nonna, or if that's limited to the ghosts who live there? Guess I'll find out soon enough.

The rest of the journey passes in three-way conversation. Nonna has a lot of instructions she wants to pass on, many of them accompanied by back-handed compliments or outright insults. Tom is both laughing and exasperated by the time he turns the car into the estate's driveway.

As the crackle of energy washes over me, Nonna's form becomes subtly more *real*. I've always had to look twice to tell the difference between living and dead people, but I noticed last week that it's even more tricky here on the estate. Tom half turns his head to say something to me and shrieks, running the car off the driveway and onto the lawn.

I guess it's not just ghosts who live here that can benefit from whatever the fuck is here.

"Tommaso, what are you doing?" Nonna shrieks. "You drive like your nonno, all over the road!"

Slamming the car into park, Tom jerks around in his seat. "Nonna?"

She gasps. "You see me?" Her hands rise to tidy her hair—which, just saying, she didn't care what she looked like when it was only me who could see her—and she fades a little.

"Where did you go?" Tom demands in a panic. "Nonna, come back!"

"You need to concentrate on being here," I tell her. "He can only see you if you put effort into it. It will tire you out," I warn, but I don't think she cares, because in the next second, she's so solid, I would swear she was alive.

"My Tommaso!" she exclaims, stretching out her arms. He reaches toward her cautiously, eyes going wide when he touches her hand and feels how solid it is.

"Ma'am, maybe tone down the solid body," I suggest. "It will use up all your energy and then you'll fade sooner."

Instantly, Tom's fingers sink into his grandmother's palm, and he yanks back. "That's creepy. But I'm so glad you're here, Nonna." His eyes get wet, and I decide it's time for me to go.

"Sorry to interrupt, but I'm just going to leave you now. Feel free to stick around and talk—I'll make sure Kieran and Skye know what you're doing."

They both turn glassy gazes on me. "Are you sure? Let me drive you up to the house, at least," Tom protests, and I laugh.

"Dude, it's like fifty feet away. Just pop the trunk so I can get my stuff. You have some catching up to do."

"Thank you," Nonna says sincerely. "You are a good boy, even if the devil is inside you."

"Um… thanks." I slide out of the car while Tom exasperatedly tells her she can't go around saying people have the devil in them. Leaving them to it, I collect my stuff and trudge up the driveway to the house. It's a lot busier today than when I came last week, with groups of people standing out the front and walking around. As I approach, I can see the paved parking area at the side of the house, where an assortment of cars and two tour buses are parked. Deciding to be smart, I avoid the front entrance and go around the side of the building to where the staff door is. I don't have a pass to open it, but if I recall correctly, it's about ten feet away from the kitchen window. Maybe I can get someone's attention and get them to let me in.

But as I get closer to the door, it opens and a man steps out, phone in one hand and coffee cup in the other. A big man with muscles that make my tummy feel funny. Who I know. Biblically.

Fuck.

Now what? Do I wait for him to go and then hope to find someone else?

Or do I act like a big boy and pretend this isn't awkward as fuck? Nothing good ever comes from sleeping with a coworker, even if he's not shacked up with another coworker.

I sigh. I'm going to have to work with him and his

boyfriend, so I guess I should start adulting now. Professional distance is the key.

"Hey," I call. "Ewan!"

He turns and looks at me. "Josh. You made it back."

Did he think I was going to disappear and leave Kieran in the lurch? Wow, what a great impression of me he has. So glad I let him fuck me.

"Yeah. I did. I was just wondering if you could let me in? I didn't want to drag this stuff through the front, but I need somewhere to stash it until I find Skye or Kieran and get some keys." I try not to sound as bitchy as I feel right now. If he wants to pretend it's no big deal to fuck around on his boyfriend, I can too. And, I mean, maybe it's not? For all I know, they have an open relationship. Maybe Daniel is cool with Ewan going to town once a week or whenever and boning a stranger. But I personally don't like getting involved in situations like that, so a heads-up would've been nice.

The worst part is that I don't know what their normal is. Like… even if they do have an open relationship, has Ewan told Daniel it was me he fucked? Do they talk about what they do with their… I don't know what to call it. Side pieces? Am I a side piece if it was a one-off? And does the situation change if Daniel has to work with the side piece, i.e. me? This is so complicated. I lift my hand to rub awkwardly at the side of my neck.

"No problem," he assures me, either not picking up on my antagonism or not giving a shit about it. His eyes are caught on my hand, and I drop it back to my side. "Cool nail polish. Kier said you were coming today and to keep an eye out for you. He's got your keys in the office. Let's go in, and I'll get them for you."

"I don't want to interrupt you," I blurt, closing my

hand in a fist, nails tucked inside. Did he mean it, or was he goading me? "If you can just let me in, I'll figure out the rest. You can go on your merry way."

For a second, he just looks at me. "Do you have a problem with me, Josh?"

"Why would I have a problem?" I challenge, then force a smile. Professional distance.

"I really don't know. Yeah, it's awkward finding out you now work with a guy you fucked, but it's not like we're exes. I thought we both had our expectations met and left on a good note."

My jaw drops.

"Are you not out, is that it?" he continues. "Are you worried I'm going to out you? Because I won't. But if you want to be out at work, this is a safe place to do it. I'm gay, so's Skye, Kieran's bi, and Arissa's ace. And that's only the senior staff. Intolerance isn't accepted here."

"I'm not closeted," I manage. Does he seriously not get why I might be a bit mad at him? That I don't appreciate being the "other guy" without prior knowledge? That it's damn awkward having to work with him and his boyfriend after we fucked?

"So what's the problem, then?" He stares me down. Like an asshole.

"You want to know my problem?" I begin, truly angry now. "Fine, I'll—"

"What's this? What's this? Surely both of you know better than to be shouting like children when there are guests around," hisses Freddie, appearing beside us suddenly enough to make me gasp.

"Where did you come from?" I ask. Sure, ghosts can zoom all over the place, including through walls, but he had to be pretty close to be able to hear us, and surely I would have noticed that.

He points up at the window one story above. "I was inspecting the housekeeper's work and overheard your very unprofessional behavior," he scolds.

Ewan sighs. "Leave the housekeepers alone, Freddie. They don't need you checking their work."

Freddie draws himself up to his full height—which is well short of Ewan's—and somehow manages to look down his nose at him. "Leave the affairs of the house to me, young man, and you worry about the smithy."

Shaking his head, Ewan rolls his eyes. "Show Josh where Kieran left his keys, would you?" He switches his coffee to the hand holding his phone, managing to hang on to them both without disaster, and digs into his pocket. A second later, the electronic lock on the door has released and he's holding it open for me.

I scramble to get my bags inside, mumbling, "Thanks."

"Whatever. See you round."

As he walks away and the door swings closed, Freddie shoots inside to join me in the combination mudroom/storage room. "Well," he says, sounding very self-satisfied, "allow me to convey you to the office."

Shaking off my anger at Ewan, I make myself smile. "That's very kind of you. Can I leave my bags here, do you think?"

Freddie eyes them. "I suppose so. They're not very attractive. Why don't you have a nice set of matched luggage?"

"For the same reason I need to work for a living. I have no money." I shove my stuff into a corner. "Come on. It's this way, right?"

Keeping pace with me as I stride through the staff-only area and into the main hall, Freddie says, "When do you officially begin working? Kieran said we're not to bring our problems to you until then, but I have an issue of some urgency that needs attention at once."

Uh-huh, I bet he does. "Will a delay of two days result in death or bodily harm to anyone or damage to the estate?" I ask.

He tilts his head and squints, considering it. "I suppose not."

"Then it can wait until I officially begin work on Monday. After nine in the morning," I add, just so I don't have him waking me at 12:01.

He sighs. "Very well."

We go through the guest parlor into the public part of the house. The living room has people in it today, a small group getting snacks and drinks, and a few couples sitting and chatting. Probably waiting their turn for a guide, or maybe resting between activities. I make sure the door to the private area closes properly behind me, smile vaguely at the people who've looked up, and walk into the front entrance. There are a lot more people here, some standing around, looking at brochures, others waiting in line at reception, where Skye and Kieran are efficiently looking after them. There's a woman in period costume, who I assume is one of the guides, counting heads, and then she instructs the group to keep close and leads them down the hall toward the museum, which clears out the space a bit.

"Uh…" I turn to Freddie, then realize I'm not sure if he's manifested or not. "Can everyone else see you right now?" I whisper out of the side of my mouth.

"No," he says, "but I would be happy to manifest if that's your preference."

Suddenly appear in the middle of a room full of people? I'm beginning to see what Kieran meant about needing a ghost wrangler.

"That's fine," I whisper, trying not to move my lips. "Did Kieran leave my keys in the office?"

"Indeed he did. In the top desk drawer, I believe. Allow me to show you."

We walk toward the reception desk, getting a snarky comment about cutting the line. Kieran looks up, but then smiles when he sees me.

"I'm not cutting," I assure the annoyed visitor. "I work here."

"Hey, Josh," Kieran says. "Here to get your keys? Give me a few minutes, and I'll—"

"It's fine," I tell him softly. "Freddie will show me where."

He blinks at me, then his eyes widen and shoot to the space beside me—unfortunately, not the side Freddie's standing on. The ghost huffs in disapproval.

"He's on my right," I mutter, and Kieran's gaze flicks over.

"Apologies, Freddie," he says quietly. "Josh, get settled, and we can chat later. Tell Arissa and the others that your lunch is on us today."

"Thank you." I sidle around the big desk and go into the office, grateful for his offer. I may have forgotten that I'll need to stock my brand-new kitchen with groceries before I can eat. Hmm… I wonder if the grocery store delivers out this far? If not, I'll be making a regular Uber trip to the store and back. If I end up keeping this job for as long as I'd like to, it'd probably be cheaper to learn to drive and buy an old banger of a car.

Something to think about.

Freddie's hovering impatiently beside Kieran's desk. There are two in the room, but his is the one covered in clutter. I'm not sure if he's naturally the kind of person who has a messy workspace or if this is a reflection of how busy he's been lately.

"Top drawer," Freddie prods when I don't move fast enough to suit him.

"Thanks." I slide the drawer open and find an assortment of pens, a box of paperclips, some Post-it Notes, and a set of keys on a blue lanyard. Attached to the lanyard is a silver rectangular name tag with my name engraved in black. Kieran must have raced right out to the key place or wherever to have that made up so quick. "Got them," I declare, closing the drawer again and slipping the lanyard over my head. The weight of the keys settles against my chest, and I love it. Belonging, here I am.

I sneak back out of the office, waving to Skye when he smiles at me, then use my very own fob to let myself back into the guest-only part of the house. Freddie follows, chattering about how he's always liked the elegance of the silver name badges, but they just don't have the same *class* and *distinction* that a matte gold would, don't I agree?

"I never thought about it," I tell him. "Different types of name tags aren't high on my priority list."

"Sorry?" a female voice asks, and I whirl to see a woman standing in the doorway of the library.

Uh-oh.

"Apologies," I say as cheerfully as I can manage. "I didn't mean to interrupt you."

"Oh, no, you didn't… I thought I heard voices…" Her gaze darts around as though trying to see who I was talking to.

"And came out to listen? How terribly rude." Freddie sniffs.

When better to try out my new life? "That was me," I tell her. "Just chatting with one of our ghosts. I'm Josh, and I work here." It gives me a little thrill every time I say that.

"Oh! Well…" She laughs uncertainly. "I guess we *were* told this place was haunted. Is… is the ghost still here?"

Freddie puffs himself up.

"Nope!" I declare, hoping he'll take his cue from me. His chest deflates. "He got bored when we started talking. But I'm sure you'll see at least one ghost during your stay. Have a great day!" I give a little wave and keep walking in the direction of the staff-only area.

"Lying is a contemptible habit, Josh," Freddie lectures me. "Why didn't you tell that woman the truth?"

I wait until I'm through the door to answer. Can't have her overhearing again and realizing I bold-faced lied to her. "The thing is, Freddie, even people who like the idea of ghosts get a bit unsettled when said ghosts just pop out of thin air. It makes them wonder if they're being watched *all* the time."

Freddie takes a moment to consider this while we duck back into the mudroom, and I load myself up with my bags.

"But they often are being watched all the time," he points out.

"Yes, but they don't want to know that. They prefer to think of ghosts as beings they might encounter and not realize aren't living until after the fact."

"Ahhhh." He nods. "Is that why gentlemen are perfectly happy to flirt with that jezebel, Maisie, and invite her back to their rooms, but then curse up a storm when they discover she's a ghost?"

Note to self: be prepared for male guests to call me swearing in the middle of the night.

"Something like that. If they don't realize at first that she's a ghost, to have her seemingly disappear when, uh… at a key moment is quite confronting."

Tapping his finger to his lips, he says, "You've given me much to consider. I'll take my leave of you now, if you know where you need to go next?"

"By all means," I assure him. "Thank you for your help."

With a polite nod, he strides back toward the main hall, walking right through the door. I've seen it happen a million times, and it still makes me blink.

Okay… next stop, food. I poke my head into the kitchen, where Arissa greets me warmly.

"Kieran said I could grab lunch here today, if that's okay?" I ask.

"Absolutely. What do you want? We've got salads and sandwiches, or the hot option is dumplings."

"A sandwich would be perfect. Is takeout possible? I don't want to get under your feet here, and I want to start getting my stuff settled."

Two minutes later, I've got a wrapped turkey sandwich, chips, and a cookie tucked in my laptop bag and am heading for the elevator. I make a mental note to do something nice for the kitchen staff. I definitely want to stay on their good side.

I let myself into my apartment with a sigh of relief, to find that someone's opened the windows and a fresh breeze is wafting in. A huge smile overtakes my face. I can't believe I get to live here.

My attention is caught by a bunch of stuff on the island, and I divest myself of my bags and go to check it out. There's a small basket of whole fruit, a loaf of bread, and a jar of peanut butter, along with a card.

Welcome aboard, Josh! Here's your starter pack. Bottomless coffee and tea downstairs for all staff. We're so glad you've joined us.

Your new workmates

I think this smile might be permanently etched into my cheeks.

Chapter Six

JOSH

"Knock knock, dear! Can we come in?"

I glance toward the door. Was that…? Sighing, I give in to the inevitable and get up. Before I even reach the door, I can hear them quietly squabbling among themselves.

"…sounds foolish. You should have manifested and knocked properly. Saying 'knock knock' lacks gravitas."

"I don't need gravitas. We're not trying to impress him with our status, we're trying to befriend him!"

"I'm not trying to befriend him. We'll be acquaintances and work colleagues only. Friends! I think not."

I pause and listen, trying to see if I can identify the voices. I'm pretty sure the first one was Hattie, but I don't recognize the person she's arguing with. Male, but his voice is too low-pitched to be Freddie or Johnny.

"Well, I'm gonna make him my friend," another voice says, and I'm sure this one is Johnny. "I want a union rep!"

"And I need a man to look after me," Maisie adds

plaintively. "I'd prefer him to look after *all* my needs, but I can settle for a gay BFF."

Oh my god. I snatch the door open before that goes any further. "Um, hello?"

Creepily, they all turn to look at me as one. Six ghosts are standing outside my door, and I'm suddenly very aware that I'm only wearing boxers and an undershirt. What? It's eight at night and I was planning to spend the evening on my couch, alone. But Maisie—who's wearing a satin hoop skirt with a midriff-baring leather bustier—puts a hand to her mouth and giggles, and I wish I'd stopped to put on pants.

"You're a disgrace," one of the ghosts I don't know, a man dressed in a suit that looks like what Skye was wearing the other day, declares. "What kind of gentleman parades around in his underwear?" He's got heavy, bushy eyebrows that give the impression he's scowling… or maybe he really is scowling. He turns to Hattie. "I don't need to talk to him. My vote is no. We need a warrior, not… this." He waves his hand contemptuously at me.

"Great," I say cheerfully. "Good night, then." I begin to close the door, but with a surge of energy I can actually feel, Freddie manifests and sticks out his arm to stop me.

"No, wait," he demands. "Please forgive us for interrupting your evening. We know you don't start work until Monday, but this is… er, that is, we wanted a chance to become acquainted outside of work."

This is weird, right? Freddie, Hattie, Johnny, and Maisie are looking at me with big, hopeful eyes. The grumpy ghost is still scowling, and the other one, a big man wearing a flannel shirt and jeans, is studying me intently, head tipped to the side.

They must take my hesitation as agreement, because Hattie pushes forward. "You've met nearly everyone, but this is Carter," she waves at the farmer ghost, "and this is Joe."

A distant bell rings in my mind. Didn't she mention a grumpy Joe the other day?

"Don't mind Joe," she continues chattily. "He doesn't watch as much TV as we do, and he hasn't seen what people wear outside the estate these days. But I watch Pride every year," she confides, "so I know you're decently attired."

What. Is. Happening.

"Uh... I wasn't expecting company, or I would have put on something else," I manage. Am I actually making excuses? "Thanks for... uh, knocking, by the way." Fair's fair, after all. They could have just floated on in.

"We's respecting your boundaries," Johnny says, with the careful cadence of a phrase just learned. Today he has teardrop tattoos under his eyes, and the mohawk is startlingly bright red.

"I appreciate it."

We stand there. Staring at each other. In the doorway.

They're not leaving. I could tell them to come back tomorrow—or that I don't want to be friends—but is it worth it? I want to work here for a long time. I need to be on good terms with these ghosts.

Finally, I sigh. "Why don't you come in for a few minutes? We can have a chat. Just a quick one," I warn. "I'm pretty tired after moving." I stand back and allow them to troop in through the door. Johnny gets impatient waiting for his turn and enters through the wall instead. Since I did just invite him in, I can't complain about it, but I don't want him getting into the habit.

By the time I close the door, they've made themselves comfortable, Hattie, Maisie, and Freddie on the couch, Johnny and Carter on the barstools, and Joe in the armchair by the window. Which leaves me the option of sitting on my bed or standing. I opt for the latter, grabbing the remote from the coffee table and turning off the TV, then hovering in front of it.

Now what? I can't exactly offer them a drink. Partly because I don't have anything but tap water to offer, but mostly because they're ghosts.

"So you're not a medium?" Joe barks at me from the window. I jump.

"Uh, no."

"Why not?"

"Because I've had no training?" Is this a job interview? Whatever it is, I don't want it.

"But you have the ability to be a medium?"

"I guess? The other medium I met said I did. And I've always been able to see and talk to ghosts."

He narrows his eyes at me. "Ever forced a ghost to cross over?"

I shake my head. "I've helped a few who wanted to. But I wouldn't know how to force it."

Turning to Hattie, he says, "He's no good to us."

"He can learn," she insists exasperatedly. "The most important things are that he has the talent and he's a nice boy!"

"Um, excuse me," I begin, because it sounds like they want me to force ghosts to cross over, and what the holy hell?

But Joe's not done with the cross-examination. He asks me my opinion of the current government, the former one, *Star Wars*—all nine movies, with a disconcerting focus on the topic of fascism—and a dizzying array of books and movies from the last century. Then he asks if I make any charitable contributions—um, what part of me being broke does he not understand?—and poses a series of "what would you do if" questions, most of which are about me choosing whether to save someone's life or assure myself personal gain.

I'm so confused. And getting really annoyed. I mean... what the heck is this? Finally, just when I'm on the verge of telling Joe to fuck off and kicking them all out, he looks at Hattie and says, "I suppose he'll do."

Maisie claps her hands, causing a multitude of bangles to clack together. "Yay! I knew my gay BFF would win you over!"

The beginnings of a headache throb behind my eyes.

The ghosts are all smiling at me—except Joe, who I don't think ever smiles.

"What's going on?" I demand.

"Just getting to know you, dear. You have such a nice aura." Hattie pats her hair.

"We all got good feelings about you," Johnny adds.

"And Ewan likes you," Carter says. "He's an excellent judge of character."

I blink. "He... does?" He barely knows me. And our encounter today wasn't exactly positive.

Carter blushes.

Oh. My. God.

Did Ewan talk to the ghosts about...?

No. Surely he wouldn't?

But the only other reason for Carter to blush while talking about Ewan liking me is if he overheard Ewan telling Daniel… right? Or did Ewan just tell everyone?

Humiliation washes through my whole body, but I shove it aside. I'll deal with Ewan and his loose lips another time. For now, I just want to get these ghosts out of my apartment so I can fall asleep in front of the TV.

As if she hears my thoughts, Hattie stands. "Well, I suppose we'll leave you to it!"

I blink. What? That's it? "Um… okay?"

They get to their feet and move toward the door, thanking me for having them over, assuring me I'm welcome to visit them at any time, and wishing me luck with my new job. When I finally close the door behind them, I stare at it blankly. I think I might have missed something important, but fucked if I know what it was.

My first full day at the estate begins with me lazily waking in a big, comfortable bed to sun-washed walls. I grin at the ceiling. There are worse things in life.

Rolling over, I snag my phone and see it's still early, just after seven, but I get up and head to the shower. Even though I don't officially start work until tomorrow, Sunday is one of the busiest days here, so this is my chance to observe, learn, and help when I'm needed.

By eight, I've showered, breakfasted, and tidied my apartment—because the novelty of having such a nice place hasn't worn off yet—and I'm in the staff break room, enjoying the coffee I just got from the kitchen, when I hear voices approaching.

A second later, Ewan and Daniel stroll in, holding coffee cups.

"Oh, hey, Josh!" Daniel greets me with a big smile on his tanned face. "I didn't know you were here already."

Ewan didn't tell him?

"I arrived yesterday." I make myself meet his gaze and return the smile. If my guess after Carter's little slip last night was right, and Daniel does know about me and Ewan, at least he doesn't seem upset about it. I'm glad—he's really open and friendly, one of those perennially cheerful people who manages not to be annoying about it. And he's hot. Not as built as Ewan, but still fit and muscular.

"Ah, so you don't have coffee upstairs yet. We ran out because we're idiots who hate to shop."

I lift my cup in salute. "At least you're not an idiot who forgot he'd need groceries. And doesn't have a car."

"Ouch," Ewan says. "That's going to be a challenge for you."

I make an agreeing noise, trying to keep my gaze from lingering on his broad torso. They're both wearing period clothes, although not like what Skye and the guides wear. No confining jackets or scarf things around their necks. Their shirts are open at the collar and down to their sternums, with seemingly no buttons, sleeves rolled up to reveal their forearms. Their pants aren't as well-tailored as Skye's, seeming a bit looser, the fabric not as fine. At a guess, I'd say these are "work" clothes, whereas Skye and the guides dress in higher fashion.

Whatever, it's disturbingly attractive. Who knew I had a secret fantasy about being ravished by a blacksmith?

"You can borrow my car if you want," Daniel offers, sliding into a chair at the table. "Just let me know when you need it."

I don't know what to say. That's really nice of him. "Uh, thanks. But I actually don't have a license. I don't know how to drive."

He shrugs. "I can give you a ride, then."

Oh my god, why is he so nice? Floundering, I look to Ewan for help. He's frowning at me.

"How come you can't drive?" he asks like an asshole.

I glare at him, then remember my professionalism. "Mostly because of ghosts. I would react a lot to people who weren't really there, and that made my driving erratic. There are a lot of ghosts in urban and suburban areas, and it was just safer for me not to drive. It wasn't a big deal in Chicago, with all the transit available."

"I can teach you to drive," he offers, then seems surprised by it.

"I… um. Really?" I want to say no, because distance is key, but I also really want to learn to drive.

He shrugs. "Sure. There's lots of room to do it here on the estate, and we'll tell the ghosts to keep clear until you're confident. Then you can apply for a permit and we can go out on some of the quieter roads. Are there many ghosts around here?"

I shake my head, still a little dazed by the idea that I could finally learn to drive. Even if it would be Ewan teaching me. "No. That's part of why I was so keen to get this job."

"Think about it. There's no rush to decide. In the meantime, I'm going grocery shopping late this afternoon, after I'm done in the smithy. You're welcome to come with me."

Oh my god, I don't think I can handle this. I'm going to have to shred my pride and just accept that whatever they've got going on seemingly has nothing to do with me. My night with Ewan is in the past and we're all just going to forget about it. I have to, because I think these guys would make good friends.

But it's just so weird.

"Thanks," I croak. "That would be great."

Ewan smiles at me and then asks Daniel if the shopping list on the fridge is up-to-date, and they chat about domestic stuff for a few minutes while I try to get my head around the whole complicated situation.

"Are you still good to settle the animals tonight so I can go out with Leanne?" Daniel asks, putting his empty coffee cup on the table.

"Sure. Things are getting pretty serious between you two. How many dates is this?"

"Seven or nine. It depends when you started counting." He shrugs. "But I think she's just using me to pass the time. She's saving to move to California. Wants to be a beach girl, whatever that means."

"You seem so heartbroken about being used," Ewan teases, and he laughs.

"I'm not the commitment type. A woman who wants to use me for sex and company until she gets a better option is basically my dream come true."

I bump the table in my shock, and my cup tips, spilling the last of my coffee. I swear and grab some napkins to mop it up, trying to make sense of this new information. Daniel's dating a woman, which, if they have an open relationship makes sort of sense, but he's not the commitment type? Who would say that to their live-in partner?

Unless I've got it wrong?

"Damn, bet you're sad about that. Want some more? I'm going to get a refill," Daniel offers.

"Please," I beg, head spinning, and he laughs as he snags my mug and strolls out.

"Do you need some more napkins? I think there's some in one of the cupboards." Ewan glances at the sodden mess in my hand, and his eyes linger. Is he staring at my green nails?

"No, I'm good. There wasn't that much left."

Awkward silence descends.

This is my chance to try to understand what their deal is. All I need to do is ask, right?

Too bad I can't think of a good way to bring it up.

Words would be a good start. Any words. Hellooooo, words?

Nope.

So we sit. In awkward silence. While Ewan sips the dregs of his coffee and I desperately wish I had some. Caffeine makes the brain work, right?

I have to say *something*. Our working relationship can't continue this way.

"Are you—"

"Can you—"

We both stop. Whaddaya know, just when I thought things couldn't get more awkward… they did.

"You go," he offers.

I swallow. "Ah, thanks. I was just, um, wondering if… if you… could tell me about your house!" It's perfect! Maybe he'll drop a clue to tell me what their living situation actually is.

"Sure," he agrees, although he seems surprised. "I hate to disappoint you, but it's just a house. Although if you're interested in the historic aspect, that's pretty cool. You should get Carter to give you a tour." He pauses. "Have you met Carter yet?"

"Last night," I say. "The ghosts came over to get to know me." My tone is dry, and he grins.

"Well, he knows everything there is to know about the house. He used to live there, when he was alive."

"Oh. He did?"

He nods enthusiastically. "Yeah. That's why he mostly haunts there. I'm kind of lucky, because he prefers Daniel's room, but that doesn't stop him from peeking into mine." He stops suddenly, and I really wish I knew what it was he was going to say.

But he's given away plenty already. I guess I might be the dumbass in this situation... but I need to be sure. "So, uh, you, uh… you and Daniel have separate rooms?"

It takes him a minute to understand what I'm saying, and when the penny—and his jaw—finally drops, we're interrupted by Daniel walking back in, balancing three mugs in his hands.

"Here we go! Ewan, I got you another one too." He studies him. "What's wrong with your face?"

"I… swallowed a bug."

"Well, you do like protein for breakfast."

Oh my god, what does that mean? Is it the kind of dumb thing friends and roommates say to each other, or is it a cutesy cum joke between boyfriends?

"Coffee will wash it down." Daniel passes Ewan a mug. "And if not, well, you still need coffee. I know what it takes to get you up in the morning."

And that! Was that an innocent comment on Ewan

liking to sleep in, or a double entendre about what Daniel does to get Ewan "up"?

"Thanks," Ewan croaks, shooting me a wide-eyed look.

"I'm going to head out and see if there are any snails in my lettuce," Daniel says, lifting his mug in salute. "See you both later."

Finally, he leaves.

"Daniel's straight," Ewan blurts. "And not straight in a 'blowjobs in the frat house don't count' kind of way. He's never even thought of being with a man. Definitely not with me. We have our own bedrooms. And beds. Alone." He takes a breath. "And if I was with someone, I wouldn't cheat." I can tell he doesn't like the idea of me thinking he would.

My face is burning hot, but I manage a nod. "I didn't think you'd cheat. Exactly. I wondered if maybe you were poly or something. And it's cool with me if you are; I just like to know upfront if the guy I'm banging has a partner already. Not that I'm looking for more than sex," I add quickly. "It's just a... thing. For me. In my head. Oh my god, why can't I just die right now?"

He laughs. It sounds a bit strangled, but it's still a laugh. "Please don't die. The last thing this place needs is another ghost haunting it."

"You have no idea." I sigh. "I'm sorry for jumping to conclusions and being an asshole."

"Apology accepted. Although, just gotta say, I like your asshole."

I grin, but then it falls away. I'm glad we've got this cleared up, so glad I don't have to worry about having ruined workplace relationships before they even began, but this miscommunication is just proof that I can't take risks like this. Mannix Estate is a dream come true for me, and I can't gamble that on sexual attraction.

"What?" He seems wary.

"We had a great night," I say regretfully. "Really, really great. Like… I think you might have ruined me for all other men." Just remembering it makes my cock stir.

From the way he shifts uncomfortably in the hard wooden chair, he might be having the same problem. "Thanks? You were amazing too. My mind is still blown."

"Yeah… but we shouldn't do it again." It almost hurts to force those words out.

"Is it because we work together? Or do you just not do repeats?"

I open my mouth to respond, then stop. "I was going to say of course I do repeats, but I don't think I ever have?" Frowning, I think about it. There was that guy… but he never called me back.

"What, never? What about boyfriends? They count." There's naked shock in his voice.

I try to smile, but I'm sure it's more like a grimace. This is so sad. "No boyfriends. There, uh, were a couple of guys I thought maybe… but the ghost thing was too much for them."

"Want me to beat them up for you?" he offers. It's a stupid thing to say, but a laugh bursts from my throat.

"Thanks, but it's fine. I'm used to it."

That was the wrong thing to say, because his face goes dark with anger. "I hope nobody here makes you feel that way?"

Oh my god, why is he making this so hard? "Nah,

everyone's been great. I finally feel like I've found my place, you know?"

"Yeah." He nods. "There's not a lot of call for blacksmiths these days, unless I wanted to work in industrial manufacturing—which I didn't. Here, I get to indulge my fascination with complex metalwork. I also get to share my love of it with others, and I'm surrounded by like-minded people." He hesitates. "Plus, from the minute I stepped foot onto the estate, I felt like I was home."

I swallow. "I know what you mean."

He meets my gaze steadily. "So, if it's not that you don't do repeats, it's the whole working together thing?"

I grimace again and nod. "This place is such a miracle for me. I can't risk that going bad by fooling around with a colleague."

"I respect that. I just want to add, though, that if you change your mind, I would never do anything to make you uncomfortable here. Well, not deliberately," he adds, clearly thinking about the whole me-thinking-he-and-Daniel-were-together mix-up.

"I don't think it works that way. But thanks. If I change my mind, you'll be the first to know."

There's another awkward lull, and then he levers himself out of his chair. "I guess I'd better get to the smithy and prep for today. I'm glad we talked."

My smile is genuinely happy this time. It's so good to know I'm not going to have work issues from the outset. "Me too. But, um, could you maybe not tell anyone about the mix-up? I'm sure I'll find it funny in a few days, but until then…"

"My lips are sealed," he promises. "Just so you know, Daniel would find it funny… and I'd be the target of his teasing. He'd be all 'you wish you could score with me.'" He rolls his eyes, then hesitates. "In the interest of honesty, he knows about you and me. It came out that first day you were here. I'm sorry."

I wave a hand, not surprised. "It's fine. I mean, I hope you didn't go into too much detail—"

"None, I swear."

"Then don't worry. I guessed he did, anyway, since Carter seems to know."

He groans. "I hope he's not being weird? He has this weird fetish about gay sex. I didn't know he was listening until it was too late."

"I'm used to ghosts, remember? It's cool."

He hovers for another few seconds. "So… see you later."

"Have a good day, Ewan."

He walks out before I can do anything embarrassing, like throw myself at his feet and beg to suck his dick. I need friends right now more than I need a convenient sex partner. No matter how good the sex was.

Chapter Seven

EWAN

I'm still shaking my head over the idea of me and Daniel being together when I pull up to the house late in the afternoon. I called ahead to let Josh know I was coming, and he's waiting for me. He gets into the car and reaches for the seat belt.

"Thanks for this," he says as I turn the car down the driveway. "It saves me getting an Uber and potentially having to deal with another grandma ghost."

I side-eye him. He's looking at the road ahead, but there's a tiny, exasperated smile on his lips as he remembers whatever the grandma ghost thing was. His hand rises to scratch his neck, and the dark metallic green color on his nails grabs my attention again. I noticed it yesterday, then again this morning, but seeing it still makes me hot for reasons I don't understand.

Stop lying to yourself.

Okay, so maybe I can't help picturing Josh's hand wrapped around my cock, those colorful nails gleaming against my skin as he works me over. Seems I have a fetish for… nail polish?

I swallow hard and turn my attention back to the road. "No problem at all," I say in belated response to his thanks. "Especially since I was coming anyway. But if you ever need a lift into town, just let me know." Even if we hadn't sorted out the weirdness between us, I would have said that. Because as great as Mannix Estate is, it would suck to be trapped there. If seeing ghosts has made something as ordinary as learning to drive difficult, I honestly can't imagine how tough he had it with everything else.

Sneaking another sideways glance, I'm glad to see his smile is a little broader. He looks relaxed and happy. Granted, I've only met him a couple of times before today, but both those times he seemed tense.

I clear my throat. "Do you mind if I ask about the ghost thing?"

From the corner of my eye, I see him turn his head toward me. "The ghost thing?" He sounds amused. "Go ahead. It's nice to be able to talk about it and not have people look at me like I'm nuts."

"I'll bet." Man, that would suck. "Have you always been able to see them, or was there something that happened… or, like, did it come with puberty…?" I should have paid more attention to movies about this stuff.

He chuckles. "Nah, nothing like that. I've always been able to see them. When I was little, my parents used to joke that I didn't have one imaginary friend, I had a whole army of them. They found it less funny when I got older and it didn't stop, and then when I told them it was ghosts, not my imagination, they put me in therapy. That didn't change a lot. I stopped talking about it as much, but the ghosts would still pop up, and I'd get a start, or one of them would talk to me on the street and I'd answer before I realized it was a ghost, so my parents knew I was still seeing them. They talked about having me medicated for hallucinations, but Mom read up on some of the side effects of those drugs and decided she didn't want to do that." He's silent for a second, and when I look over, his face is sad.

"We don't have to talk about it."

He sighs and musters a smile. "It's fine. I was just thinking I was pretty lucky. I only ever met one or two aggressive ghosts when I was a kid, so it wasn't a negative thing, you know? Just like having people constantly around. They'd tell me stories and sing me to sleep—I was never afraid to sleep, because the ghosts would keep me company. And then when I got older and decided I wanted privacy, I got online and read that ghosts won't cross a salt line, so I convinced my mom to let me salt my bedroom. It gave me a space where I could be alone. When she saw how that worked, she salted the whole house. School and other places were still hectic, but at least at home I had peace. It could have been worse. I could have been haunted by aggressive ghosts constantly, or medicated, or even institutionalized. As an adult, it's easy to see how lucky I am, even if it doesn't feel like it sometimes."

I hold back my shudder. I've never thought about people who see ghosts, but he's right. Our society isn't designed to protect them. I wonder how many other mediums—is that the right word?—weren't as lucky as Josh growing up.

"It's funny," he continues, his voice hardening, "that

after everything with the ghosts, the reason I don't see my parents anymore is because I'm gay."

The words fall like a stone between us. "I'm so sorry," I say instinctively. It's not the first time I've heard something like that—without the ghosts—but it still makes my chest ache. I know how incredibly lucky I am to have parents who love and accept me for who I am, even more so after having met so many people whose families turned their backs.

"It could have been worse." He shrugs. "I came out when I was fifteen, and they told me never to bring it up again. So I didn't. And when I turned eighteen, two weeks after I graduated from high school, they suggested it was time for me to leave. It was all very calm and civilized… if you can call cutting ties with your only kid civilized."

"It's not." I clench my hands around the steering wheel.

"It's not," he agrees. "But that was when I realized how easy I'd had it with the ghosts. I crashed with a friend for a while, but without the salt to keep the ghosts away, I wore out my welcome fast. I never had many friends, because they all thought I was twitchy and weird"—I cough to cover a laugh. It's not funny, damn it—"so I had to become independent very quickly. I wasn't a kid for the ghosts to dote on anymore, and they were a lot more demanding with an adult. I kept losing jobs because the ghosts would startle me, or my boss would catch me talking to 'myself.'" He makes air quotes with his fingers. "Chicago has a dense population, which means a lot of ghosts. I've been trying to get together enough money to move to a small town for years. This job is…" He trails off. "It's a miracle."

I guess it would be. "Have the ghosts been nice since you arrived? Our ghosts, I mean." Not that I can do anything if they haven't. Maybe lecture them? Also, I wish someone had told me about the salt thing earlier. It would work better to keep Carter out of my room than threats of exorcism. I mentally add a lot of salt to my shopping list.

The smile is back in his voice when he says, "They're great. Friendly and very respectful of my space. It's only been one night, but they waited to be invited in, which is a good sign."

"You'll have to teach me that trick," I mutter dryly.

"I'll talk to them," he promises. "Maisie doesn't bother you, does she? I've heard about her search for a man."

"She visited me the first night I moved in." And dispelled any idea I might have had about women from the nineteenth century being prudish. I've never blushed so hard in my life. "But I made it very clear that women aren't my thing, and she's left me alone since. I think she still makes an appearance in Daniel's room sometimes. He convinced her he's not relationship material and that anything else would make things awkward between them, but she likes to check if he's changed his mind."

He groans. "I'm definitely going to need to talk to her. I feel sorry for her, but she can't keep harassing people like this." He pauses. "Speaking of Daniel…"

It's my turn to groan. "He said you'd talked to him. Why? I thought you wanted to keep it quiet." Dan laughed so hard when he told me, tears were streaming down his face.

"I did, but I was kind of an ass to Daniel last week, when I didn't know what the fuck was going on, and I thought I should apologize. It all came out somehow. He's very easy to talk to."

"It's his superpower," I grouch. "People like him, and they tell him things." Though why he wants to spend that much time with people is something I'll never understand.

"That makes sense. I didn't plan to do more than apologize, but he smiled and said it was fine and he hoped we could be friends, and suddenly the whole stupid story was just blurting out of my mouth." He sounds disgruntled. "Johnny was there, so the rest of the ghosts will know all about it by now."

I wince. "They do like to gossip." Which is how they all know my dick size and that I prefer to top. Why Carter thought that was information worth sharing, I'll never know. I always just assumed that people in the nineteenth century were prudish about sex, but these ghosts have taught me otherwise. Either that, or death has caused them to lose all respect for boundaries.

"Okay, you've heard my story. Now tell me yours. How'd you become a blacksmith? That's not a common career path."

"It's really not," I agree. "But the story's not exciting. My uncle runs a dressage school and riding stable. I've always loved animals, spent as much time in the stables as I could, and my first part-time job as a teenager was there, cleaning tack and mucking out. One time when I was about seventeen, the farrier was there at the same time as me, and we got talking. When he saw how interested I was, he suggested I spend some time shadowing him, see if an apprenticeship was something I wanted to consider."

"Mmm," Josh says. "A farrier? That's like a blacksmith for horses, right?"

I laugh. "Kind of. These days, they're mostly about hoof care and health. A lot of farriers don't make their own horseshoes anymore, since it's easier and cheaper to buy manufactured ones. Albert, the farrier I shadowed, was old-school about stuff like that, though, and said learning basic forge skills was part of the job, though of course it was a modern one, not like the one I have in the smithy. He showed me how to make horseshoes, and I fell in love with the forge." It sounds stupid saying it out loud like that, and I feel my cheeks get hot, but Josh makes an encouraging sound, so maybe he gets it. "I started doing some hobby classes whenever I could, and when I graduated high school, I apprenticed to a blacksmith artist. She taught me most of what I know about finer metalwork and also got me into the Renaissance Faire circuit."

"Whoa," Josh interrupts. "Whoa, whoa, whoa. Are you talking about those fairs where everyone dresses up and talks like olden times?"

Grinning, I answer, "It's not that simple, but yes. There's a big market for metal crafts there."

"Did you, uh, wear a whatchamacallit… a codpiece?" He sounds a bit dazed at the thought.

"I did," I confirm. "Still have it, in fact."

"Mmm." When I look over, his eyes are glazed. Then he shakes his head and meets my gaze. "Sorry. Just… thinking. Um, you were talking about your apprenticeship."

Just thinking, my ass. Or about my ass, more like. "Yeah, well, at the Ren Faire I got to meet smiths who specialized in old-style smithing. The two main streams for blacksmithing work these days are art or industrial, and I was already pretty sure I didn't want to do industrial work, but then I started learning about the history of blacksmithing and how to craft things that we make with machines these days, and that was it for me. I finished my apprenticeship and joined the Faire circuit in my own right, focusing more on the history side than the crafts. I also started my own online store. My reputation started to build, and things were going well. Then after six years, Kieran contacted me and said they were looking for a new blacksmith at Mannix Estate, and would I be interested in an interview."

"He just contacted you? There was no ad or anything?" Josh sounds dubious. "Does that mean you're like blacksmith royalty?"

I snort. "No. There's no blacksmith royalty. But my rep was good, and the pool of blacksmiths who do old-style stuff and know all the history is pretty small."

"Right, but I bet there aren't many jobs like this available, so the competition would still be pretty fierce."

My cheeks are getting hot again. "Maybe," I concede.

"If I ask Kieran about this, is he going to tell me you're blacksmith royalty?" There's a note of teasing now, and I can't deny how much I like it.

"No. But he might tell you I'm considered one of the top experts in the country," I admit. It's not boasting if he asked, right? Besides, part of me wants to brag a little, maybe impress him.

"Ha! I knew it. After I watched your demo today—"

"You watched?" I blink in shock. "I didn't see you."

"That's because you were all focused. And that loud woman up front kept distracting you with stupid questions like 'do you ever burn yourself?' Jesus fuck, lady, he's working with an open flame and meltingly hot metal. Of course he's going to burn himself sometimes." He mutters the last bit, and I can't help chuckling.

"I get that question at least twice a week."

"People are dumb," he scoffs. "But anyway, your demo was so good, I knew you had to be better than average."

I don't know what to say. "Uh, thanks."

Fortunately, the grocery store is just up ahead, so this sudden awkwardness isn't going to last. As I park the car, a thought strikes me.

"Hey, stay close in there, yeah? That way, if you end up talking to a ghost, people will think you're just talking to me."

The look he gives me is so full of gratitude, my whole body flushes.

"Thank you."

I clear my throat. "Anytime." I mean it, too. I'd do anything to make him look at me like that.

After Josh's first full day at work, Daniel invited him to our place for dinner. Just a casual, friendly, welcome-to-Mannix dinner. No reason for me to get excited.

But I am.

Sighing, I check that the chicken coop latch is firmly in place and turn for home. Technically tonight should have been Dan's turn to settle the animals, but I was so thrown when he told me Josh was coming over that I said I'd do it and then ran out of the house. Like an idiot.

He's never going to let me live that down.

When I walk into the house, I smell food and hear voices coming from the kitchen. Either one of the ghosts has dropped in, or Josh is here. So I sneak down the hall to the bathroom. Gotta wash up, right?

I don't know why I'm being this way. Sure, I'm wildly attracted to Josh and would love to fuck him again, but I've been attracted to men I couldn't have before. It's never made me act like a teenager.

Under the hot spray of the shower, I give myself a mental pep talk about acting normal. Josh needs friends. It would be good for me to have another friend. We need a positive working relationship. I can do that. I managed at the store, didn't I?

I think about the grocery store as I get dressed. The half hour I spent there with Josh gave me a tiny taste of what his life must be like. All the relaxation he'd had in the car was gone the second we walked in. Twice, he jumped like someone had goosed him. A few times, he turned his head and looked at nothing, but in a way that I knew he was seeing something. And three times he spoke to people I couldn't see. The whole time it was happening, he kept giving me wary looks, and he apologized twice. But I just kept smiling at him and telling him not to worry, and I think it helped? I hope it did. He was less tense by the time we got to the checkouts, though I'm not sure if that's because we were close to being done or because I helped him relax.

Regardless, when Josh isn't tense and jumping at ghosts, he's good company and easy to talk to. I like him, and I can make myself ignore how much I want to bone him if it means we can be friends.

I keep telling myself that as I walk down the hall to the kitchen.

"Hey, Josh," I say casually. "How was your first day?"

He looks up, smiling brightly, and I give a little cough, feeling like the air's been knocked out of me.

"It was great. I'm going to love this job. Thanks for having me over."

I wave dismissively, trying to channel casual and chilled. "That was Daniel's idea. I mean, we're glad you could come." Could I have sounded any more ungracious?

His smile has dimmed somewhat, and I'm casting about for a way to bring it back when Daniel swoops in to rescue me.

"Ewan was worried that you'd judge us for not cooking. I had to convince him you'd be cool with it." He glances at me. "I told Josh about how Jorge keeps us stocked."

I manage a laugh. "Yeah, well, now that Josh knows we're just bachelor roommates, I didn't want him thinking we were a total cliché." Oh my god, why am I making this worse?

For the first time ever, I'm grateful when Carter pops into being in the middle of the kitchen.

"Fuck!" Daniel gasps. "Please stop doing that!"

"Sorry," Josh says. "I should have warned you he was here. But he just came in a second ago."

"Not your fault," I declare. "Carter, we talked about this."

"I tried the ghostly wind," he protests, "but you've

got the windows open, and it just blended in with the breeze."

Uh-huh.

As annoying as Carter can be, he's broken the tension I caused with my runaway mouth, so I don't scold him more. Dan dishes up the food, and we're sitting down to eat in just a few minutes.

Josh is good company, and he, Daniel, and Carter carry the conversation while I focus on eating and only commenting occasionally, when I can be sure I won't say something stupid. By the time our plates are clean, I'm confident that I'm back in control of myself, and we chat about the changes to the estate over the past few years and what Kieran has planned for the future. Josh wants to know everything.

"…like the idea of a fete or festival, but the scale Kier wants would mean a lot of people tramping around the estate, and I'm worried about damage," Daniel's saying. He means damage to his fields and kitchen garden. Kieran's plan calls for us to set up a temporary camping area.

Josh nods thoughtfully, tapping a fingertip against his lip. Sometime between last night and now, he changed his nail polish from green to a deep purple, and I swallow. Of all the weird fetishes for me to develop…

"Aside from all the tents and porta potties, you'd also need somewhere for people to park. Then the space for the fete itself… I don't know that the estate is big enough," Josh muses.

"It's not," I say bluntly. "We've told Kieran to think smaller, but he says the event needs to be big to make the effort worthwhile. He's still trying to think of a way to make it work."

"It would be a grand affair, if there's a way to make it happen." Carter sighs wistfully, reminding us that he hasn't seen a fair or festival for a hundred and fifty years.

Josh pats his hand sympathetically before asking, "Does the campground need to be here? What if the estate rents a field from one of the farms nearby, or the school football field? Then shuttle people to and fro so they don't need to bring cars to the estate at all."

Daniel and I exchange glances. "That might work," I concede. "It's definitely worth mentioning, in any case."

Josh's smile lights up the room.

"It would be a better option than having people wreck the lawn and fields with car tracks," he says.

"Speaking of wrecking things with car tracks, how do you feel about a driving lesson?"

"What's this?" Carter asks, smiling delightedly, eyes wide. "I would love to learn to drive!"

"No," all three of us say. He pouts.

"Now?" Josh asks. "Aren't you tired?"

"It won't take long. It's still mostly light out, so let's see what you still remember. Maybe do a very slow lap around the dorms. There aren't going to be any ghosts to startle you." I give Carter a hard look. "Are there?"

He has the nerve to be indignant. "We would never!"

"Carter's going to stay with me," Daniel interjects. "We'll watch from the front porch, and if any of the other ghosts come this way, we'll stop them from interrupting."

"We will?" Carter asks.

"Exorcism," I tell him, and he nods at Josh.

"We certainly will."

"Well, you remember where everything is and what it all does," I say ten minutes later, after making sure Josh is familiar with being in the driver seat. "Start the engine, and let's see how you go."

He does, grinning nervously. "It's dumb that I'm this excited and scared, right?"

"Nope. Now pull out slowly and follow the driveway along to the end of the house." I backed the car in under the portico when I parked last night, so all he has to do is drive forward and turn. And it's an automatic transmission, so it should be a piece of cake.

Swallowing, he puts the car in Drive and eases down on the gas pedal. At first it's not enough, then he gets worried and presses too hard, so the car jerks forward before he panics and slams on the brakes.

"You're doing fine," I assure him. "Did you get a feel for how much pressure you need now?"

He nods. "I think so. Just so you know, I'm really grateful for this."

"How grateful?" I ask, then realize how that must sound. "I mean—"

But he's laughing. "Grateful enough to cook you dinner. How's Wednesday?" With some of his attention on me, he puts his foot back on the gas and smoothly pulls the car out of its parking spot, turning into the driveway. I can't hold back my grin.

"Wednesday sounds good," I confirm as we draw even with the front of the cottage. The driveway curves again here, leading up toward the main house, but this first time, I'd rather we didn't get too close to anywhere there might be guests. "Okay, let's go off road. See the dorms?" I point, but he'd need to have his eyes closed to miss them. "One lap."

"Got it." His confidence is back, and he doesn't need any further guidance from me, taking the car at a steady speed around the dorms and then back to our starting point.

"Wanna try parking?" I ask, my eyes on his happy expression.

He pulls a face. "Reverse in? I don't think I can."

"What about pulling in forward? That's just a turn. You don't have to if you're not comfortable," I add when he bites his lip.

"No, I want to. I've done that before, and the space isn't too tight." A small furrow of concentration appears between his brows, and I take a deep breath, restraining the urge to kiss him. *Friends. We're friends.*

He turns a fraction too late and ends up needing to reverse slightly to adjust the car's position. I keep my mouth shut and let him do it. He'll ask for help if he needs it, but he doesn't. When he finally turns off the engine, the car is dead straight and perfectly centered in the space.

"How'd that feel?"

The wide grin on his face when he turns to me is all the answer I need, but he lunges forward and smacks a kiss dead on my mouth.

Then pulls back, eyes wide with horror. "I'm so sorry! I just wanted to thank you and… I guess I got carried away. I didn't mean to cross any lines."

I muster up a smile and try to ignore the way my lips are tingling. "It's fine. This is an exciting moment. No lines crossed. I promise."

He eyes me in a way that makes me think he can tell

it's a lie, but then his smile comes back. "Thank you. Dinner Wednesday? Maybe we can make it a trade—a meal for a lesson."

"Sounds good," I manage, pretending I'm not tingling all over from the memory of his lips on mine and the thought of more time with him.

Chapter Eight

JOSH

I sink onto my couch with a deep sigh and a low-grade headache. Three weeks into my new job, I'm still loving it, but that doesn't mean I don't wish some guests to hell. Who complains because the cutlery at dinner isn't the same pattern as *one* picture on the website? I had to zoom all the way in to even see the pattern, since the photo was of the dining room, not the cutlery.

But apparently it matters to some people, so I had to go and find the right set before the man would eat his dinner.

Thankfully, the meal is done, the after-dinner scavenger hunt through the house is done, and most of the guests are in their rooms. There were only two couples left in the parlor when I checked before coming upstairs.

Glancing at the clock, I try to decide if I'll stay awake long enough to watch a movie, or if I should just go to bed. It's only nine thirty, but Saturdays at Mannix Estate are chaotic, and Sundays not much better. We haven't had a big weekend event since I started, but there's a murder mystery retreat coming up, and Skye told me it'll make me want to cry. Then he laughed and assured me it would be fun too. I think whatever he uses to dye his hair might have affected his brain. I told him that, and he just laughed harder. Skye and I have become good friends already. He's fun to talk to, open-minded, and really sweet. He's also got a mind like a steel trap, though he hides it behind a sometimes ditzy façade. I think he might have a crush on Daniel, but he hasn't said anything, and I don't want to risk our friendship by asking… yet. If he does, it's doomed to be unrequited.

Much like my thing for Ewan.

Don't get me wrong, I'm pretty sure Ewan would happily go to bed with me if I gave him a sign. But what if it made things awkward between us after? Things are so good for me here. I don't want to mess that up. He's been such an amazing friend to me since I got here, right down to buying me a new bottle of nail polish last week when he went to the drugstore, just because I whined about having broken one of mine. Without fail, he notices every time I change the color and always comments. I've never had anyone notice me like that before, and I don't want to risk it.

Even if I do get tingles every time he catches hold of my hand to inspect my nails.

So I'll keep having dinners and driving lessons and coffee breaks with Ewan (and the others, but I don't want to strip them naked and lick every inch of their skin), and we'll be friends, and nobody has to know that for the first time ever, the imaginary boyfriend of my wistful dreams now has a face.

Wow, I'm so good at killing my own mood.

Hauling myself off the couch, I'm turning toward the bed—that'll kill this headache better than a movie—when someone knocks on the door. I groan. It has to be one of the ghosts. The guests can't get up here. I guess it could be Ewan or Daniel, but they've never just dropped in before, and if there was an emergency, they'd call.

The knock sounds again. Dragging my feet, I go to open the door. I've learned that the ghosts won't go away if I ignore them. Yes, they respect my space by not just coming in, but they'll stand there knocking all night.

To my surprise, it's not just one, or even a few, but all six crowded around the door, reminding me of my first night here. Maybe Joe wants to question me some more? I've seen him the least of all the ghosts, although Kieran tells me that's not unusual. There's a reason he's called Grumpy Joe.

"Hey," I say warily. "Something wrong?"

Hattie smiles, but it's a little unsure. "Of course not, dear. We just wanted a word."

Hesitating, I study them. I'd like to tell them to come back during work hours, but they seem... edgy. Something's going on, no matter what they say. I sigh and hold the door open. "Just a quick one. I was about to go to bed."

None of them comments about how early it is as they file past me, and my worry escalates. Since I got here, they haven't hesitated to lecture me on my sleeping habits, my eating habits, my clothes, my choice of nail polish colors, whether I should flirt with people, who I should flirt with, whether I should exercise, what kind of exercise it should be, and so much more. I was certain they'd have something to say about me going to bed at nine thirty on a Saturday night.

When I turn back from closing the door, they've all found seats and are staring at me.

"So… what's up?" I ask.

"Have you had a nice day?" Hattie counters.

I sigh again. "A busy one. And tomorrow will probably be the same. I'm tired. What was it you needed?"

"You've been here nearly a month now," Freddie says congenially. "How are you liking it?"

Oh my god, do they seriously want to chat? "It's great. I love it." Maybe if I keep my answers short, they'll get the hint.

"We like you too," Maisie assures me. "You're nice to us."

Hello, guilt. "Um… thank you. I mean, it's easy to be nice to you."

She smiles weakly and looks away, solidifying my certainty that something is wrong. Maisie stood toe-to-toe arguing with me when I told her she couldn't hook up with guests anymore without telling them she's a ghost. She's not the type to look away because of a compliment. Her clothes are remarkably subdued tonight—skinny jeans and a gauzy black blouse over a bright blue bra, and a normal amount of jewelry. I don't think I've ever seen her wearing an outfit from a single time period.

I glance at Johnny. He has no tattoos, and his hair is only half an inch long all over his head… and brown.

"Okay, I don't know what the issue is here, but you need to tell me. Now."

Hattie sighs and glances over at Joe. "It's a long story, dear. We were going to wait until you'd settled in more and we could get a better idea of your mettle, but you have such a nice aura."

"Just tell me what you want." I sound tired.

Hattie leans forward. "It's simple, dear. We want your help saving the world."

HALF AN HOUR LATER, my headache has become a dozen angry men with hammers pounding at my skull.

"Okay, wait, let's go over this again," I insist from where I'm sitting on the coffee table, rubbing my temple.

Joe heaves a sigh. "We've been over it already."

"Yeah, and it's still as wild as a motherfucking acid trip," I snap, "so we're going to go over it again." Then I wince. "Sorry for cursing."

Hattie snorts. "Don't you worry your motherfucking mind about that."

A laugh bursts from me. It sounds kind of like a sob, but I promise, it's a laugh.

"So… the land this estate is built on is mineral rich."

"Yes," Hattie agrees.

"And the particular combination and… I don't know, density of minerals makes it a good place for ghosts."

"Oh yes," Maisie says. "That's why so many of us chose not to cross over. It's lovely here."

I nod. "So you all died here on the estate, enjoyed the energy the minerals give, and decided to hang around for a while."

There's a flurry of agreement. Except from Joe, who just glowers.

"And you were just… here, haunting the hotel guests and staff in a low-key kind of way, back in the

1970s when one of the guests decided to hold a séance."

"We don't know for certain," Freddie interjects. "I don't think it was a séance. Séances don't have that kind of result. But she definitely did something."

"That resulted in her death," I clarify. That information didn't show up in my research, and Kieran didn't mention it. "And the hotel closed a few weeks later."

"Yes." Hattie frowns, sadness written all over her face.

"Why?"

They all blink at me in unison. It's creepy.

"What do you mean, why?" Carter asks.

"Well… if the death of one guest was enough to close a hotel, there would be no hotels left open. The only reason I can think of is if it could be shown that something in the hotel caused her death. You're telling me she died because of whatever ritual she conducted, right?"

They just stare.

"If that's the case," I continue, "why was the hotel closed?"

"Because of the dark spirit," Freddie says, as though it's obvious.

"The…" I stand and pace away, rubbing the back of my neck and praying for patience.

"What's he doing?" Maisie whispers.

"Probably thinking it all over," Freddie says sagely. "He's a smart one. He'll think about it, then come back with a brilliant solution."

I snort. Brilliant solution? I don't even know what the problem is yet.

"Okay." I pace back toward the coffee table but

don't resume my seat. "This is why we're going over things again. Because you left out the dark spirit the first three times."

Johnny makes a tsking sound. "We did, didn't we? Darn it."

"Language!" Hattie snaps, and I try not to choke on my own saliva.

"Tell me about the dark spirit," I insist, not wanting them to get off track. "The guest who did the ritual died—do we know her name?"

They all shake their heads. "I barely remember her," Maisie volunteers. "She just wasn't very interesting. Until the vortex opened."

I close my eyes for a second. "Vortex?" Another thing that didn't come up during the first telling. "Why don't you walk me through exactly what happened the night she died?"

They trade dubious glances, then turn as one to look at Joe. Oh, joy.

He shrugs. "The first sign we had that something was wrong was when the whole hotel was filled with dark energy."

"It was like cold slime all over us." Maisie shudders. "And it sticks. You feel like you can never be clean again."

"It was easy enough to find the source. The air on the second floor was so thick with evil, the guests could feel it. One of them went to get the manager, convinced there was something wrong with the ventilation system," Joe continues. "We knew it wasn't the air-conditioning causing it, though, and we followed it back to her room."

"Which room?" I grab my phone and start taking notes. I have a feeling I'm going to need them later.

"It's the Garden Suite now. Back then, it was 203," Maisie says helpfully. "That's the room I died in."

What am I supposed to say in response to that?

Fortunately, Joe isn't waiting for platitudes. "Inside the room was a cesspit of darkness. It was almost too thick to move through. The guest was already dead when we got there, lying in a heap on the floor, and she'd opened a vortex to the spirit world."

I hastily add *spirit world?* to my notes. I don't know what that is, but I don't want to interrupt the story again.

"Her soul was gone," Hattie adds in a hushed voice. "Normally they linger for a little while after death, even if the person wants to cross over. It can take time to adjust to being dead, you know. But hers was just… gone. The dark spirit consumed it."

A chill races down my spine. That doesn't sound good.

"We were unprepared," Joe says grimly. "None of us had dealt with the spirit world before. We didn't even know what the vortex was at first. The dark spirit struck at us while we were still trying to understand what we were seeing."

"That's when we lost Mona." Freddie's voice cracks. "I'll never forget the look on her face when the dark spirit consumed her."

Oh my god. This is getting way darker than I expected. "Mona was… one of you?"

Freddie nods. "She was a dear woman."

Okay, so the dark spirit, whatever it was, ate souls, including ghost souls. What a happy thought.

"What happened then?"

"We fled," Joe says simply. "We didn't know what to do, how to fight, or even what we were fighting. So we fled."

"Yeah, but… to where? Was the, uh, dark spirit bound to that room?"

All six of them shake their heads. When things are a bit less tense, I'm going to ask them to stop doing things in unison like that.

"No, it was free to roam about. That's why the hotel closed. In the course of the first week, it caused two serious accidents and several minor ones. We were all so afraid, hiding at the manager's house with Carter and hoping it would stay in the main hotel and not venture to the grounds." Joe's gaze goes distant, like he's remembering. He sighs. "It was then we realized we had the ability to fully manifest."

I blink. "You'd never known that before?" I just assumed that they'd always been able to do it—wasn't that why they told me about the "mineral-rich land"?

"We'd never been able to do it," Joe corrects in a tone that implies I should have known that. "The energy here allowed us to partially manifest for brief moments —allow people to catch glimpses of us, or for us to knock small items off tables—but we were never able to fully manifest and actually interact with the living. The opening of the vortex changed that. It took us a few days to notice, because the dark spirit was tainting the air and we were so afraid, but there was so much more energy. There *is* so much more. And we hoped that a medium or an exorcist would be drawn by the changes and be able to help us."

Makes sense. I nod encouragingly, hoping this is

when he'll say "and someone did, solving all the problems. Now you know the history of this place, the end," and then they'll leave, and I can marvel over what they've told me while I snuggle in my bed.

"But then the dark spirit knocked a guest over the third-floor gallery."

Okay, maybe not.

"He fell two stories to the ground and cracked his head on the floor."

I swallow hard. "He died?"

"No," Hattie hastens to assure me. "He was rushed to a hospital before he could die. We found out later that he'd slipped into a coma, but the hotel was closed and abandoned before we could learn if he survived or not."

"It was then that we realized the dark spirit couldn't merely snatch souls from living bodies. It had to kill them first. And with the hotel closed and all other sources of souls out of its reach, it came after us."

I've gotta hand it to Joe, he's one heck of a storyteller. Even knowing they're all here, obviously safe and not consumed, I'm still freaked out about what comes next.

"We discovered we could fight it off when we were fully manifested, and we outnumbered it. So we stayed together all the time, stayed fully manifested all the time. Our hope of someone coming to help us was gone—why would anyone come to an abandoned hotel?"

"We began to seriously consider crossing over," Carter says somberly. "But with all the dark energy the spirit was emitting, we weren't sure it would work. What if we ended up in the wrong place?"

"And then the young people started coming." Maisie shakes her head. "An abandoned building outside of town? It was the perfect place for them to meet and… do things."

I blush, though I'm not sure why. It's not like I've never "done things" before, and I know Maisie has.

"We couldn't let the dark spirit kill them and take their souls," Hattie declares. "Not on our watch."

"And it was too hard to run interference for all of them," Joe continues. "We had to be on alert at all hours, and sometimes there would be a lot of teenagers here. So we decided we had to get rid of the dark spirit. Send it back where it came from."

I swallow. It sounds like the kind of plan a bunch of teens in a horror movie would come up with. But they must have succeeded, right? Because the place is open now and teeming with people most days, and there's no dark spirit trying to kill anyone and harvest their souls.

Is there?

I'm pretty sure I would have noticed that.

"It was difficult." Joe sighs, suddenly looking less grouchy and more like a tired old man. "We didn't know what we were doing. One time, we managed to force it back through the vortex, but unfortunately, the vortex isn't directly linked to the spirit's presence here. So it didn't close, and the spirit was able to come right back through."

"Wait," I interrupt. "What do you mean, the vortex isn't linked to the spirit's presence? I thought they appeared at the same time?"

"They did. But we think the vortex opening was one thing, and then the dark spirit coming through wasn't connected to that. The vortex isn't a door specifically for the dark spirit; it's just a door, and the dark spirit happened to use it."

The implications of that are terrifying. "So potentially this vortex, which you said is still open and you need my help with, could be used by hundreds or even thousands of soul-eating entities to gain access to Earth?" My voice is rising. "*Why* haven't you mentioned this to Kieran or anyone? Why wait, when another dark spirit could come through at any moment and *eat all our souls?*"

"Chill, bro," Johnny says, and we all stop and stare at him. His expression turns uncertain. "Did I use it wrong? That's how they says it on TV."

I start to laugh. It sounds a bit hysterical, but I don't think anyone can blame me for that. "You said it right," I manage, and he beams.

"Great! Anyway… chill, bro. It's still open, but it's mostly blocked. And we think the dark spirit keeps other ones away."

"Fair…" Wait. *Wait.* "Did you just say the dark spirit's presence keeps other ones away?"

He gives me a questioning look, nodding.

"As in… it's still here?" My head whips around so I can stare at Hattie and Joe, who I think are the oldest in the group. "There's a soul-eating spirit in the building?"

"If you'd pipe down and let us finish the story, we'll give you all the details," Joe gripes, and I snap my mouth closed. Huffing, he continues, "When the spirit came through the vortex the second time, we realized we needed to learn more about… everything." He waves a hand as though to encompass the universe. "All of it. We couldn't fight something we didn't understand. So Hattie went to the library in town to try to find out more, and the rest of us started watching the spirit to learn whatever we could."

"The library was mostly a dead end," Hattie admits. "There were very few books on spirituality, much less dark spirits. The librarian at the time was very religious and would have eliminated the section on alternative spiritualism altogether if she could." She sniffs. "If there's one thing a hundred and fifty years of afterlife has taught me, it's that we should be learning everything we possibly can."

"To be fair, I don't think there are a lot of readily available books on dark spirits and vortexes. Vor…tices? Whatever. And if there are any, they possibly wouldn't be that accurate." Fuck knows, most of the books about being a medium aren't.

"That's true. Even now, with the internet, there's a dearth of useful information. We've been looking." She sounds so tired on that last sentence. "But while I was at the library, I did some research into why the energy at the estate has always felt so nice for us. Turns out there's a lot of quartz in this area, which is an energy amplifier. It's also a stone of healing and some say purity."

"Which ended up being valuable information," Joe adds. "We noticed the spirit didn't like to leave the house much, not after we fought it off the first few times. And it absolutely wouldn't go down to the basement."

An image of the basement door and the memory of the creepy feeling I got when I went near it rise in my mind. I have a sudden hunch I know where he's going with this, and I don't like it. "Would it have had any reason to go down to the basement?"

They all smile at me in that creepy unison way I'm going to force them to stop. "I knew you were a smart boy," Hattie says approvingly.

"We asked ourselves the very same thing." Freddie

nods once. "And the answer was, probably not. It's not finished down there and was only ever used for storage. Coldstuffs and vegetables back in the days before refrigerators, and then old furniture and tools after that. But because it's unfinished, there are places where the bare rock is exposed."

I blink. "Whoa. That's *really* unfinished."

"We thought there might be a chance the spirit was avoiding the basement because of the quartz content in the foundations," Carter says. "There really is a lot of it around here, even in the soil. But we had to test that theory before we could implement a plan to use quartz against it. So Joe pretended to quarrel with us all and then very loudly stomped off to the basement to sulk alone. And then the rest of us pretended to go back to the manager's house."

"But really we was hiding outside, waiting to see what happened," Johnny interjects hastily. "We would never of left Joe alone like that."

I muster up a smile for him, because not abandoning a friend to soul-death is something that should be encouraged.

"And the spirit didn't go into the basement," Joe confirms. "What it did do is wait at the top of the basement stairs. All day, and all that night."

"How did you get out?" I'm kind of in awe of these ghosts right now.

"I'd stolen some quartz pieces when I was in town," Hattie says. "There was a woo-woo shop there at the time. Two hippies ran it. They sold candles and tie-dyed shirts and crystals, and if you knew the codeword, marijuana." She whispers the last word. "The shop didn't last long, just a few years, but I only needed to steal quartz that one time, so…" She shrugs.

Freddie picks up the story. "We had those half-dozen chunks of crystal, and we used them to herd the spirit into the basement. It was hard," he admits. "It didn't want to go in there, and it fought back, tried to get away. But finally we got it down there, where Joe had used some of the stuff left behind to chip out a hole in the rock. We forced the spirit into the hole and blocked it up with the quartz and some more bits of rock."

Heaving a huge sigh, I wonder idly why I didn't stock any alcohol when I went grocery shopping. A bottle or six of tequila would be good right now. "So there's a dark spirit entombed in the basement?"

"Yep!" Maisie declares. "Sometimes it tries to escape, but we keep an eye on it. And the quartz weakens it a lot."

Oh my god.

"We're going to come back to that in a minute," I promise, because I'm pretty sure it's a health and safety violation for us to have a being that tries to kill people and eat their souls on the premises. Although, silver lining, it's unlikely the inspector will ever notice and file a report about it.

Am I getting hysterical? I feel like I might be getting hysterical.

I just wanted somewhere I could talk to ghosts without being ridiculed. Was that really so much to ask?

Clearly it came with a price tag.

Chapter Nine

JOSH

"I want to talk about the vortex some more. Before, you said it was mostly blocked. What does that mean? Mostly? Can other spirits get through?"

They exchange doubtful looks, and my heart sinks. "We don't actually know," Hattie confesses. "We're fairly certain that the vortex is the reason we're able to manifest so easily. That ability began after it was opened, and when we blocked it, manifesting became harder."

"So you think the energy is flowing here from the spirit world? And what is the spirit world?"

Hattie shrugs. "The world where the dark spirit came from?"

Wow.

"When the dark spirit was contained, we were able to spend some time examining the vortex. None of us were able to enter it—"

"You *tried*?" Holy crap. "What if there were a bunch of soul-eaters on the other side? That's such a dumbass thing to do." The thought of these annoying yet sweet and caring ghosts being consumed really bothers me for some reason. Am I… getting attached?

"We had to determine our options," Joe huffs. "For all we knew, there was a spiritual sheriff on the other side who could take the dark spirit off our hands."

Ha! If only.

He shakes his head. "But of course, since we couldn't check, we'll never know. What we did learn, without the dark spirit's taint distracting us, was that energy was flowing out of the vortex. We think that's what allowed us to manifest so easily, though we're not sure if it's because the energy is a different type to what we have here or just the volume of it. But a few days after we locked up the dark spirit, we felt a presence on the other side of the vortex."

"A presence? What kind?" My voice is sharp. This story just seems to be one nightmare after another.

Freddie shrugs. "We don't know. It didn't feel dangerous like the dark spirit, but who's to say that's not because the vortex was between us? Maybe it would feel completely different once it came through. So we decided we needed to close the vortex, for safety's sake."

"Only we couldn't." Maisie pouts. "We just couldn't work out how to do it. The best we've come up with is a kind of plank of energy pressed right up against it. That seems to have stopped anything else from coming through, but it also reduces the flow of energy from the spirit world."

"Which makes it harder for you to manifest," I say slowly, the pieces finally slotting together in my head. "Does it ever seem like anything is trying to break down your barrier and get through?"

Maisie looks at Hattie, who shrugs and looks at Joe.

"No?" she says. "If they are, we've never noticed the difference."

"Okay, so... can we think of the vortex as a doorway? Somehow, a doorway was opened between here and the spirit world. The energy flow from there is like, um, like a strong wind, right? It blows right through the doorway. Or actually, let's say it's water."

"Is it water or wind?" Johnny whispers to Carter, who shrugs.

"It's water," I insist. Fuck, I hope this analogy pans out. "There's a lake on the other side with currents and everything, and once the doorway opened, the water started pouring in."

"Are you saying we're draining the spirit world?" Maisie asks in alarm.

"No, I—look, just let me finish. The water is pouring in, and all the creatures living there have noticed the resulting shift in current." I can barely remember learning this stuff about water pressure and currents in high school, so I hope I'm not making it up. "And they come to check it out. Like the dark spirit did. It found this doorway with energy flowing through and a tasty soul on the other side, and it decided to see what was up."

"And then once it was here, there were lots of other souls nearby!" Maisie's excited by my analogy, even if Joe still looks doubtful.

"Right. Maybe there weren't any on the other side. Or they were harder to get to?"

"That could be it," Freddie says slowly. "We're positive nothing else came through the vortex while the dark spirit was roaming around free—what if other spirits can sense its nasty aura like we can? And they know to stay away and fight back. That would make hunting harder for it. But here, most living humans can't even sense that it exists, and if they can, they think it's an air-conditioning malfunction. So even though it has to kill its prey first, it's still easier for it to hunt."

"Because its prey doesn't even know it's there," I finish. It's just a theory, but it seems to fit. And makes me want to vomit, especially when I think about how many guests are currently asleep and vulnerable in this building… and how many have been over the past twenty years. If the spirit had ever gotten free…

"You said before that it's been trying to escape. How high are the chances of that happening?"

Hattie seesaws her hand. "We're pretty sure it won't get free again."

"How sure is pretty— Wait. *Again?*"

They exchange glances.

"Well, when the estate was sold and they began renovating—how long ago was that?"

"A little over twenty years," I tell her. Weirdly, it's something the guests ask about a lot.

"The owners thought they could finish the basement and use it for the guests. We didn't know anything about it until one day the workmen went down there and started poking around."

A vague memory wriggles to the surface. Didn't Ewan and Daniel say there was a mean ghost when the renovations first started? And that the other ghosts had kicked it out?

"Let me guess—they unbricked the dark spirit."

Joe harrumphs. It's so weird hearing a ghost make that kind of visceral sound. "They did. And the only reason they're still alive is because it was so weak after nearly thirty years surrounded by quartz. It tried to smash their skulls in with the tools they were using but didn't have the strength. They both had broken bones, though—an arm and some ribs, if I recall correctly."

"We were able to get it sealed back in before it could regain enough power to do more harm," Hattie adds. "And then we had a serious talk with the owners and made them promise to leave the basement alone. They were talking about hiring an exorcist and getting rid of all of us, but they also wanted to use the estate being haunted as part of the attraction, so we were able to convince them we had it all under control."

"Why did you do that? You've asked me to help you close the vortex—why didn't you let the owners hire an exorcist or a medium and get the job done then?"

Silence.

"Not gonna answer me?"

Nothing.

"Fine. We'll come back to that. Let's talk about the vortex. You said that when you blocked it, you lost the ability to manifest quite so easily."

"Yes," Maisie, Johnny, and Freddie all say, obviously eager to make up for not answering me before.

"So that fits with the energy-as-water analogy, right? If the water can't flow through as easily, you're not going to be able to access it."

"And it explains why nothing else has tried to get through," Carter says thoughtfully. "If we think of the vortex as a doorway and the block as a door, the energy can still seep in around the edges—it's not watertight—but there wouldn't be such a big change in current on the other side. So beings over there might not even notice it until they happened to be very close already." He nods. "This makes sense."

"It's still just a theory," I caution. "Okay. So… now what? You want me to close the vortex? I have no idea how I'd do that."

There's another exchange of glances.

"Stop doing that," I snap. "You need to talk to me. You've come here and unloaded all this on me for a reason, so now you need to tell me what that is."

"We're tired," Hattie says quietly. "It's hard work keeping an eye on the dark spirit and maintaining the block on the vortex. We worry all the time. We just want to make sure everyone here is safe. And that means getting rid of the dark spirit and closing the vortex."

My annoyance and anger drain away. They've been doing this for nearly fifty years. That's a long time, even for centuries-old ghosts. Of course they're tired and worried. I'm tired and worried just thinking about it.

"I know you don't want to talk about it," I start quietly, "but why did you refuse the owners' offer to hire someone? And why haven't you told Kieran? He told me there have been several mediums here over the years. Surely one could have helped? Did none of them ever notice the vortex or the dark spirit?" I sure didn't, but I'm not trained. Would that make a difference? I got a bad vibe about the basement, but that's in an area guests don't have access to, so presumably a medium wouldn't have gotten close enough to sense it?

I did feel the difference in energy here, though, and from what Kieran's said, others have commented on it. Did none of them look into why?

"How can we know who to trust?" Joe asks. "Before the renovations, people would come. Not just young people—adults, ghost hunters. Some were harmless with their silly rituals they saw in a movie, and we'd put on a show for them. Well, they'd put on a show," he adds, jerking his thumb toward the other ghosts. "It's a waste of time, if you ask me. But there were others too, talking about the energy here and how if they could work out how to channel it, they could use it to influence others. They could use it to become wealthy and powerful. They talked about using ghosts as industrial spies, or military spies. How do we know any medium or exorcist we asked for help wouldn't get a taste of the power on offer and decide to do the same?"

"We needed time to get to know the right person," Maisie says earnestly.

A combination of pride and utter horror floods through me. "And… you think I'm the right person? You barely know me."

"We know enough. You're a good boy who treats us with respect." She purses her lips. "I'm not quite sure why you're determined to be single, though. You should be nicer to Ewan. Flirt with him. He's a good catch. A blacksmith can always find work."

"He's not a catch. We're colleagues. I'm perfectly nice to him. I'm not going to flirt!" My face is hot, and I avoid looking at Carter. The last thing I need right now is for him to mention that Ewan and I have already hooked up.

Maisie claps her hands. "Do you have a crush on Ewan? Oh, this is wonderful! We can have an estate romance! Like in that movie—only not in an office."

My eyelid begins twitching. "No, I don't have a crush. And there will be no romance. What movie?" I can't help adding the last bit. I'm a sucker for a good rom-com.

Maisie waves her hand. "I don't remember names. It's that one with the boss who's an asshole and the assistant he can't live without. And they go to a conference? I don't know. Are you sure you don't have a crush on Ewan? That would be soooooo perfect."

"I'm sure," I insist.

"Why are we talking about this?" Joe asks nobody in particular.

"Excellent point, Joe. There are other things to discuss right now."

Hattie backs me up. "True. We can talk about why Josh and Ewan would be good together another time. What I was saying before is, you might've only been here a few weeks, but you've been very respectful to us. You told us honestly what your boundaries are and then gave us the chance to adhere to them. That's important. Some mediums don't ask; they just assume we won't respect their wishes."

"We're people too, you know." Carter sniffs. "We might be dead now, but we still have feelings."

"Some of them tell Kieran he should do more to monetize our presence here," Joe adds with a glower. "As though we're circus performers!"

"Most of them don't stay long enough for us to be comfortable with them." Hattie takes back the reins. "There was one who might have been okay, but Maisie didn't like her hair."

I blink, then turn my gaze on Maisie. "Her hair?"

"Hair is very important. How can we trust someone with our souls and all of humankind if she doesn't have a good hair care routine? At least put it in a ponytail if you don't want to waste time on it."

I give that comment a wide berth—and somehow manage to resist the urge to smooth down my hair. "Fine. So you weren't comfortable with any of the random mediums who have visited. But why didn't you tell Kieran? You trust him, don't you?" *Please say you do.* There's no way I can make this work if we have to sneak behind Kieran's back.

Not that I think I can make this work at all.

"Of course we trust Kieran!" Freddie declares, looking affronted that I'd even suggest otherwise. "And Skye, and Arissa."

"And Daniel and Ewan," Johnny adds. "All the senior staff are proper good. We made sure of it."

That seems like something else I don't want to ask about.

"So why am I hearing about this from you instead of him? He might not be a medium—which, remember, I'm not either—but he could invite some mediums for you to check out. Or do some research."

"And if none of that worked out? He'd be just as worried as we are. We didn't want to inflict that on him unless we had some hope."

No pressure or anything. I rub my hand over my face.

"Let's go down to the basement," I say abruptly.

Hattie's face lights up. "Really?"

"I just want to look," I clarify. "I can't check out the vortex tonight because there's a guest in that room"—oh my god, the *liability*—"but let's see how the basement feels." I take the time to grab some ibuprofen for my headache, and then I lead the way down three floors to the main storage room.

The fluorescent light bounces off the shelves of pantry goods and stacks of folding chairs and boxes. It feels different at night—I don't know why. It's not like there's even a window in here.

"It's this way," Freddie says authoritatively, heading toward the back of the room.

"I know." It's not like I'd forget. With each step I take closer to the basement door, the feeling of wrongness increases. It's an itch in the middle of my back—ever-present and annoying. "Is it locked?" I say as we reach it, half hoping it is. Although that wouldn't make a difference, since I have keys to every room in this house. I doubt Kieran would have left the basement off the list.

Joe rolls his eyes in exasperation. "Of course it's locked. We want to keep people out."

My keys are still in my hand, the lanyard I keep them on trailing, and I lift them. "Which one is it?" Most places in the house are accessible by fob. My apartment has a separate key, as does the main door. I also have keys for the outbuildings that require them, and for the key cabinet in the museum, where the keys to the locked cases are. But there isn't anything extra.

"This one," Joe says, pointing to the key that unlocks the front door. "It's the same lock. Only you and Kieran have this key."

That makes sense, since one or both of us are always on site, and the rest of the staff can gain access via the staff door. Pushing down the strong sense of foreboding, I stick the key in the lock and turn it.

The click seems obscenely loud.

The room beyond the door is invisible behind its cloak of darkness, the light from the storage room only illuminating the first few steps.

"Wait... how unfinished is this basement? Are there lights?" No fucking way am I walking into a dark basement that contains a soul-eating spirit. I might not be the smartest guy alive, but I'm smarter than that.

"No lights," Freddie reports. "You need to use a flashlight."

"There's one over here," Hattie says, much to my disappointment. Damn Kieran for having a stock of heavy-duty flashlights to pass out in case of power outage. I grab one, check it works—and nearly blind myself—then sigh and muster up my courage.

The flashlight's bright beam leads the way down the steps. I was worried they'd be rickety, but they seem secure enough. I guess they don't get enough use to be worn out. Is that how it works?

Who cares? I'm just trying to distract myself from the fact that I might be descending to my doom. What kind of idiot knowingly walks into a room with a demon?

Dark spirit, I remind myself. It sounds less imminent-deathy than demon.

When I get to the bottom and both feet are safely on solid ground, I shine the light around the room. It's pretty big for a basement dug out before modern machinery, and cold as balls down here. I can see why it would have been ideal for cold storage. There are a few bits and pieces of garbage left strewn around—some old, half-rusted tools, a broken chair, what looks like a rat carcass—but it's otherwise empty. Interestingly, the overall vibe here isn't any worse than it was upstairs in front of the door. It's not fun, but it's definitely not a swamp of bad things, like I was worried it would be.

The nearest wall looks to be made of bricks, with crumbling mortar between them, but when Joe steps out in front, he walks toward the wall directly ahead, about twenty feet away, which is bare, uneven rock.

Except for a square of neatly fitted-together stones, approximately a foot high and wide. Even if I didn't know what was behind it, I'd know it was *wrong*. Here, I can feel the darkness. It beats against me, furious and hungry, desperate to be freed, and the taint of it, the utter foulness, makes me want to flee.

But I don't. The ghosts have withstood this for fifty years. The least I can do is take a look.

The vault is at chest level for me, and I stoop to examine it. I honestly can't tell if the stones themselves are any different from what you'd find on the side of the road, but if I remember the geology unit from high school science, quartz is one of the most common minerals in the world, and particles of it can be found in pretty much any dirt or rock. I *can* see the small chunks of pure quartz embedded in the cement used to hold the stones together. And I can feel the miasma of darkness trapped behind them.

But I have no fucking clue what to do about it.

I hadn't realized until this very second how much part of me was hoping that I'd *know*. That I'd get here, and it would be like one of those "chosen one" movies, where the good guy gets thrust into the bad situation and instinctively knows what to do to save the day.

That didn't happen.

So now I'm just a scared shitless guy in a mostly dark basement with a bunch of ghosts and a soul-eating demon. And no idea how to get rid of said demon. Because let's be real, whatever the ghosts want to call it, it's probably a demon.

"Let's go back upstairs."

Back in the storage room, I turn off the flashlight and set it back on the shelf, then carefully lock the basement door. I check the handle twice—we definitely do *not* need any of the kitchenhands wandering down there.

Then I leave the storage room and head for the office, ghosts in tow.

"Where are we going?" Maisie asks.

"The office."

"Why?"

"Because I need to check something on the computer and send an email."

"To who?" Joe demands sharply.

"All the senior staff. We're having a meeting about this. They need to know. I can't deal with it on my own." We need a plan. We need research and resources. And we need a buttload more quartz. I want that thing so weak and locked down, it won't even try to get out. Plus, on the off chance it does, I need Ewan and Daniel fully informed and ready to come to my aid in the middle of the night.

The ghosts whisper among themselves as I unlock the office and turn on the lights. They're still arguing when I boot up the computer. But by the time I log in and open the reservation system, they're lined up in front of the desk, watching me.

I glance up at them. "Well? What did you decide?"

Hattie clears her throat. "We're willing to trust your judgement on this."

The warmth of acceptance settles in my belly, going

a long way toward easing my panic about the whole situation. "Thank you."

First, I tab through the reservation system, looking at the occupancy rate for the Garden Suite. I'd rather not have guests in the same room as a vortex to the spirit world if we can help it. Plus, if we're going to try to close the damn thing, we'll need access. It looks like I can rearrange all the reservations during the week—we're rarely full then—but for weekends, I'm shit outta luck. We're fully booked for the next four months.

Fuck. Well, not much I can do, at least not until I've spoken to Kieran. I block out all availability in the meantime, so nobody books it by accident—or before I can tell them not to—and then open a new email.

If I had my preference, I'd be waking them all up right now to share in my turmoil. Instead, I try to be logical. The dark spirit and the vortex have been here for almost fifty years, mostly without issues. Tomorrow is Sunday, one of the busiest days here, when everything is chaotic and everyone is running at full speed. I'm better off waiting for Monday. That means calling Kieran in on his day off—he and Skye and I rotate taking days off from Monday to Wednesday so there's always someone here to oversee things—but this can't wait until the full staff meeting on Thursday.

I shoot off an email to all the senior staff, telling them the ghosts have brought a non-emergent but urgent situation to my attention and requesting they all be here for a meeting at nine on Monday. Most guests have either already checked out or aren't ready to check out at that time, and it's early enough that there aren't likely to be any tourists dropping in. Monday is our quietest day in that regard. There's a school group scheduled to come, but not until around ten thirty.

"Monday at nine?" Hattie says, reading over my shoulder. "We'll be there."

I stop typing. "Actually, if you don't mind, I think only one of you should come. It's going to take them some time to absorb this, and I'd rather not have you all exhausted from manifesting when I'm sure we'll need you at your best later in the week."

Freddie opens his mouth indignantly, then pauses. "I suppose that's a valid point."

"But who will go?" Maisie asks plaintively.

"That's up to you to decide among yourselves." No way am I getting dragged into that. Although I do have preferences. I hit send on the email and shut down the computer. "Okay, I'm going to bed. I probably won't sleep, but I'm going to pretend to." And I'm *not* going to spend half the night hovering in the hallway outside the Garden Suite, trying to tell if the energy from the vortex is doing anything different.

I'm really not.

Chapter Ten

EWAN

I come in from feeding the animals on Sunday morning to find Daniel frowning at his phone instead of getting breakfast started. Damn it. I'm starving.

"What's wrong? Did you lock yourself out again?"

He shakes his head, not looking up. "It's this email from Josh."

"What email?" I look at the clock. "And what's he doing sending emails at six thirty on a Sunday? Did the guests keep him up all night?"

"I think he sent it late last night. Listen to this: 'Apologies for the inconvenience, but I need everyone here for a senior staff meeting at nine on Monday. It's not an emergency, but it is important and time sensitive. The ghosts have made me aware of something that needs our attention.'" He finally looks up. "What do you think that could be about?"

I grab my phone from my back pocket and check my email. I have the same one, and there's no more detail. I look at the clock again. It's still early, but I need to clean up, eat, and be ready for the first demonstration in the smithy at eight thirty. After that, I won't have time for more than water breaks and a quick lunch until after Daniel and I get the animals settled tonight, and by then I'll be too tired to traipse up to the house.

"Wanna beg breakfast at the house and see if we can corner Josh?" I ask.

"Yep. Who's on duty in the kitchen this morning? I'll call and sweet-talk them while you wash up."

Twenty minutes later, we wander into the kitchen.

"Look, it's a ravening horde," Arissa says dryly. "Come to steal food with puppy dog pouts."

"Guilty," Daniel says. "What are you doing here? I thought you were off today." Arissa's the only member of the senior staff who doesn't work both weekend days.

"I was, but Ray's sick, so I've been demoted to cook for the day. We've got waffles if you want them."

"Yes," I reply instantly. "Can I go help myself to the buffet, or do you want me to wait in here?"

She shakes her head as Daniel pours us both coffee. The hot drinks station is one of the only things we're allowed to touch in the kitchen. Since the kitchen is licensed for commercial use, Arissa is hella strict about untrained people using it. "None of the guests have come down yet, so I haven't got the buffet set up. I'll dish up for you—the bacon and sausage are ready. Do you want eggs and toast too?"

My stomach growls. "You're my favorite," I tell her. "Poached, please. I could do the toast?"

The assistant on duty—I can't remember his name—laughs. "Dude, no. Why are you even asking that?"

Arissa points at him. "What he said. Go wait in the staff room. Daniel, what do you want to eat?"

"I'll have the same as him. Has Josh been down this morning?"

"I haven't seen him." She casts a sideways look at her assistant and lowers her voice. "The email?"

We both nod. "It's weird, right?" I ask.

"Is that why you're here? To ask him about it?" She grins. "Really? You can't wait *one* day?"

"Your amazing cooking is also a big attraction," Daniel says.

"But mostly we can't wait one day," I add, and she rolls her eyes. "Don't forget to add our breakfast to the bill," I throw over my shoulder as Daniel and I walk out. All staff get a certain number of free meals, and of course we're welcome to help ourselves to the snack stations whenever we want, but because Daniel and I live on the property, we don't get as many freebies as most of the others. It's so easy for us to dash home for lunch, and our salaries are plenty generous, even with the reduction for rent and utilities. We can still eat at the house whenever we want, but each meal gets added to a monthly tab.

We settle into the staff room with our coffee, leaving the door open so we can hear if Josh comes down. If he doesn't, we're going to have to go up and knock on his door, and I'd rather not. He might still be sleeping, since he barely has a commute, or he might open the door in his underwear or something. Which, don't get me wrong, I'd love to see, but I've been in that apartment before. It's spacious, but the bed is *right there*. I don't want to risk being overcome with lust at the sight of him mostly naked near a bed.

Arissa brings our breakfast five minutes later.

"Marry me," Daniel offers, and she smacks his shoulder.

"Josh just stumbled into the kitchen," she says in a low voice. "His eyes were barely open, and he went straight for the coffee. I promised him breakfast and will send him in here."

"Thank you," I say through a mouthful of waffle.

She pulls a face. "You're gross."

"We'll report back," Daniel assures her, and she goes back to the kitchen.

Josh sleepwalks in—swear to god, if the guy is awake, I'll eat my boots—a minute later.

"Whoa, dude, what happened? You look wrecked," Daniel says, kicking out one of the empty chairs. Josh sinks into it wordlessly and gulps from his mug.

Daniel and I exchange glances. "Was there a problem with the guests last night?" I ask. "You know you can call us when shit happens. Don't stay up all night dealing with it alone."

He lifts his gaze from his mug and blinks slowly, seeming surprised to see us. Then he startles. "Oh my god, what time is it? Am I late?"

"Relax," Daniel soothes. "You're fine. We came up for breakfast."

He slumps forward. "Thank fuck."

"Didn't you sleep well?" I try again.

"One hour," he mutters.

"You only slept for one hour? Why?" Daniel sounds aghast. He needs a solid eight hours to function. It makes him unbearable when we have a problem with the animals in the middle of the night.

Josh waves his free hand. "Ghosts."

That seems to be all we're going to get out of him,

and I'd totally respect his right to privacy if not for the fact he's requested a meeting because of something the ghosts said, and now it seems the ghosts kept him up all night.

Arissa brings his food, giving Daniel and me a chance to wordlessly communicate about who asks the next question. We know each other pretty well, so we manage to get the points across with wiggling eyebrows and grimaces.

"Are you both having strokes?" Josh asks, fork in hand as he studies us. The coffee must be kicking in, because he seems more alert.

"Nope," Daniel says cheerfully. "Just wondering what the meeting tomorrow is for."

Josh puts his fork down, buries his face in his hands —his nails are a bright yellow that makes me smile— and groans. When he looks up again, he says, "Please don't ask me now. I'm too tired to tell it properly. And we have a lot of work today. Trust me, it's better to wait until tomorrow."

"But," Daniel begins, and I kick him under the table. It doesn't take a genius to see Josh is at his limit.

"Just tell us this," I say instead. "Is there anything we can do right now?"

He seems surprised at first, then takes a deep breath and shakes his head. "No. There's nothing we can do right now. I should have slept last night, but I was… processing."

Okay, fuck, that's not a good sign. He's right, though —if he needed a sleepless night to process whatever this is, I don't need to be thinking about it while I'm working the forge. Blacksmithing can be dangerous even when you're giving it your full attention.

"I'm not feeling a whole lot better about this," Daniel says. "But okay. We trust you."

Josh blinks. "Thanks? That's, uh, really... nice."

"Eat your breakfast," I chide. No way is he going to be able to deal with people all day if he doesn't fuel himself. He looks down at his plate, then picks up his fork and begins shoveling in scrambled eggs.

Daniel and I talk quietly while we eat, mostly leaving Josh to his own devices. There's a list of things that need doing in the barn that we've both been putting off, so we discuss which ones can continue to wait and which need attention ASAP.

By the time we're done with breakfast, Josh seems a bit more awake. Arissa sticks her head in to ask Daniel how much fresh lettuce is available from the garden, and he leaves with her. I study Josh.

He lifts his head and catches me staring. "What? Do I have food on my face?" Grabbing a napkin, he wipes his mouth.

"No." I shake my head. "I'm just worried about you." My face gets hot, but I push on. "Is there any way you can catch a nap?"

He scoffs, but he's smiling at me. "Not on a Sunday. I'm okay, Ewan, I promise. I did get some sleep." A laugh huffs from him. "I must look pretty shit for you to be worried."

The words are out before I can stop them. "You look pretty, but never shit." I reach out and grab one of his hands, tilting it so the nail polish gleams in the light. "Great color. Sunshiny, like you."

Those big hazel eyes blink at me, and then color stains his cheeks. "Uh... that's sweet. Thanks."

And I've made it awkward again. Clearing my

throat, I get up. "Well, gotta go. There's stuff to do in the smithy before the crowds arrive."

"Yeah, bye." The relief in his voice is clear.

In the hallway, I run into Freddie. He's fully manifested and rummaging through the linen closet.

"Fred, what are you doing?" It's impossible not to sound exasperated. The housekeeping staff hate Freddie because he's always checking up on them.

"I'm inspecting the linens," he says. "They have been shelved in a most haphazard manner."

I glance into the closet. The shelves are filled with stacks of sheets and towels that look plenty tidy to me. "They're fine. But if it concerns you, you can rearrange them."

He gasps and throws up his hands. "I? Rearrange the linens? That's a job for *staff*, not guests."

I give him a level look, and he has the grace to look abashed. "Since you're neither, it's up to you whether you do it or not. But leave the housekeepers alone."

He sniffs. "Very well."

I take three steps down the hall, then turn back. "Freddie?"

"Yes?" He closes the closet door.

"Do you know what the staff meeting tomorrow is about?"

"Of course!"

Satisfaction curls my lips. "So what's it about?"

He shakes his head. "I'm not permitted to speak of it. I'm not the elected representative."

The… Do I even want to know?

"Thanks anyway."

I'll find out in one day. It's not worth getting into a complicated conversation with a ghost over.

Chapter Eleven

JOSH

"...And that's where we are," I finish. At my request, they let me tell it all without interrupting, although I think it might have caused Kieran physical pain to keep his mouth shut once I started. Skye sat there with his mouth open for the first minute, then started scribbling notes at a speed that actually scared me. "Joe is here to answer your questions." I gesture to the ghost, who's scowling from a chair at the end of the staff room table.

The silence is deafening. I glance around at the shocked faces. Yeah, that's pretty much what I was expecting.

"So..." Kieran stops and clears his throat. "So what you're saying is that there's a demon in the basement and a doorway to hell in one of the guest rooms?"

"Yes. No. Maybe?" I flounder. "We don't know exactly where the vortex goes. Or what the thing in the basement really is. So... not sure about what terminology to use?" I look at Joe to help me.

"What I want to know," Skye says, "is have you been

in the Garden Suite? What does the, uh, vortex look like? Feel like? This is so weird."

I spread my hands. "I don't know. I've never had to go in there before. I did stand outside it for a couple hours on Saturday night," I admit. "But I couldn't sense anything, really. Maybe a tad more energy flow? But that could have been my imagination."

Kieran sucks in a deep breath. "Okay. Okay. There's a couple in there, right?"

I nod. "The Himmels. They haven't checked out yet, but they're due to leave this morning."

"First thing we need to do is rearrange reservations for that room," he orders.

"I've done everything except the weekends. We're full for months."

"Leave it with me," Skye says confidently. "We'll tart up the cabin teachers use during school camps. We can call it the executive suite or something and tell people they're getting an upgrade."

Kieran points to him. "Yes. Excellent idea. What do you need to get it done?"

Skye bites his lip. "I can take a lot of the stuff from the Garden Suite and storage, but I might need to buy a few bits and pieces. It could probably do with some paint? And furniture needs to be moved, so maybe muscle?"

"We'll help," Daniel volunteers, and Ewan immediately nods. I can't hold back the mental image of his broad back flexing as he lifts furniture. Maybe the veins on his forearms will show themselves.

"I will too," I say, my voice a little hoarse. "I don't have a lot of muscle, but I can paint and follow directions."

"There's a kitchenette in the cabin, isn't there?" Arissa muses. "We can stock it with some basics so the guests don't feel like they're missing out, being so far from the house. And we could do optional basket deliveries for meals. Make it the honeymoon suite and allow the guests to choose how much interaction they want with other people."

"Good plan," Kieran says, making a note on his tablet. "If you all can pull this off before the weekend, I'll double your Christmas bonuses."

"Consider it done," Daniel declares. "I'll even plant a little garden out the front, make the outside pretty."

"Okay." Kieran runs his hands through his hair, leaving it sticking out at funny angles. I'm beginning to think "okay" is a mantra for him—a word he says to organize his mind. "So we're getting the guests out of the Garden Suite. I'm changing the code on the lock panel, and only the people in this room will have access. And the ghosts," he tacks on, turning his gaze on Joe. "Is there anything we can do to make it easier for you to maintain the block?"

Joe shakes his head. "If there is, we don't know about it."

"It seems like not knowing is a big part of our problem here," Ewan says quietly. "How do we increase our knowledge?"

Everyone looks at me.

"I don't know." I try not to look at Ewan. Ever since our conversation yesterday, when he called me pretty and sunshiny, I've felt… vulnerable about him. I'm not ready to deal with those feelings yet, and fuck knows they're not the priority right now. "I can start with some internet searches, see if I stumble across anything. I want to call the medium who offered to train me a few years back. I won't tell her what's happened," I rush to add when Joe opens his mouth to protest. "I get that we need to be careful about who we trust. But I can tell her I've been reading stuff online and need help working out what's true and not."

"That might work." Kieran taps his fingertips on the tabletop. "I don't know any of the mediums who've stayed here before well enough to know if they can be trusted, I'm afraid. But I think one of them might have stayed in the Garden Suite?" His brow furrows. "I remember him saying the room had great energy. I'll check on that." He makes another note on his tablet.

"What are our goals?" Skye asks. "Get rid of the bogeyman and close the portal so it can't come back?"

Joe grumbles, and I know it's because of the words Skye chose. I shoot him a warning look. Terminology really isn't important right now. For all we know, the ghosts have been using the wrong labels for the past fifty years.

"Those seem like sensible goals," Daniel says dryly.

"They're certainly my goals," Kieran mutters.

"But won't closing the portal or whatever mean the ghosts won't be able to manifest anymore?"

Silence falls. I can't believe I didn't think of that. Maybe because I don't need them to manifest for me to talk to them.

"We know," Joe says heavily. "We'll miss talking to all of you, but it will be nice not to have to worry all the time. And Josh is here now to interpret for us."

Be the mouthpiece of half a dozen ghosts? No pressure or anything. But they're making a real sacrifice here, so the least I can do is pass on messages.

Kieran sighs. "Let's see what we can find out before we make any major decisions. This is your home too, and we want you to be comfortable here."

"Maybe we'll be able to find a way to get rid of the dark spirit without having to close the vortex," Ewan suggests, winning an approving glance from Joe for using the right words.

"But then others might sneak in," Arissa points out. "Still, Kieran's right. We don't need to decide right now. We might not even be able to do anything."

"There's a depressing thought." Daniel looks across the table at me. "You're going into the Garden Suite as soon as the guests check out?"

"I'll be in there while they're still at reception," I confirm. "Why? You wanna come?"

"Yes. And then I want to go down to the basement."

"Me too," Ewan adds. "Maybe there's something I can build to make it more secure."

"You work with metal, not crystals or stone," Daniel points out. "But yeah. We should check."

"You're not getting me down there," Arissa declares. "I don't know anything about demons anyway."

Joe shifts in his chair, scowling irritably.

"Could you watch reception?" Skye asks her. "I want to see, and I don't know if this thing will work in the basement." He gestures to the baby-monitor-type thing that allows him to see if anyone is at reception.

"No problem."

"Okay," Kieran says, and I bite the inside of my cheek to keep from laughing. This really isn't the time for it. "First step is for Josh to have a look at the vortex and hopefully discover there's a really easy way to close it. Don't make that face, Josh. Until you see it, I'm living in my bubble of hope."

I smooth out my doubting grimace and nod. "Bubble of hope for the win."

He snorts. "From this moment, the only people permitted into the Garden Suite are senior staff, even if that means we need to cancel some reservations. Which leads to the next step, converting the teachers' cabin into a honeymoon or executive suite. Skye's taking the lead on that."

"Got it," Skye promises. Not for the first time, I wish I had his confidence. Although moving furniture and painting is probably not comparable to closing a vortex to hell.

"Concurrent with that, we're going to start researching what the thing in the basement is and ways to get rid of it. I'll stop by the library and see if I can find any books that might help." He holds up a hand when Joe opens his mouth. "I know you've already tried that, but I can speak to the librarian and get some help. Maybe we can find something via inter-library loan."

"We should check out Amazon too," Ewan suggests. "The library might not have some of the more niche books, and if we're looking for a how-to on banishing demons, we probably need something pretty specific."

Kieran points his pen at Ewan. "Yes. Good thinking. We can also contact some of the paranormal investigation groups. Most of them are whack jobs, but some are genuinely doing research."

"What'll you tell them we want it for?" Joe demands. "Remember, you can trust *no one.*"

"I promise, Joe, I won't let anyone use this place or you to achieve nefarious ends," Kieran says solemnly, and Daniel mouths "nefarious." "I'll come up with something to tell them. Maybe that we're putting together a pamphlet on paranormal activity for our guests, since we're recognized as being a haunted building."

Joe doesn't look happy but doesn't argue.

"Josh, are you happy to take the lead on research? Since you're the one who'll have to implement whatever plan we come up with?"

I'm nodding before he finishes speaking. "Yeah, definitely. I won't object to help, but I'll coordinate the research."

"Good. Let's reassess at the staff meeting on Thursday, see how we're going. For now, while we're waiting for the Himmels to check out, let's go look at the basement."

Arissa reaches across the table to take the monitor from Skye. "That's my cue to go find the charm my sister gave me that's supposed to ward off the devil."

"They make those?" I wonder. "I mean, legit make them? It's not a velvet bag of herbs or anything?" We all get up and start moving toward the door.

"Not a bag of herbs," she confirms. "Her Italian mother-in-law gave it to her. It's supposed to be a horn or something, but the first time I saw her wearing it around her neck, I thought it was a dick."

I stop dead. "Seriously?"

"Yup. It doesn't actually look much like a dick," she adds. "I just didn't get a good view."

"I'm so disappointed by that." I would have liked wearing a dick on a chain around my neck. There's gotta be someone making cock-shaped jewelry, right? I'll get on Etsy later and see what I can find.

We part ways with Arissa in the hallway outside the staff room, and Kieran leads the way to the basement door, where we stand and stare.

"So you can feel that there's something bad down there?" Skye asks dubiously, hand up, palm toward the door, as though he's trying to feel something.

I shiver. "Yes. It's not that strong up here—a sense of wrongness. Like a danger sign? It makes me want to avoid this area."

"Danger signs don't have that effect on me," Daniel says absently, studying the door, and Skye elbows him in the ribs. "Oof. Thanks for that."

"You're welcome," Skye says sweetly. "Come on, are we going down?"

"Yes." Kieran grabs the flashlight and unlocks the door. "Ewan, can you put a deadbolt on this door?"

"No problem," Ewan assures him.

"Do we really need to?" I ask. "I mean, you and I are the only ones with keys to get in. And if that thing gets out, I don't think an extra lock will stop it."

"What a comforting thought," Kieran murmurs, peering into the basement. "We really need to, if only so I can assure myself I took all possible steps to prevent a demon from eating souls."

Also a comforting thought. I try not to dwell on the fact that as someone who lives in the house, my soul would probably be one of the first the dark spirit would go after.

I'm not sure what everyone expected to see, but as I show them the section of rocky wall the dark spirit is trapped in, they all seem disappointed.

"That's it?" Daniel asks.

"That's it," I confirm. "You can't feel the darkness?"

He hesitates. "I was going to say no," he says slowly, "but I guess I feel like I don't like it? It doesn't give me the creeps or anything, but I just don't... like it."

"Same," Ewan says from directly beside me, and I jump. When did he come to stand there?

"I'm creeped out when I look directly at it," Skye says, taking half a step closer, then shivering and stepping back. "And when I get too close. But just standing here and looking somewhere else?" He shakes his head. "Nothing."

We all look at Kieran, who's shining the flashlight along the edges of the small tomb. "I'm with Skye," he says. "Looking at it gives me the heebie-jeebies. What can we do to make this more secure? Aside from buying a shit-ton of quartz and filling the room with it?"

"No idea. Joe?" I ask.

He harrumphs. "If we knew, we'd have done it already."

"Salt, maybe?" Ewan suggests. "Isn't that supposed to be a deterrent?"

"That's for ghosts," Daniel reminds him, and Joe glares.

"Are you implying that we are in any way kin to the dark spirit?"

Ewan holds up his hands. "No way. But all those movies that have demon summonings use a salt circle, right?"

"You have shit taste in movies," Kieran tells him. "But that's right." He looks at me. "Would salt help?"

I rub my jaw. "I really don't know," I admit. "I don't think it would hurt, but it would prevent the ghosts from getting in here."

"Do they need to get in here?" he counters. "If this thing gets out, what would they do that we can't?"

We all turn to Joe, who appears to consider it. "If anything, you're better equipped to deal with it," he concedes. "We have to be manifested, which takes a lot of energy. It would have to kill you before it could take your souls, and from what we saw when it first arrived, it can't directly do that. It has to push you down stairs or throw something at your head and hope that works."

There's an awkward little silence while we all mull over how much we don't want to be shoved down a flight of stairs by a dark spirit that's hoping we'll die so it can eat our souls.

"Okay," Kieran says at last. "We put a salt line down here and hope that helps. And we stock up on quartz. Everyone carries a piece with them at all times, so you'll be ready if we need to herd this thing somewhere." He turns back to me. "Is there a ritual or something needed with the salt?"

I shrug. "I've never used one for ghosts. It's the actual salt itself that does the work."

"Let's do that now, then."

"I'll grab the salt. There's some in the storeroom," Daniel volunteers, heading back to the stairs. Skye starts asking Kieran about bedding for the new honeymoon suite, and Ewan edges closer to me.

"Are you okay?" he murmurs in a low voice, and for the first time this morning, I look at him properly. His gaze is warm and concerned, and that hidden, deep-down part of me that's so tired of always having to get by really wants to snuggle up against his big body and let him take care of me.

Which is stupid. For one thing, he's never given any indication he *wants* to take care of me. Our connection was about a good fuck and nothing more. And even if he did want to, I don't need to be taken care of. I've spent my life looking after myself, and I don't need to change that now.

"Sure."

He puts one of his big, warm hands on my forearm, and I curl my toes in an attempt to keep from shivering. "You're allowed to not be okay, you know. This is a huge mess to get dumped on you, and you haven't slept enough since you found out."

I swallow and try to laugh. It comes out broken. "Are you saying I look shit?"

His smile is slow and seems to convey a special message. "I don't think you could ever look shit." He grabs one of my hands and inspects my fingernails. Even in the crappy light down here, the yellow is bright. "I really like this color," he says.

What do I say? "Thanks," I croak, then am thankfully rescued by the sound of Daniel thumping down the stairs, a ten-pound bag of salt slung over his shoulder. We all turn toward him as he reaches us.

"What do we do?" he asks me.

"Open the bag and pour out a line of salt." It's not really that hard.

Although the looks he and Ewan both give me suggest I've oversimplified things.

"How thick should the line be?" Daniel asks.

"And how high? Do we need to pile it up?" Ewan adds.

Oh my god, way to overthink this. "It doesn't matter, and no. All you need is an unbroken line. If you had the patience to line up individual grains of salt, that would probably do the trick."

Ewan's eyes widen, and they exchange a glance that I think means they want to try that. "But we're in a hurry today," I add hastily, "so just a regular poured line will do."

Daniel pouts but obediently rips open the bag and starts pouring, with Ewan hovering by his elbow. Skye's sniggering, and when I look over, Kieran meets my gaze and rolls his eyes. He's smiling, though, which makes me feel better.

In fact… everything about this morning has made me feel better. It's weird, because the situation hasn't changed since yesterday, but telling people and knowing they've got my back is such a relief. Last night I lay awake for hours, fretting about whether I'd be able to handle any of this, but now, with Kieran's to-do list and Skye's upbeat confidence and Ewan's and Daniel's steady capability—not to mention Arissa's go-get-'em attitude—I'm not as worried. Even if it's not easy, we'll find a way to get this done.

I'm not alone anymore. And fucked if that's not weird.

BY THE TIME we leave the basement and lock the door securely behind us, the Himmels have checked out of the Garden Suite. Arissa must have shoved them out the door, because she's waiting for us in the storage room.

"Vortex room. Let's go," she announces. "I need to get back to the kitchen soon."

"Bring the salt," I tell Daniel. "It might not make a difference, but it can't hurt to use it."

So we troop along the hallway and upstairs, trying to seem casual in case the last lingering guests are around. Hattie meets up with us on the second-floor landing.

"Is the meeting done? What's been decided?" she asks anxiously.

"We're going to look at the vortex," I tell her.

Kieran shoots me an odd look. "We know, you don't... Oh. Ghost?" He glances around. I guess that means Hattie's not manifested.

"Hattie," I tell him as Joe pulls her aside and begins muttering. I'm not sure if he's telling her about the meeting or just complaining that nobody used the "right" terminology.

We stop in front of the door to the Garden Suite, and Kieran uses his fob to open it. Inside, the bed is unmade, and a glance into the en suite bath shows towels on the floor, but the room is otherwise tidy. I've heard the housekeepers complaining about guests who leave trash—or worse—strewn around, and I'm glad we don't have to deal with that right now.

"Well, where is it?" Ewan asks, glancing around as we all crowd in. The room is a decent size, but not really meant to hold so many people.

I walk over to the closet and throw open the doors. I don't need the ghosts to direct me—this close, I can feel the rushing whisper of energy. And once the closet is open, I can *see* the vortex. Just faintly—a slightly glowing outline—but it's there.

"Is it in there?" Skye asks, coming to stand at my shoulder. He holds his hands out toward it. "I can feel...

kind of like a breeze?" He steps back and glances around. "Or is that the air-conditioning?"

"It's here," I confirm. There's definitely a flow of energy coming through, seeping around the edges of the ghosts' block—which is itself a big lump of energy, but it feels different.

Still, I have no idea how to close it.

I study it a bit longer, hoping something will catch my attention, but other than the energy flow making me feel great, there's nothing. I turn to face the others and shake my head. "I'm sorry, I don't know what to do."

Disappointment flashes across their faces, and I hate to have let them down.

"Never mind," Ewan declares, grabbing the salt from Daniel and moving forward. "We were pretty sure we'd need to do some research first anyway." He smiles at me. "Should I just salt the whole closet?"

Spinning to look at the vortex again, I hold out a hand, palm up. "Hang on. Give me some salt, please."

The fine grains fill my palm as he pours it, and I close my fist around them. I need to do this carefully. I'm not sure how the salt will affect the ghosts' block, and we definitely don't want to accidentally pull that down.

Pinching a few grains of salt between my fingers, I toss them at the block. There's no change.

"Did you feel anything?" I ask Joe and Hattie, who are hovering near the door.

"No," Hattie says, and Joe shakes his head. So I try a bigger pinch of salt.

Still nothing.

Then I throw the whole fistful at it.

"I don't know what you're doing, but it's making a mess," Kieran observes.

"We were going to pour salt there anyway," Skye reminds him. "And the housekeepers won't be coming in to complain. Which reminds me…" He turns toward the bed. "I guess it's up to us to strip the linens."

"Dammit," Arissa whines.

Blocking them out as they begin discussing whether they should leave the old sheets on to protect the mattress while it's being moved out to the cabin, I reach into the bag Ewan's holding and grab another handful of salt.

"Do you need anything?" he murmurs to me, and I shoot him a grateful smile. It might be weird, but I can't help liking it when he tries to take care of me.

"I just want to see if the vortex will react to the salt."

This time, I adjust my aim away from the block and toward the faint outline of an opening. The salt hits it squarely, and then some of it *blows back into the room*.

"Whoa!"

"What the fuck?"

Ewan's and Daniel's voices grab everyone's attention.

"What happened?" Arissa peers over Daniel's shoulder, trying to see.

"It was like a wind," he tells her, "blowing the salt."

Skye's eyes get big. "Really?"

"Can you do it again?" Ewan asks me as they all crowd around. I want to say something about it not being a party trick, but I don't since I want to try it again anyway.

This time, I use a bit more salt, and the effect is

clearly visible, the salt floating on the energy current for almost a foot before dropping to the floor.

"Holy fuck," Kieran whispers. "Fuck fuck fuck."

"So, uh, there's definitely something there." Arissa takes a big step back. "You don't need me in here anymore, do you? I'll just, uh, head back to the kitchen."

"Go," Kieran tells her, not taking his eyes off the spot in the closet where the salt had been. "Could you take the monitor from Skye and keep an eye on reception again? I want to get everything we need for the cabin out of this room now."

Skye passes the device over to her, and she flips us a wave as she dashes out the door. I can't blame her—I'm used to paranormal crap, and this still makes me nervous.

"Did the salt affect the vortex?" Ewan asks, laying a big hand on my shoulder.

"I don't think so. The flow of energy is undisturbed, and there was no change in shape or size." I glance over at the ghosts. "Right?"

"Agreed." Hattie speaks for them both.

Kieran sighs. "There go my hopes of chucking enough salt at this thing to close it."

"The vortex itself doesn't appear to be dangerous—more what comes through it. And the salt might help to deter that." I take the bag from Ewan and pour a thick line of salt around the vortex, getting into the closet to reach behind it too. Its energy brushes up against my skin when I get close, and I can't lie: it feels amazing. The ghosts were right to be cautious about who they trusted.

When I step back, there's a circle of salt in the closet. "Could we get some quartz stones in here too?" I suggest to Kieran. "Now that there won't be any guests to question it, they might be useful."

"Definitely." He whips out his tablet and makes a note. "So… that's it?"

I spread my hands. "There's nothing else I can do until I know more."

He nods. "Then let's get the furniture out of here."

Chapter Twelve

EWAN

This week has lasted for eternity, and it's only Thursday. Our busiest days are still ahead.

I sink onto the couch and rest my head against the back, closing my eyes just for one second. I promised to flip through some of the books that arrived today. Kieran must have ordered everything Amazon had on the subject of demons and spirits. He and Josh already went through everything the library had on offer, and aside from the usual talk of demons being bad, there was nothing there.

"Want a beer?" Daniel offers from the doorway to the kitchen.

"No, thanks." A beer would likely put me to sleep right now. I haven't been getting enough rest this week. Aside from the extra work we've been doing to set up the cabin, and the mind fuck of having a soul-eating demon and a gate to the underworld or wherever on the property, I've been worried about Josh. He seems to be taking it personally that there's no easy way to resolve this.

Prying my eyes open, I nab the top book from the pile. It has a very homemade-looking cover, but we're hoping the less-mainstream books will have some tidbits we can actually use.

I'm flipping pages slowly, scanning my gaze down each one, when I sense a presence beside me on the couch and look up to see Carter.

"Didn't we talk about you announcing yourself somehow?" I grumble, returning my gaze to the page. It's only halfhearted, though. Now that I know how hard he and the other ghosts have been working to keep us all safe, I'm inclined to cut them some slack.

"Hattie thinks you should come to the house and talk to Josh," he informs me, and my head snaps up.

"Why? Is he okay?"

Carter shrugs. "I think he's fine, but Hattie says he's depressed. Maisie thinks he needs a good seeing to, so I said I'd come and get you."

I blink even as Daniel bursts out in loud laughter.

"Carter," I protest, "you promised to keep it a secret."

"I did! I didn't say you'd seen to him before—"

"Okay, wait. You've gotta stop saying it like that," Daniel interrupts.

Carter huffs. "—I just suggested that if he needed a s— er, *company*, you would be a good person to do it. Give him… company. And they all agreed."

"Even Josh?" I ask pointedly, and he pulls a face.

"We didn't ask him."

I sigh, close the book, and stand.

"You're going to proposition Josh because the ghosts suggested it?" Daniel asks incredulously.

I glare at him. "No. But if Josh is feeling down, he

might like some company. And some bourbon. Or maybe just the bourbon. Either way, I can take it over and check on him."

Daniel loses interest once he's sure the possibility of salacious gossip is past. He's a simple man.

I put shoes on and grab a nearly full liquor bottle from the cabinet over the fridge. We don't drink much of the hard stuff here on the estate, but my sister gave me this for my birthday.

The walk up to the house is lovely—quiet, since Carter has either stayed behind or done his zippy ghost thing to beat me there—and I'm humming with good feelings when I let myself in through the staff door. I'm not sure how many guests we have tonight, but it's still early enough that I can hear people in the kitchen, probably cleaning up after dinner. I slip past, not wanting to answer questions, and head up to the attic.

Josh answers the door on the first knock. He's changed into sweatpants and a faded old tee that's clearly shrunk in the wash, and he looks delectable.

"Ewan." The note of surprise is clear. "Is there a problem?"

I shake my head. "Nope. It's been a bitch of a week, and I thought you might like to forget it for a while." I hold up the bottle, and a smile breaks over his face.

"You have the best ideas. Come in." He takes a step back and gestures, but I hesitate.

"Are you sure? If you want quiet, I don't mind leaving the bottle and going."

He bites his lip. "If that's what you prefer…"

Something slams into my back, shoving me hard, and I stumble forward into the apartment.

"Johnny!" Josh scolds. I turn to look just as Johnny disappears from my sight.

"Is he gone or just not visible to me?"

"Gone." He scowls at the empty hallway, then reaches out and takes the bottle from me, the sparkly blue of his fingernails looking great against the amber liquid. "C'mon, let's drink."

I close the door behind me and obediently follow him to the kitchen island. The last time I was in here was when I helped Adele move, and even though the furniture is mostly the same, it feels different now. Maybe because Adele loved floral cushions and throws and tchotchkes, and from the looks of it, Josh would be fine living in a cave with a single military surplus blanket. But he brings out two plain glass tumblers, the kind they sell in a four-pack at the grocery store, and grabs the ice-cube tray from the freezer.

What more can a man ask for?

We move to the couch, and he pours with a heavy hand. I have a strong feeling I'm not going to be at my best tomorrow. Luckily, it's Daniel's morning to get up for the animals, so I can have an extra hour in bed.

"Cheers," he says, holding up his glass. "To a totally fucked-up week. May it end soon."

"Hell, yeah." I clink my glass to his and then take a bigger gulp than I probably should. The liquor burns pleasantly all the way down my esophagus.

For a long moment, we sit in silence. Josh is staring into the distance, a contemplative look on his face. Maybe he'd rather be alone after all? Did Johnny force his hand?

Should I offer to leave?

"What's on your mind?" I venture. That gives him an opening to tell me he's tired, right?

Dragging his attention back, he looks over at me and smiles wryly. "I was just thinking that if I drink enough of this, I'll be able to suck your dick and then tell myself I did it because of the alcohol."

Um.

"Really?" I ask weakly. What the heck else can I say? Not that I'd let him if he was drunk—not when sober Josh made it clear he didn't want anything more to happen between us.

He nods. "Yup. But then I realized that would be a crappy thing to do. And that if I want it enough sober to get drunk to do it, then I should just get over myself and do it sober. Right?"

I'm not even sure if that sentence made sense, but if he's asking me if I think he should blow me, there's only one possible answer. "Yes. Definitely."

He sets his barely touched glass on the coffee table and slides off the couch to kneel in front of me. Oh my god, this is really going to happen. Coming here tonight was the best decision I've ever made.

Except…

I catch his hands in my free one as he reaches for my pants. "Wait… is this going to make you uncomfortable with me again? Because even though you give the best blowjobs I've ever had, I don't want things to be awkward between us."

He heaves a big sigh. "Why'd you have to say that? Now I have *feelings*."

Say what?

"I won't hate you," he promises. "We'll be friends."

Who am I to say no to that? I let go of his hand, toss

back the remainder of my bourbon, and set the empty glass on the arm of the couch while Josh opens my pants and pulls out my cock.

"Mm, hello," he murmurs. "Remember me?"

I snort. "Are you seriously talking to my dick?"

He licks the head, making me break out in a sweat, then smiles wickedly up at me. "Shh. We're having a moment."

I don't have the chance to answer before he swallows me whole and I lose every ounce of brainpower I've ever possessed. I'd almost forgotten this from our night together—if Josh has a gag reflex, it's so miniscule it might as well not exist. Which is how he takes me halfway down his throat in that first moment.

"Fuck!" It bursts from me in a harsh exhalation as my hand finds its way to Josh's hair. The cool, silky strands slide through my fingers as he draws back, working the head with his tongue, tracing along the vein that runs along the underside, then plunging back down.

I force myself to keep my eyes open, wanting so desperately to watch. Josh holds my gaze, his mouth stretched wide around me, and I emblazon this image in my memory. It's what I want to envision in future while I jerk myself raw.

He pulls back so only the head is in his mouth, cool air whispering over my spit-damp flesh, and sucks lightly. A deep moan is torn from my chest. Distantly, I notice Josh's arm moving and realize he has his hand in his sweatpants. Good. Although I really want to take a turn getting him off later.

His mouth slides back down the length of me, and for a second, my eyes fall closed. I pry them open, not wanting to miss anything, and slip my hand from his hair to lightly clasp around his throat, feeling the way he's working my cock from yet another angle. Each breath is being torn from my lungs, desperate, needy. I can't hold on much longer.

But then, judging by the glazed passion in his gaze, neither can he. His arm is moving faster now, almost frantically, as he slowly draws back up my dick, the clasp of his lips so tight around me.

Then he places his other hand low on the sensitive skin of my abdomen, right above my cock, and a tremor runs through me. Almost involuntarily, I look at his hand. The sparkly blue of his nails is bright against my skin… and pushes me over the edge. I come so hard, I think I black out.

I open my eyes in time to see Josh wiping his mouth with one hand and his other hand down the leg of his sweatpants. He's breathing even harder than I am.

"Come here," I gasp, patting my lap. "Let me—"

"No need," he declares, scrambling to his feet. "Gimme a sec. Help yourself to another drink."

I twist my head around to watch him go into the bathroom, then lever myself forward and grab for the bottle, refilling my glass and topping off his. By the time he comes out, wearing a different pair of sweats, my breathing is almost back to normal.

He throws himself onto the couch, sprawling along the length with his head in my lap, then takes my glass out of my hand and knocks back the contents in one go, his neck craned at an awkward angle to avoid spilling or choking.

"Hey," I protest, though mostly it's because it's a sin to treat good bourbon like that. He hands me back the glass.

"I couldn't reach mine," he explains with a faux innocent smile. There's something different about him—he seems… relaxed?

As if he can hear my thoughts, he gives a contented moan and stretches. "That was amazing."

"It really was," I agree. "Though I feel like I didn't pull my weight."

"Oh, you totally did. Although next time we'll sixty-nine or something. But that was just what I needed." He sits up and looks me in the eye. "There's not much in my life I've had control over. Since I came here, it's been better, but still… But this, this was perfect. It's good to know I can trust you to let me be in charge. Thank you."

I feel guilty about the pride that bursts in my chest, because really, all I did was get a fucking awesome blowjob. But if it gave him what he needed, I'm not going to be the asshole who argues about it. "Anything you need."

We smile at each other, and then he grabs his glass off the table with one hand and passes me the bottle with the other.

"Wanna watch a movie?"

"No, but see… see… seeeeeeeeeeeee. Wow, that's a great word! Why have I never appreesated it afore?" Josh seems delighted by his new discovery.

I squint, trying to see his face clearly. It's hard. There's some kind of weird blurry fog distorting my vision. A tiny voice at the back of my mind tells me it's because I'm drunk, but I ignore it. Drunk people aren't capable of thinking as clearly as I am right now.

"Seeeeeeeee," I repeat, trying it out for myself. "Wow, it *is* a great word!"

"We should make it the word of the day." He raises his voice from where he's lying half under the coffee table. "I heretoforeby declare the word of the day to be… what was it again?"

"What was what?"

"The word! What was the word?"

"Ohhhh. The word. It was… a good word. See! It's see." I smile smugly. Hah! I can't possibly be drunk.

"See is declarated to be the word! And we shall… say it. A lot. See!"

"See!" I echo cheerfully.

"Anyhoodles, what was I saying?"

"Not saying, *see*ing." He must be much more drunker than me.

"My mapogolies. Ampogolies. Ma-pog-logies. Why is that word wrong?"

"Is it wrong, though? Is it? Maybe all the words are right and *we're* the ones who're wrong." I tip my head back to contemplate the ceiling, and the room spins. "Whoa. Are you okay?"

"Maybe? It's hard to know, y'know? Is anyone really okay?"

Wow, he's so *deep*. "You're so deep. I just want to plunder how deep you are." I squint. Wait. "I mean I want to pillage your depths."

"Thank you," he says gravely. "I've never been pillaged before. I think I was plundered once, though? It was at Burger King."

"I like Burger King. Can I tell you a secret? I like McDonald's."

His eyes widen. "Me too! Oh my god, we're like… twins!"

I scrunch up my face. "I don't wanna be your twin. That would make the things we've done icky."

He heaves a big sigh. "Yeah. Twincest is not as good as McDonald's. So it's official… we're not twins."

"Deal!" My attention is caught by what's happening on the screen. "Oh, this is the best part!"

Josh sits up abruptly and smacks his head on the coffee table. "Owww!"

"Dude, you need to ask it nicely to move! Say you're sorry."

He wriggles out from underneath, then pats the table. "Sorry, friend." Hauling himself up onto the couch beside me, he says, "See, this is the *thing* about this movie. People watch it and they don't understand it. They think it's just fun, and it *is*. It *is* fun. But it's also got more. It's… it's… it's *nuanced*. Nuuwwannnced. There are *nuances*. And people don't get those. They don't get how *subtle* and nuanced this movie is."

I nod, fascinated, while on the screen Ricky Bobby tells his father that he's lived his whole life based on the principle "if you ain't first, you're last."

"I get it. I get the new-antsing," I tell him. That doesn't sound right somehow, but it's probably because Josh is drunk.

Sometime later, we both must fall asleep, because I wake in the soft glow of dawn with a sore neck and Josh's head in my lap. And a pounding headache.

The groan that's ripped from my throat hurts my head even more. Josh whimpers.

"Why are you being loud?" he whispers.

"Coffee. Is there coffee?" I beg.

"Shhh. Loud."

Slowly, I turn my head to look over at the kitchenette. There is no coffee machine. Please let Josh be the type to use a french press. Please.

Somehow, I don't think I'm that lucky.

Swallowing down bile, I force my weak and achy muscles to work and ease Josh's head off me as I heave myself to my feet… and sway. *Please don't fall.* I don't think I could manage to pick myself up again.

Thankfully, I don't fall, and with slow, shuffling steps, I drag myself over to the kitchen and begin checking cabinets.

There is no french press.

There is no coffee.

There is no cola in the fridge.

Or chocolate.

No caffeine. At all.

A sound that might be a sob bursts from me.

"Whyyyyyy are you loud?" Josh moans from the couch.

Ignoring him, I find a glass, fill it with water, and then help myself to the ibuprofen in one of the cabinets. Next stop: bathroom.

When I come out after relieving myself and splashing a lot of cold water on my face, Josh has hauled himself to a sitting position and has his head buried in his hands. I get him some water and ibuprofen, and he manages a scratchy, "Thanks."

Collapsing on the couch beside him, I stare blankly at the TV. The screen is dark, but I think it's still on? So we must have passed out while we were watching…

It floods back to me. Did… did I actually agree that *Talladega Nights* is a meaningful movie?

Wait.

Did Josh actually mean it? Because that's terrifying.

"Um…"

"What?" he mutters.

"Do you remember last night?"

His head turns in slow increments until he's looking at me. "Maybe? I remember sucking you off. I was sober then. I don't regret it. We should do it again sometime. Did you do something weird to me after I passed out?" He wriggles his body. "I don't feel like you did."

"I'd be offended by that if I had the energy. No. And yes, we should do it again sometime. Let's talk about it when thinking doesn't hurt."

"Agreed. What am I trying to remember then?"

"We watched *Talladega Nights*," I prompt.

He blinks. "Yeah? So? Did—" His eyes widen. "Oh my god. Please tell me I didn't say 'nuanced' fifty times."

I close one eye. "Fifty sounds about right."

"I am *such* an idiot. I should never be allowed to watch that movie drunk. Last time, I got on eBay and tried to buy a kids' bike to deliver pizzas with because that seemed like such a good idea."

He… wow.

"Well, this wasn't as bad as that. Unless you really do think it's a subtle movie." Don't get me wrong, I enjoy it as much as the next guy, but I don't think I could take him seriously if he believes all that. And I really want to—take things seriously with him. You know, now that we're friends. Who give each other blowjobs.

And share each other's hopes and dreams.

He gives me a disbelieving look. "It's pure comic relief and about as subtle as the sledgehammer pounding inside my skull. I need coffee."

"You don't have any," I tell him helpfully. "What time is it? Would someone be in the kitchen yet?"

We both squint at the wall clock. It's just before six.

"No," he groans. "The breakfast shift doesn't get here until six thirty. Do you know how to use the machine downstairs?"

I snort, then wince and wish I hadn't. That bastard vibrated right through my brain. "I don't even know how to turn it on. What are the chances that the thermos in the parlor still has something in it?" It'd be stone cold, but worth it.

He shakes his head. "Low. The guests we have now like to stay up late talking." Taking a deep breath, he drags himself off the couch. "Let's shower. That might help. If nothing else, by the time we're done, someone who knows how the coffee machine works will be downstairs."

"You have good plans." And I can maybe have a catnap while he showers first.

He stares down at me. "Are you going to make me pull you up? Because I didn't do great in high school physics, but I know you're twice my size and it's not likely I can do it."

I blink at him a few times while his meaning sinks in, then scramble to my feet, ignoring the way that makes my stomach lurch. I'd be an idiot to pass up a joint shower. And despite all the evidence to the contrary right now, I'm no idiot.

"Lead the way."

Chapter Thirteen

JOSH

By the time Friday night finally arrives and I can slink off to my room—and hope none of the guests need me—I feel like a wet rag. No, not just a wet rag—a *dirty* wet rag.

Getting drunk last night was a huuuuuge mistake. Because of how I feel today, obviously, and if one of the guests had called during the night, I would have been screwed. I get nights off, but that wasn't one of them. So… yeah. Mistake.

There was a good part, though, and that was Ewan. I'm not even talking about the part where we both came, great as that was. It was so good to just talk to him. Even when we were off our faces and saying stupid stuff, it was nice. Comfortable. Secure. And the same this morning.

I feel like Ewan sees who I am without all the ghost stuff. That's scary enough, but worse? He likes it. He likes who I am.

I don't know if I'm okay with that. Nobody's ever really liked me that way before. While part of me really wants this, wants him, I'm terrified I'll get used to it and then it will go away.

This probably isn't the time to worry about that, though. I have a nagging headache still, I'm tired, and I'm hungry. Plus I have a bunch more research to do tonight, because we're not finding the information we need.

An hour later, hunger satisfied and headache thankfully fading, I squint at my laptop screen. Ewan sent me an email ten minutes ago with a link to a website about demons.

Not sure if this will be of any use, but the forum has a few threads on summoning and stuff. Let me know if you want me to dig through them. And get some rest. Dinner tomorrow night? I'll cook.

I click the link and try not to think about what him cooking me dinner means. Is that like a date? Or is it beyond a date? Are we… boyfriends? We can't be. I'd know that, right? There has to be a category between dating and boyfriends.

Wait… how do you know when you're boyfriends with someone? Is there a list of criteria?

Fuck it. I'll ask Skye tomorrow.

Pushing the thought aside, I scan the website. Most of it looks pretty hokey, wannabe demon-worshippers, which surprises me. I hadn't thought of approaching it from this angle, but I guess people who want to summon demons would need to have a fair bit of information about them. Hopefully including how to make them go away.

If the spirit in the basement is, in fact, a demon. Urgh. How am I going to get rid of it if I don't know what the fuck it even is?

I click over to the forum page on the site, which looks like a question/answer knowledgebase type thing. Anyone can ask a question, but it looks like only registered site members can answer. That's okay. I'm just looking for answers, not giving them.

Skimming down the threads, I get more and more frustrated. Are people really this fucking stupid? Half these questions are about summoning demons—how to, where, will they appear with clothes, and if not, what kind of clothes would they like, what to feed them (um, the souls of your enemies, you nitwit), where they're most comfortable sleeping... it's like these idiots think demons are well-behaved houseguests. I don't know much about summoning demons, but I'm pretty sure you don't just invite them into your home without setting some serious boundaries. Does salt work on them?

Curiously, I click into one of the "How do I summon a demon" threads. Maybe the answers will include instructions for sending them back.

Half an hour later, my headache has intensified and I'm wondering if this whole site is just satire. If not, the future of humanity is bleak. On the plus side, none of the answers about summoning demons look anywhere near realistic. If standing in a dark room and calling out "Demon Lord, I summon thee" works, then high school slumber parties probably would have wiped us out decades ago. There are a few vague answers involving pentagrams drawn with chicken blood and chants in Latin, but none of them are detailed enough to make me worry that people are actually summoning demons. Some people who've commented must agree with me, because there's a few instances of "This isn't helpful" and "Does anybody have a drawing of the exact symbols needed" and, my personal favorite from someone called NotEvenDemonsDeserveThis, "oh my god why do you all even exist, I can't handle how stupid you are." There's a barrage of responses to that for daring to call upon a god. Sadly, there's nothing about sending demons back.

I'm just about to close out of the site when another thread catches my eye. *How do I know what kind of demon I've summoned?*

Ooh. Maybe someone's said something that would help us to work out what the spirit in the basement actually is. Because while Joe and the other ghosts have insistently been calling it a dark spirit, the humans in the know are leaning pretty heavily toward demon. Personally, I don't care what we call it as long as we work out a way to get rid of it for good.

I click into the thread and am immediately disappointed. Most of the answers are unhelpful, telling the original poster that they can't have summoned a demon without first knowing all the details about it. One suggests torturing it with holy water until it identifies itself, but that has a flurry of responses decrying it because that would upset the demon, and an upset demon won't help to overthrow enemies or whatever.

My skimming gaze lands on an answer from NotEvenDemonsDeserveThis.

I can't believe I'm doing this but you're all so dumb I feel compelled to try to save you. Listen up. YES, it's not easy to summon a demon without knowing exactly what you're doing, but there are some morons out there who manage it anyway. Usually because they're too stupid to exist and the universe is trying to balance that out. If you have somehow summoned a demon within a circle and don't know how to identify it, here's a tip: ask for its true name. Within the circle, summoned by you, it will be compelled to respond. Don't bargain with it until you have its true name, and for fuck's sake, don't release it from the circle. If you somehow summoned it without a circle, you won't need this advice, because you'll be dead. But thanks so much for unleashing a demon on the world before it killed you.

I read it three times, trying not to get excited. It might sound like they know what they're talking about, but whoever this person is might just be making up bullshit.

Putting down my laptop, I go in search of a ghost. For the first time *ever* in my life, I wish there was one in the room with me. They've been so respectful of my personal space since I set boundaries, but right now, I need to talk to them.

I find them just down the hall in the room for staff to crash in overnight. They're watching reruns of *The Bachelor* from two seasons ago for reasons I don't want to ask about. I knock lightly on the doorframe. "Do you have a moment?"

They all blink at me. "Josh? Is everything okay?" Hattie zooms forward, shedding the pretense of being corporeal in her worry that something might be wrong.

"Everything's fine. Sorry, I didn't mean to worry you."

There's a general round of sighs and grumbles as they settle back onto the beds.

"What can we do for you?" Hattie beams at me, thrilled that I've sought them out after hours.

"How well do you remember the night the dark spirit arrived?"

"Vividly," Freddie says dryly.

"Burned into my brain," Maisie adds.

"Do you remember seeing any kind of circle or drawing on the floor of the room?"

Blank stares are the only response.

"It might have been in chalk or salt… or blood. And it would have been near the vortex. Or maybe around it?"

Hattie shakes her head slowly, glancing over at Joe. "I didn't see anything like that. But we might not have noticed that night."

"The dark spirit and the vortex itself had all our attention," Joe adds.

"I guess they would. That's fine. Thanks anyway."

"I think," Maisie begins slowly, her brow furrowed, "I think the housekeepers might have said something?"

I freeze. "Really?"

She purses her lips and shrugs, making the bodice of her perilously low-cut Regency-style dress slip a little more. "Maybe? I went back to check on my room after the police said the owners could use it again—that's the room I died in, you know—and there were two of them in there cleaning up after the dark spirit's rampage. One was complaining that whatever the guest had been doing to end up dead, she'd left a mess everywhere, even in the closet." Maisie waves a hand casually, rings catching the light. "Maybe that was salt or something?"

"Maybe," I agree. "Thanks, Maisie." Although I'm not really sure what this proves? That the dark spirit is a demon and the guest—whose name I still don't know, despite Kieran trying to find out—let it out of the circle without being able to control it? Or maybe her circle was accidentally broken? But where does the vortex come into it?

"There might be more information in her diary."

This time, I'm not the only one who freezes. The whole room goes still, and then we all look at Maisie, who blinks innocently.

"Di—" I clear my throat. "Diary?"

"What diary?" Joe demands.

"There's a *diary*?" Johnny claps hands covered in tattoos of smiley faces. "This is just like *Murder, She Wrote*!"

"Why didn't you ever mention this diary before?" Joe barks, and Maisie jumps, her lower lip trembling.

"Don't snap at me," she whines.

Hattie holds up her hands. "Now, now. Let's all just stay calm. Maisie, dear, how do you know about the diary?"

Maisie sniffles. Which, considering she's a ghost and can't actually cry, is something special. "The housekeepers were talking about it. The police took all her things, but they mustn't have searched the room too well, because after her death was declared a heart attack and the housekeepers were allowed to go into the room again, they found her diary on the floor under the bed. The owners called the police, who said they didn't need it. But the housekeepers felt it was wrong to throw it away, so they put it in the lost-and-found."

I take a deep breath and reach down deep for patience. "So the diary got thrown out when the hotel was closed?"

"No," Freddie says excitedly. "The owners moved out most of the furniture and valuables, but a lot of things got left behind. The dark spirit was active then, remember. They just wanted to get out as soon as they could. When the new owners bought the place, they found the old lost-and-found box in a storage closet. They were excited, remember?" he asks Hattie, who nods slowly.

"Yes… there were some things that had been there for a long time, and they thought they'd be good for the museum. History of the hotel and all that."

"And the diary was in there?"

Hattie shrugs. "I'm not certain, to be honest."

"I am," Maisie declares. "I have an *affinity* with everything that was ever in Room 203. That's where I died, and part of me will always infuse that room."

I make a mental note not to ever get between Maisie and the Garden Suite.

"Maisie," I begin as calmly and sweetly as I can, "do you know where the diary is now?"

She nods. "Of course. I have an—"

"Affinity, yes, I know. I'm so glad for that. You'll have to tell us all about it one day. Where's the diary?"

"And why did you never mention it before?" Joe growls. Obviously he can't hold himself back any longer.

"But mostly where," I add desperately, not wanting her to get upset and distracted.

"In the museum, of course."

My heart sinks. I might not have been here that long, but after having to help out with some museum tours, I know what's in the displays, and a hotel guest's diary from the 1970s is not there.

"Well, not *in* the museum." She giggles. "In the storage room. When the owners curated the display, they didn't think the diary was historic enough just yet. So they put it away for the future."

My heart starts beating double time. "Maisie, do you

know exactly where?" I've glanced into that storage room. It's fifteen feet by fifteen feet, lined with box-filled shelves, and has additional rows of shelves in the center. I'm sure there's some kind of indexing system, but it's not something anyone ever showed me, since curating new displays and packing up old ones isn't anything I'm trained to do. If Maisie doesn't know where it is, I'll have to wait until morning or call Kieran.

Maisie pouts. "Not *exactly*," she says. "I know which wall it's on, but I lose track of which shelf."

That still cuts the amount of work needed dramatically. I could potentially find it tonight and actually have some answers by the time Kieran arrives in the morning. I bite my lip.

"Come on," I order, deciding abruptly. "Show me which wall."

An hour and a half later, I'm wondering if this was a bad idea. Maybe I should have waited until morning. Kieran or one of the museum guides could have looked up the diary in the index and pointed me to the exact box it's in, instead of me having to go through every one on the west wall.

That's if Maisie even got the wall right. She's very sweet, but not exactly bright.

I've only gotten through a dozen boxes so far, and that's only because four of them were filled with clothes and easy to check. The rest… let's just say there are a lot of people in the county who were so thrilled about the idea of a local history museum that they sent every piece of garbage their ancestors ever hoarded. Right down to electricity bills from only a few decades ago. The ghosts got so bored that they all wandered off ages ago.

There are another four dozen boxes at least, and if the diary is in the last one, I'll be here most of the night just looking for it. Maybe I should just give up and go to bed. My head is pounding, I'm tired, sore from sleeping on the couch last night… and weekends are always chaos around here. I need to be on my game, not exhausted from pulling an all-nighter.

Sighing, I lift my hands to rub my eyes, but stop myself at the last second. My hands are covered with dust and grime right now, and the last thing I need is to make my eyes more sore and itchy.

"Josh?"

Shrieking, I spin toward the door, raising my fists as though to defend myself.

"Whoa," Ewan says. "It's just us."

I blink at him in surprise as he steps into the room, followed by Daniel. "What are you doing here?"

"Carter told us what you're doing," Daniel says, looking around the room. "It's bad that I didn't even know this existed, right?"

"You don't know anything exists if it doesn't grow," Ewan points out, then smiles at me. "We thought we'd come and help."

Tears sting my eyes. It has to be because I'm so tired. Not for any other reason, like people giving enough of a shit about me to help me.

"But—" I swallow the lump in my throat. "But you both must be exhausted after moving furniture around at Skye's whim."

Daniel snorts. "Bossy, isn't he? I thought he'd never be happy with where the bed went."

"You've been working hard all day too," Ewan says gently, coming over and wrapping me up in a hug. "And we're all invested in this. Let us help."

It feels so good to be able to lean on him that I don't bother to argue, just nod. He leans down and kisses me gently.

"Whoa!" Daniel yells. "What's this?" A delighted grin stretches his mouth as heat washes up my face.

"Uhh…"

"Don't be a dick," Ewan orders. "Josh and I are… something." He looks down at me. "Did you still want to be casual? Because I was thinking it would be nice to date."

Do I have heart eyes right now? It feels like I might. He wants to date me?

"I guess that would, uh, be… nice. Thank you," I add, then want to kick myself. *Thank you?* I thanked him for wanting to go out with me? Why don't I just tattoo LOSER on my forehead right now? I smooth my hands down his arms, marveling over how defined they are.

He breaks out in a grin, but it's not an I'm-laughing-at-you grin. More like a you're-so-adorable one. I like it. "You're welcome," he says solemnly. "You never emailed me back before… does this mean I can cook dinner for you?"

"Yeah, that—oh, wait! I didn't email you back!"

"Dude, you need to get some sleep," Daniel says, looking up from the box he started going through while Ewan and I have been doing our awkward mating dance.

"No… well, yeah, but what I meant was, you don't know what started this whole search for the diary." I explain what I saw on the demon site, the words coming so fast, they trip over each other.

"So finding out there's a diary is just a side benefit of finding out this thing might actually be a demon we can… what, control? Banish?" Daniel looks confused.

I spread my hands. "I don't know. At first I just wanted to get an idea about whether it could be a demon or if we still don't know what we're dealing with. But once I heard about the diary and started looking, I thought, maybe she made some notes about what she was trying to do? And I could, I don't know, contact this person on the site and use the diary as a basis to ask questions?" Wow, it sounds super lame when I say it out loud.

They must agree, because Ewan says, "Well, let's find the diary first and go from there. If nothing else, we might get a better idea of why she came here."

We settle back in to work. Ewan stays close enough to me for me to feel the heat radiating off him, and where before I was focused on steps I could take once I found the diary, now my thoughts are full of him. Like… he smells so good. Does he like how I smell? I'm sweaty and grimy from going through boxes and probably stink. And I've chipped my glittery blue nail polish. He said last night that he liked it, so I'll have to make sure I fix it before our date. Nervous trepidation fills me at the idea of a date. He wants to cook for me, which seems so sweet… but does it actually mean he doesn't want to be seen with me in public?

No, Ewan's not like that. Besides, he was perfectly fine being seen with me in the bar the night we met.

"This might be it," he says, breaking into my thoughts, and Daniel and I both abandon our boxes to crowd around him. He's holding a notebook covered in dusty green velvet. It doesn't look like the diary of a woman who wants to summon demons. Although… what would that look like?

Ewan opens the cover gingerly. Written on the first page are the words "Emma Marie Harper, 1973 vol. I."

"The date's about right," Daniel says. Ewan flips through the first few pages, which seem to be the usual kind of stuff you'd find in a diary. A happy New Year message to herself, a list of her resolutions for the year, and then summaries of her day, of things people said, some gushing over a guy she had a crush on.

"Look at the last entry," I suggest. We can always read the whole thing later if we need to, but if it turns out this isn't what we're looking for, I don't want to waste time we could spend going through more boxes.

Ewan fans through the blank pages at the back, then nearly drops the book when a folded piece of yellowed paper falls out. Daniel grabs it and carefully unfolds it.

"Whoa," he breathes.

We stare at the detailed drawing of a pentagram with weird symbols at each point and arrows leading to handwritten notes. The clincher, though, is the heading at the top of the page: DEMON SUMMONING CIRCLE

"I guess this is it," I whisper, and then my brain snaps back to attention. "Let's put everything away in here and take it upstairs. I want to wash my hands and drink about a gallon of water."

"Coffee?" Daniel asks hopefully, packing up his box and shoving it back onto the shelves.

"No," Ewan and I say in unison, then grin at each other.

"The cute factor is fading," Daniel warns sourly. "How can you not have coffee?"

"It's nearly midnight," Ewan reminds him. "If you drink coffee now, you won't sleep at all. And tomorrow's Saturday."

Fuck. "Maybe we should wait until morning," I suggest glumly. "None of us is exactly well rested after everything that's happened this week."

"I can't wait until morning to know what's in this," Ewan says, tapping the cover of the book. A tiny plume of dust rises from it, and he grimaces. "But we don't have to read it all. Let's just check out the last few entries. It'll take half an hour or so, tops."

"I'm in," Daniel agrees immediately. "I'll be up all night wondering otherwise."

Yeah, me too. "Okay. But I'm setting a timer, and after half an hour, we stop." After all, even if it turns out Emma Marie Harper included instructions for banishing a demon in her diary, it's not like we can do anything tonight. Not with guests here.

Upstairs in my apartment, we take turns using the bathroom and settle on the couch with a jug of water and a bag of chips. Because digging through archive boxes is hungry work. If I was still in Chicago, I'd order a pizza, but nowhere in town is open this late, and they don't like to deliver out this far even when they are open.

"Okay," Ewan says, scanning the last entry in the diary, then flipping back a few pages. "We're going to need to read from the beginning to get the full picture, I think. The tone seems a bit different here to what was in those first entries. But it sounds like she came here specifically because she knew this was a good place for the paranormal." He looks up at me. "The ghosts said that, right? That the minerals in the soil and rock here were ghost friendly?"

"Yep. And even back then, the hotel was known to be haunted. Not as actively as now, since the ghosts couldn't manifest, but the research Kieran and Skye did shows that people used to come specifically for the ghosts."

"Just the ghosts? Because I don't think she was interested in them." His gaze skims down a page. "She's talking about the conditions being right tomorrow night… and that vengeance will finally be hers."

"Because that's not creepy," Daniel says with a shudder.

"It seems pretty obvious that she deliberately summoned a demon and it got away from her," I concede. "Does she mention anything about the vortex? Because nothing on the site made any reference to it, and I can't work out where it fits in. We've been working with the premise that the vortex opened first and the dark spirit or demon came through it, but this seems to disprove that."

He turns a page and shakes his head. "I'm not seeing anything. But maybe it's in an earlier entry?"

We go back to the beginning, but don't get through more than the first few weeks of January before the timer goes off.

"Well, that was boring," Daniel says, standing and stretching. "I mean, she seems like a nice enough woman, but I really have no interest in Greg from her office. He sounds like a douche."

"Agreed," Ewan and I say in unison.

"You've *got* to stop doing that," Daniel orders, pointing at first me, then Ewan. "You've only been dating two minutes. Brain-syncing is forbidden this early on."

"We'll try," I assure him, because it *is* kind of weird and embarrassing.

That doesn't mean I don't like it.

"I'll talk to Kieran as soon as he gets in," I add. "We need to adjust the inventory for the museum storeroom to show we took out the diary. And then I guess find some time this weekend to talk about it all?" Fuck knows when, though. There aren't usually any lulls on nice weekends in spring, although I've been assured there are fewer random tourists during the winter. You know, when most of the estate is buried under snow.

Ewan hesitates. "If you don't mind delaying our date, we could see if the others want to do a dinner meeting?"

The tiny pang of disappointment is accompanied by relief. "That might be the sensible option. We could have our date one night during the week? I think there are no guests on Tuesday, so I wouldn't be distracted or interrupted." Oh crap, maybe that's a bad idea. What if I fuck things up and need an excuse to escape?

But it's too late to backtrack. His whole face has lit up. "That's a great idea. I can take you out instead of you having to be on call, and all your attention can be on me."

"You're killing me here," Daniel says. "So dinner tomorrow night? At our place, since we won't all be comfortable squeezing in here, and if we use the staffroom, the dinner shift in the kitchen might overhear."

"I'll check with the others in the morning," I promise.

"Great!" Daniel takes off for the door, pausing when he gets there to cast a wicked smile over his shoulder. "Can I lock up, Ewan?"

Tingles go through me at the thought that Ewan might stay, sober this time, and not on the couch. But… it's late, and we're not sure what we're doing, and both of us need to sleep.

I just don't want to tell him to go.

He must be thinking the same thing I am, though, because he casts me a regretful look and says, "No, I'm coming. Wait for me."

Daniel rolls his eyes and goes out into the hallway, and Ewan takes my hand, lifting it to his mouth. I think he's going to comment on my nail polish, or maybe kiss it, a romantic, old-fashioned gesture, but he shocks me by sucking my index finger into his hot, wet mouth instead.

I make a sound that would fit right into a porn movie and lift my gaze to lock with his. If this is a hint of what dating him will be like, I'm so in.

When he finally releases my finger, a slow, suggestive grin quirks his lips. "I'll miss you."

"Meep." That was supposed to be "me too," but I appear to have lost the power of speech.

He leans forward, kisses me gently on the lips, and then stands and walks out.

Holy fuck.

Chapter Fourteen

EWAN

Kieran's hair is standing on end in what might be the most comical visual known to man. Although, he's lucky it's just messed up. With as many times as he's run his hands through it, it should be falling out in chunks by now.

I bite back my smile as I mop up the last of the spaghetti sauce with a chunk of bread. I'm not the fanciest cook, but I excel at some of the basics, and this was the easiest thing to do after a long day to feed five people. Arissa begged off for a date with her new guy, but we have her approval to proceed with whatever the group decides on.

"I don't approve of this plan," Joe declares, frowning so hard it looks like his bushy old-man eyebrows might actually touch his nose. "Consulting a stranger will only bring disaster."

"We're not going to tell them anything about us," Kieran says for what must be the dozenth time, a lot more patiently than I would have. "Josh is going to have a cover story. This Demon person won't even know his real name, much less anything about Mannix Estate."

Joe, the only one of us not eating—for obvious reasons—doesn't look convinced. Josh told me that he and the other ghosts were excited that we'd found the diary. Carter, Johnny, and Maisie wanted to try "reversing" the ritual Emma Marie Harper performed so long ago in the hope that doing so would suck the dark spirit back through the vortex and then close it. Thankfully, Joe, Hattie, and Freddie have slightly more sense and explained to them that it wasn't a good idea.

Kieran hasn't let the diary out of his sight since.

"Let's go over it again," Skye suggests. "Emma had a crush on Greg, who was an associate at the law office where she worked in the typing pool."

"Right," Kieran agrees. "The first month or so of the diary make her seem sweet, maybe a bit shy?"

"And then Greg notices her back," Skye continues. "She's excited when he asks her out, and their first few dates are good."

"She mentioned more than once what a gentleman he was," Josh volunteers. "Never pressured her for anything, not even a kiss. Held all the doors, pulled out her chair, ordered for her."

"Did people really do that in the seventies?" Daniel grimaces. "I get not letting a door slam in someone's face, but when I was at college, I tried to impress a girl by racing ahead to open the door, and she was not impressed."

We all look at Joe, who's the only one of us who was around during the seventies. He scowls. "I haven't left this estate for nearly two hundred years. You're asking the wrong person."

"*Anyway*," Skye says, "Emma was obviously impressed by it. She and Greg were dating, and she thought he was something special."

"And then it all started to change." Josh sighs in frustration. "Whatever was happening, Emma was writing less in her diary and her tone was very different. She mentions Greg's friends a few times, and I can't tell what's going on there."

"It sounds like she's impressed by them but also hates them," I agree. "Intimidated, maybe?"

"I wish she'd written it all down." Kieran's frown is epic. "She just starts writing regularly again in the middle of April and says she'll never speak of his betrayal but is determined to wreak vengeance."

"She should have just keyed his car," Skye says sagely. "Or 'accidentally' spilled coffee on his suit right before a meeting. Summoning demons seems like overkill for a guy dumping you or sleeping with someone else."

A terrible thought strikes me. "It couldn't have been worse than that, could it? Like… he didn't…"

Wide eyes and horrified expressions meet mine. "Fuck, I hope not." Daniel shudders. "Is there any way to find out? If he did, I vote we find this Greg guy and introduce him to the demon."

Joe grumbles, but since we're now fairly sure it actually *is* a demon in the basement, he doesn't insist we call it a dark spirit.

"I don't think that's it," Josh muses, paging through the diary. "Look, here she says she doesn't understand how he could betray her like this while still being such a gentleman. 'Shouldn't someone who'd plan something so vile behave like a lout? He was always so respectful to my face but plotted behind my back.' She wouldn't still think he was a gentleman if he'd assaulted her, would she?" He looks up. "Maybe we need a woman's perspective on this."

"I think you're right," Kieran says slowly. "That part about being nice to her face but plotting behind her back… that implies that he was using her, right? Maybe for something at work? Did she have access to information that he wanted?"

"She was in the typing pool. What even is a typing pool?" I ask, but I'm met with shrugs and confusion. Skye gets out his phone to look it up.

"'A collection of people, usually women, who undertake typing and secretarial tasks for executives and managers who don't have a permanently assigned secretary.' I guess that's the kind of job that disappeared when people started doing everything on a computer."

"So potentially she might have known something, seen something while typing letters or whatever that Greg wanted to know."

"Yes! He was an associate, right? If I've learned anything from watching *The Good Wife* and *Suits*, it's that law firms are cutthroat and associates will do anything to get ahead." Skye sounds way too excited about this.

"I think we're getting off track," I interject, even though I'd love to know what Greg did to Emma. "Regardless of what he did, and I really hope it was just use her for information, it's not important now. What we need to focus on is what Emma did once she'd vowed revenge."

Skye pouts, but nods. "Fiiiine. But in my head, there was some epic drama at the law firm."

"Mine too." Daniel winks at him before turning to look at me. Over his shoulder, I see Skye blush.

Uh-oh. It's looking more and more like he has a crush on Dan. Poor guy. Crushing on straight men never works out well.

"Okay, Ewan," Daniel drags my attention back to him. "What do you think Emma's plan was?"

"That part's pretty clear. She wanted to summon a demon to… how'd she put it, Josh?"

He flips a few pages and clears his throat. "'I hope whatever foul being responds to my call rips his guts out and feasts on them while he cries and begs for mercy.' Emma was definitely pissed off."

"Yep. I thought my ex who had all her friends spread a rumor that I was impotent was vicious, but at least she didn't summon a demon to murder me." Daniel grabs another roll from the bread basket, then glances up to see us all staring at him. "What?"

"Is it actually a rumor?" Kieran teases.

Dan rolls his eyes. "Of course it is."

"If what Carter says is true, it's definitely a rumor," Joe adds, then scowls at Daniel. "And you should be stricken with the clap."

"Gee, thanks."

"Speaking of things I wish I didn't have to think of," I break in, "why did Emma decide to summon a demon?"

"We've covered this," Skye says patiently. "Greg betrayed her, and she wanted revenge."

"Yeah, I get that. But why revenge by demon? At the beginning of the year, she was this kind, shy young woman with hopes of becoming an executive secretary or even a paralegal. She talked about Sunday dinner with her parents and sister and maybe going with her friends to the beach for a week in the summer. Do people like that immediately think 'demon feasting on his guts' when someone hurts them?"

Silence.

"Well," Skye says slowly, "it's not my go-to. It seems like a lot of work? Like… where do you even find out how to summon a demon? We've all been looking hard for this information for a week, and the closest we've gotten is someone online who maybe seems like they know what they're talking about. And Emma didn't have the benefit of the internet."

"Demon summoning is still considered garbage, right?" Kieran asks, looking around the table. "I know I thought it was. I wish I still did," he mutters. "So what I'm saying is, there probably aren't many—if any—reputable publishers who would put their name on a guide for summoning demons."

"Makes sense," Josh agrees. "And this was before the days of self-publishing being so easy. So even if someone had written a guide like that and paid a printer to run off a few hundred or thousand copies, they'd have to hand sell them. The only way to get a copy would be to know someone who knew the author… or if the author convinced a bookstore to stock some?"

Kieran shakes his head. "I worked at an indie bookstore during college. Even then, at the beginning of the self-publishing revolution, we'd rarely stock anything self-published, even on consignment. Shelf space is at a premium, and there are already so many publisher books that have serious marketing dollars behind them. Those were the ones that got priority. Something as obscure as a demon-summoning manual would never get a look in."

I bite my lip and think about what Josh said about Hattie getting quartz from a store in town. "What about new age shops? Or somewhere that focused on the occult?"

"Maybe." Kieran shrugs. "But that still doesn't answer your original question of why she went looking for a store like that to begin with. January Emma didn't have any interest in the occult. Heck, the only candles she mentions are the ones she lit so she could write in her diary during a blackout. I don't think she was spending a lot of time in new age stores."

Josh gasps and grabs the diary, flipping pages in search of something. "We're so dumb."

"Probably," Daniel agrees. "Why?"

"We even said it before, that she was writing less, that her tone changed. It's Greg. He introduced her to the idea of demons. Look, here, where she's talking about his friends. 'I'm not quite sure what to make of them. Like Greg, they're very sophisticated, talking about things I don't always understand. My sheltered upbringing never prepared me for this, and it makes me uncomfortable but also makes sense? I think. I'm so confused. I wish we didn't have to see them this weekend.'" He looks up triumphantly.

"How did we miss that?" Kieran wonders, and then we all jump when Joe slams his hand on the table.

"You missed it because she could be easily talking about politics instead of demons. It's only when you look at the context that it becomes clear. You're idiots, but not *that* stupid."

Wow, Joe's in top form tonight.

"So we're agreed? Greg introduced Emma to the concept of demon summoning, or at least to the occult in general?" Josh looks around the table. We're all nodding. "Which makes her plan for vengeance even more personal—she was going to use his own, uh, hobby against him."

I grin. "Hobby?" I tease.

"Shut up. What else would you call it?" His scowl is so adorable, I can't resist the urge to lean over and kiss him.

"Um, hello!" Skye's shriek makes me wince. "What the actual fuck just happened and why didn't I know anything about it?" His eyes go wide. "Is this who you're dating? Ewan?"

I smile at Josh. "You told him we're dating?" That makes me all warm and squishy inside.

His face is beet red. "I needed advice. But I didn't mention your name yet," he mumbles.

"No, he did *not*," Skye snaps. "And we'll be having words about that. But first I need to know everything." He jerks his head around to look at Daniel. "Did you know about this?"

My best friend and roommate shrugs, somehow still eating even though he's already consumed enough food to sustain an army. "Of course."

The sound of indignation Skye makes is high-pitched and wordless.

"He's only known since last night. After we found the diary," Josh rushes to assure Skye. "And we've only been dating since... are we even dating if we haven't been on a date yet?"

"If I may interrupt," Kieran says dryly, and it occurs to me—with a sinking feeling of dread—that we possibly should have mentioned to the boss that we were planning to officially get together. Josh goes pale, and I know he's worrying about losing his job. I take his hand and squeeze it reassuringly. Kieran's not an asshole.

He proves me right by saying, "We keep getting off track. Could we *try* to stick to the important stuff, please?"

Josh blinks at him. "Y-You don't care that Ewan and I are... dating?"

"Of course I care," Kieran rushes to assure him. "I'm happy for you both, seriously. And if you want to talk about it, we can. Totally. But can we deal with the demon in the basement first? Because I haven't slept properly all week, and I'm going to have to buy shares in Pepto if this goes on for much longer."

The deep sigh of relief Josh gives makes me bite back a smile. "That's great. I just... I don't know the policy about it. So... but yeah. If you're fine with it, there's nothing to talk about. Let's get back to demons."

"There definitely *is* something to talk about," Skye mutters. "And we'll be talking about it later. But fine. Demons."

"Where were we?" Josh asks, ignoring most of what Skye said.

"Greg was Emma's gateway to demon stuff, and she was going to use it against him," Daniel summarizes, finally pushing his plate away. "It could even be likely that she got that diagram thingy from him. The handwriting on it is different from the diary."

I lean over Josh's shoulder to look again. He's right.

"Whether she got it from him or bought it or copied it out of a book isn't as important as what happened next and what *we* are going to do next," Kieran says, his patience seeming to fray. "We can't help Emma. She's been dead for fifty years. We need to act to prevent that from happening to anyone else." He pauses. "Maybe after we've done that, we can track down this Greg guy and slash his tires or something."

"Keying his paintwork is worse," Skye volunteers. "If you do it right, it costs a hell of a lot to repair. And you can write words to let everyone who sees the car know what an assmonkey the owner is."

Note to self: don't piss off Skye.

"So… we're going to contact the person from the website?" Josh asks.

"No!" Joe snaps. "No strangers."

Kieran sighs. "Joe, it's an option we can't ignore. This person seems to have information we can use."

"I swear I'll make it as hard as I can for them to find out anything about me," Josh promises. "We'll get a VPN and create a special email account with fake information. From a different state. Or even a different country. There are tons of haunted castles in Scotland, yeah? I'll say I found a diary and the diagram in a haunted castle in Scotland and now I want to write a book about it."

Joe's scowling, but it's his thinking scowl instead of his "fuck no" scowl. "What's a VPN?"

"It hides where you are on the internet," Skye says. "Someone who knew what they were doing could still find out, but most people have no idea. Including us. Otherwise we could do some fancy hacker thing instead of paying for a VPN."

The scowl now seems more confused than anything else, but Joe nods grudgingly. "Fine. But I still don't like it."

"Noted. Thanks, Joe." Kieran looks around the table. "Any other objections?" Silence. "Okay, so what are we putting in this message? Aside from Josh's new identity as a Scottish wannabe author."

"Keep it simple." Daniel drums his fingers on the table. "Hi, I noticed you seem to be the only person here with brain cells. I'm writing a book about a woman who goes to a haunted castle in Scotland to try to summon a demon. The research I've been doing is really vague on what she'd need to do that, but I found this drawing. Can you tell me what kind of demon this would summon? And once she's summoned it, how does she send it back? I want this book to have a happy ending."

"That's good," Josh says, scribbling notes, "but they're so going to think I'm trying to summon a demon."

Dan shrugs. "So? Do you care what they think of you?"

"I care about them deciding not to reply to my message because they think I'm a crackpot who wants to summon a demon."

"Good point." Dan looks at me. "How does one ask about summoning demons without sounding like one wants to summon demons?"

"Don't refer to yourself as 'one,' for starters. It makes you sound like the kind of douche who'd want to summon demons," I advise. "Uhhh… What if we come at it from another angle? You've bought a house in Scotland or wherever that you know is haunted, but since you moved in, the 'ghosts' have been nasty—violent. Aggressive. You found this old diary and drawing under a floorboard or something, and now you're worried that what's in the house is not actually a ghost. Can NEDDT tell you if the drawing would summon an actual demon and if so, would they act like that? Describe some of the stuff our demon was doing before the ghosts trapped it."

"Who?" Daniel asks.

"Not Even Demons Deserve This. NEDDT," I explain.

Kieran points at me. "Yes. This. I like it. The acronym and the plan."

"And it's a great opener to ask if they know how to get rid of the demon," Josh adds, scrawling down the idea. "I'm kind of bummed I don't get to be a wannabe author, though."

"You still get to be Scottish," Skye says consolingly. "And if you want, you can say that you bought the haunted house because you're a wannabe author who wanted inspiration."

"Good idea." Josh smiles, seemingly happy to have a backstory for his fake self, and I kiss him again.

"Awww." Skye puts his hand over his heart. "You're so cute together."

"That's one word for it," Daniel mutters, and Skye's eyes narrow.

"What other word would you use?" he asks dangerously... if a kitten with unicorn hair can be considered dangerous. Fortunately, Kieran intervenes again.

"Stay on topic," he reminds them. "Josh is going to message this person and hope they have more information we can use. In the meantime, now that the honeymoon suite is up and running—eternal gratitude to you all for everything you've done, with special thanks to Skye—" We all clap, and Skye stands and gives a half bow. "—but now that it's up and running, we need all the help we can get trying to find information."

Daniel grimaces. "I'm not great with the internet."

"Unless it's a hookup app," Skye mutters, and Dan grins.

"True."

"There's still a bunch of books to go through that you could help me with," I offer. "We'll leave the online searches to people who know what they're doing." I'm also not great with the internet. I can handle social media sites and basic searches, but anything that requires more than a surface-level Google search is beyond me.

"You found this site," Josh protests. "I'd say you know what you're doing."

"Thanks, but it was a total fluke. I was looking for exorcists."

Kieran closes one eye. "You searched for exorcists and a site about summoning demons came up?"

"Yep."

He nods slowly. "Sounds about right. Anyway, I've been buying all the quartz I can find. We're reinforcing the barrier in the basement, and I've also put some in the Garden Suite. If anything else tries to come through the vortex, hopefully the salt and quartz will contain it."

"Some of the other staff are asking questions," Skye says. "Especially the housekeepers, who know very well there aren't any plumbing issues in the Garden Suite."

"I know. What have you been telling them?"

"That you're the boss and I have no idea how your brain works." He grins.

"Thanks," Kieran replies dryly. "Okay. Okay, I'm going to tell them we wanted to get the honeymoon suite going before the summer season begins, but that we're only licensed to operate a certain number of rooms and

I had to close one to do it until approval comes in for the extra room."

"Is that true?" Josh sounds dubious.

"Fuck no. And it's got more holes in it than swiss cheese if you really think about it. But hopefully nobody cares enough to think about it that much."

Josh and Skye, who spend the most time with the house staff, look doubtful.

"What about the vortex?" Joe demands. "Are you going to ask the demon person about how to close it?"

Josh pulls a face. "I'm hoping they'll mention it as part of their answer. Like, maybe it's normal for a vortex to open when a demon is summoned? But because Emma died, it never got closed. Hopefully the instructions on how to banish the demon will also close the vortex. If not, I'll figure out a way to ask. I don't want to be too memorable, though, in case the vortex is actually a separate thing from the demon that Emma somehow managed to do."

"There are no notes about the vortex in the diary?" Daniel asks. We talked about this before, but he was busy eating.

"Nope. Nothing that sounds like it at all. She talks a lot about her vengeance and a bit about the things she needs for the 'ritual,' but the focus is definitely on the demon, not anything else." Josh's frustration is clear in his voice. Finding the diary and the diagram killed our earlier theory that the demon came through the vortex by chance, so as far as the vortex goes, we're back at square one. While the diary was a fantastic find and has helped us, it would be even better if Emma had meticulously documented everything she was planning to do, why, and how. And where she got her information from.

Still, it's hard to be angry with a woman who died fifty years ago and had her soul eaten by a demon. Even if she did summon that demon.

"Let's leave it there," Kieran decides. "We've covered the new info and our next steps. There's no point rehashing everything over and over until our brains explode."

Skye pops up out of his chair and begins stacking plates. "Yay! I'll help you clean up and then I'm outta here!"

"Hot date?" Josh teases as the rest of us get up and start clearing the table.

Skye laughs. "Not tonight, but some friends are meeting at a bar. Hey, wanna come? You'll like all of them. Tom's coming."

Tom? Who's Tom, and why does Skye say his name like Josh knows him?

Josh hesitates and flicks a sideways glance at me.

"Actually, Josh and I have plans," I say, only feeling a tiny bit bad about it. I know he hasn't had a chance to make any local friends outside of us yet. That tiny bit disappears when Josh smiles.

"Josh and Ewan, sitting in a tree, K-I-S-S-I-N-G…"

Chapter Fifteen

JOSH

After an evening spent snuggling on my couch watching movies, then a night of explosive fireworks, Ewan left early Sunday morning to see to the animals while I sent a message through the demon website to NEDDT. I worked hard to achieve the perfect balance of "in need of help" yet not "crazed and desperate," and I think my message was okay.

But the wait is killing me.

Especially since I don't even know if NEDDT even *got* the message. Do they still visit the site? And if they did get it, maybe they'll decide not to bother replying. Or worst of all, maybe they'll reply, but whatever they say will be useless to us and we'll be back at the beginning.

After two full days of waiting and checking my emails every half hour, sometimes more, I'm a nervous wreck. And tonight is my first official date with Ewan.

He suggested we head to the next town over, where there's apparently a great Korean barbecue place. I haven't eaten out since I got here, unless you count dinner at Ewan and Daniel's or the few times I've had a meal in the staff break room, so I'm game to leave the estate and let a good-looking, sexy, sweet guy romance me. But I'm also scared I'll fuck it up.

Which is why Skye decided to tell me about the worst dates he's ever had. Kind of like a what-not-to-do. Technically, it's his day off, but he claimed to be bored and came in to watch TV with the ghosts.

"…and then he told me he'd pay for dinner if I jerked him under the tablecloth," Skye's saying. "Ewan's not that kind of guy, though, so you won't ever have to worry about that."

"Until the next guy," I say gloomily.

He gasps. "Why would you even think that? Things are going to work out for you two and you'll live happily ever after."

I study the dreamy expression on his face. "You're a romantic, aren't you?"

"How'd you guess?" He laughs. "Seriously, though, I know it's early days, but you have to think positive. Focus on the good and exciting parts of being together. If it doesn't work out, fair enough, but don't borrow trouble."

He's right. Just because I've never been in a relationship before doesn't mean things will fail with Ewan. He's already seen my bitchy side, *and* he knows about the ghost thing and is cool with it. That puts me on a level playing field with every other guy out there for the first time in my life. I'm still nervous, though. I like Ewan a lot and really want things to go well.

From the reception desk in front of us, my phone makes a weird chiming sound. My mind is so full of Ewan that it takes me a few seconds to realize that's the notification sound I allocated to my fake email account. I snatch it up so fast, I drop it and have to scrabble around on the floor in search.

"What are you doing?" Skye asks bemusedly.

"Phone! Email! Demons!" I gasp, finally returning to my chair with my phone clutched to my chest.

For a moment, he looks confused, but then his eyes go wide and he darts a worried glance around us. Whoops. I used the D word in a public part of the estate.

Luckily, there's nobody around, and he leans closer as I unlock my phone. Pleeeeease don't let this be an email from the VPN company… or spam. I swear, if someone's trying to sell me Viagra, I'm going to have a hissy fit.

But the email that appears on the screen is from the demon-summoning website. *You have a new message. Log in to check your messages,* it proclaims.

Skye and I look at each other and bolt for the office. There's no computer at the reception desk, because it doesn't fit with the historic vibe, and I definitely want a full-sized screen and keyboard for this.

As I log in to the site, Skye adjusts the door so it's half open and we can see if any guests need us. My hands shake as I type in my username and password, and I must have hit a wrong key, because I get an error message.

Skye groans. "C'mon, Josh. Pull it together."

Taking a deep breath, I shake out my hands and try again.

You have one new message.

"Yes!" I punch the air in victory, then click through to the private message.

> NEDDT:
>
> Sounds like you made a mistake buying that house. I've got good news and bad news. The bad news is, that circle would summon a soul-eater demon. It's trying to kill you so it can eat your soul. Get out of the house NOW.

Skye and I exchange wide-eyed looks. "Sounds like they know what they're talking about," I venture, and he nods.

> More bad news: the reason you have a soul-eater on the loose is because the circle is slightly wrong. Burn that drawing so nobody else can try to use it. That circle will summon the demon, but it won't contain it. The summoner would have no control over the demon and would likely be their first meal. It wouldn't even have to kill them first—the summoning bond would make them vulnerable.

"Checks out," Skye murmurs. "Poor Emma."

> The good news is, it's possible to banish a soul-eater. You need to find a medium—someone who can talk to ghosts and interact with beings of the otherworld. Try to get proof they can. They'll need a shitload of salt, quartz, sage, rue, and dill, and...

I read through the rest of the directions carefully. They're a lot simpler than I would have expected. There's no fancy circle needed, no chants or spells. I'm not sure what rue is, but dill and sage are herbs, so maybe it's one too? The idea seems to be to contain the demon within a circle of salt and quartz and then use the herbs and my power as a medium to banish it.

"Can you do it?" Skye asks. I can feel his gaze on the side of my face.

"I'm not sure," I admit. "I have questions." I click into the message thread and begin to type.

> HAUNTEDBYMISTAKESOFOTHERS:
>
> Thank you so much for replying! Please forgive me for taking advantage of your generosity, but I have a few more questions.
>
> 1: I know someone who can speak to ghosts, but he's never been trained as a medium, and he's never said anything about the otherworld. Would he be able to help me?
>
> 2: Where does a banished demon go? Back to where it came from?

I ask a few more technical things about the ritual, then hit Send and sit back in my chair. "Hopefully we don't need to wait another two days."

Skye stares at the screen. "More likely less than a few minutes."

I glance back and see *NotEvenDemonsDeserveThis is typing* at the bottom of the thread. "Quick, call Kieran. Tell him everything and ask if he has questions. We might not get this chance again." We each grab our phones, and while Skye calls Kieran, I shoot a text to Arissa, Ewan, and Daniel. Arissa's in her tiny office off the kitchen, but I think Daniel might be doing a farming demo. He was scheduled for one. Ewan's probably doing chores, so there's a chance he'll see the message and reply.

Skye's still talking to Kieran, making notes, when Arissa appears in the doorway, breathless. "What'd they say? You can't just text 'got a reply' and nothing else, Josh!" She comes to lean over my shoulder just as my phone chimes.

> EWAN:
>
> OMW

"Read for yourself," I tell Arissa, pointing to the screen. I should get up and let her have the chair so she can see it better, but if I hand over the control seat, I won't get it back. I haven't known these people all that long, but definitely long enough to know that much.

The reply pops up a moment later.

> NEDDT:
>
> If your friend can talk to ghosts, he can definitely help. Training to be a medium is usually just an experienced medium teaching a newbie their favorite habits. Most of the important stuff is instinctive. And the majority of mediums have never had to interact with the otherworld and don't know it exists.

> No, the demon doesn't go back to where it came from. I'm not sure why we say "banish" when we really mean "destroy." A soul-eater's energy comes from the souls it consumes. If it hasn't been eating lately (try to find out if anyone's died in the house within the last few years), it's probably already pretty weak. And they're dumb fuckers. It doesn't really occur to them to leave the place they were summoned to. So you've likely got a weak demon that you're going to trap with the salt and quartz. Then your medium is going to sort of squeeze the remaining soul energy out of it, leaving only the demon essence. The herbs will rip that apart and return it to the universe.

"Does that make sense to you?" Arissa asks. "I was following until the end bit."

I'm about to say it makes no sense at all—I mean, squeezing? WTF?—when something inside my brain clicks. Not to be all metaphorical or anything, but it's like a doorway opens and light floods in, only the light is knowledge and understanding.

"I think I get it," I say slowly, looking at her. Into her. It's not… "Where are the ghosts?" I want to test something.

"Not sure. Freddie's probably hounding one of the housekeepers. Want me to check?"

"No need for that," Hattie says, bustling in with Ewan right behind her. "I saw dear Ewan racing up here and knew something interesting must be happening. What do you need?"

"To look at you, I think." I study her carefully, and now that I'm searching for it, it's so readily apparent, I almost want to laugh. Unlike Arissa's soul, which is tethered to her physical body, Hattie *is* her soul. That's what a ghost is—the essence of a being contained in the memory of its life. I can't believe I never realized that before.

Looking at Hattie, I'm swamped by the understanding of what a medium can do. If I wanted to, I could scatter her mortal memories, and her soul would be forced to move on. Everyone calls it "crossing over," but suddenly, that doesn't feel right to me.

I push it aside. There's time for an existential crisis later.

"Yeah, it makes sense," I tell Arissa confidently. I still don't know how it'll go when we try it, but the theory fits.

"What makes sense?" Ewan comes over to the desk, playfully hip checks Arissa aside, then leans over to kiss my cheek and peer at the screen. "Ohhhhh."

While Ewan's reading, I swivel the chair around the other way and hold out my hand to Skye for Kieran's questions. He's stopped writing and is just rolling his eyes toward the ceiling, which means Kieran's just repeating himself and worrying now. Kier's a champion worrier.

I skim the list. Most of these have already been answered in the latest response, and some are more for me than NEDDT.

"I don't like this," Ewan says abruptly as I wave Skye over to take a look so he can convey the latest to Kieran. "This puts you in danger."

"Not really." I try to sound as reasonable as possible.

"Not any more than everyone else. If anything, I'm the person in least danger."

"You'd be facing a soul-eating demon head-on," he exclaims.

"Oh my," Hattie murmurs, unmanifesting so she can slip between everyone and look at the screen. I glance away. It makes me queasy to see ghosts twist themselves like that.

"It would still be restricted by the salt and quartz," I remind him. "The only difference would be that we'd actively be trying to get rid of it."

From the way he's scowling, I can tell he's not convinced. Fortunately, Skye interrupts us.

"Kieran wants to talk to you." He holds out his phone.

I take it and put it to my ear. "Hi. Sorry to bug you on your day off."

"I would have been so mad if you hadn't" is his reply. "Skye says you think this is a good idea?"

"I think it's our only option," I say frankly. "I'm still not sure what caused the vortex or what we can do about it, but as far as dealing with the demon goes, this feels like the right choice."

He sucks in a deep breath and blows it out. "Okay. We don't need to decide right away. We're not doing anything risky while there are guests on the estate. When's the next time we have nobody?"

My stomach sinks, and I swallow hard. "Tonight."

"No," he says instantly. "It's date night. Skye would never forgive me."

I laugh because it's true. "Let me check, then." I shoo everyone away from the computer and switch screens to the reservation software. It doesn't take long to check. "Monday. But after that, there's at least one reservation every night for three solid weeks." Which is good for business but not so much our need to keep people safe.

"Monday," he echoes. "Okay. Tell me again what they said you'd need?"

"Salt and quartz, which we already have tons of, thanks to you." Turns out, Kieran's a champion online shopper. The ghosts are not so thrilled to have this much salt on the property. "And herbs—dill, sage, and rue. That should be fairly easy to get. Daniel might have some already."

"Agreed, but I'll order more now, and then we'll be ready even if we decide to delay until next month. Until then, focus on enjoying tonight." He hesitates. "I know I didn't seem excited the other night, but I really am happy for you both. I'm just preoccupied."

"It's not like there's nothing going on for you to be preoccupied with," I point out. "But thanks. I appreciate it." Even if it's early days for people to be happy for us, it's still nice knowing we have support.

Kieran says goodbye and ends the call, and I toss Skye his phone, then switch back to the website.

"Well? What did Kier say?" Ewan demands.

"We do nothing until Monday at the earliest," I report. "But the decision about when after that isn't final." I stare at the last message NEDDT sent me.

HAUNTEDBYMISTAKESOFOTHERS:

Thank you so much. Would it be okay for me to contact you again if I have questions?

Arissa pats my shoulder. "I'm going back to work. Come have lunch with me later."

"Sure." The kitchen will be quiet, since all the guests have checked out and we're not expecting any tonight, and that means Arissa's going to play with a new meal option. I'd be an idiot to turn that down.

"Me too?" Skye pleads, turning his best puppy dog gaze on her. She rolls her eyes but agrees, then points at Ewan before he can ask.

"Yes. And Daniel."

"You're my favorite," he tells her, and she laughs as she saunters out. Hattie manifests and goes out with her, asking what she plans to cook.

Ewan spins my chair so I'm facing him, leans down to kiss my lips, then pulls back and looks me in the eye. "We'll continue that conversation another time. Not today, though. See you at lunch." And he follows the others out, leaving just me and Skye.

"You know," my rainbow-haired friend says thoughtfully, "Ewan's such a sweetie that I sometimes forget that others find him intimidating. Then he acts all masterful like that, and it's suddenly 'helloooooo.' That was so hot."

I blow out a breath. "It really was."

On the computer screen, a new message appears. It's one line: an email address.

"At least we have an expert consultant now," Skye says. "Even if the situation they're consulting on doesn't actually exist."

"It exists. It's just not exactly what they think it is. But the important parts are the same."

"Are you sure?" he counters. "What if geography is

important? Like what if the ritual that works in Scotland doesn't work in the States?"

I stare at him. "Are you trying to make things worse? Why would you say that?"

He shrugs. "Just trying to get ahead of any problems."

"Well, stop. I don't think geography would be a factor." I hope.

Great. Something else to worry about.

Chapter Sixteen

EWAN

I study myself in the mirror one last time. My hair isn't sticking up. I'm shaved. My shirt is neatly pressed. My chinos are clean.

I look nervous.

Why am I so nervous? I really don't know. I've been on dates before, but for some reason, this is different. Maybe it's because Josh and I work together. Or maybe it's because we've done this ass-backward, sleeping together before dating.

Whatever it is, I like him so much.

Leaving the bathroom, I stop quickly in my room and grab my keys. It's warm enough that I won't need a jacket. Sticking my head into the kitchen to thank Daniel for taking my turn with the animals so I could get ready, I freeze when I see the ghosts.

All of them.

"What's going on?" I ask cautiously.

"You look so handsome," Maisie gushes, clasping her beringed hands in front of her chest. She's wearing a green T-shirt that says Spank Me Harder over a long orange skirt with a large bustle.

"Uh, thanks."

Freddie clicks his tongue. "But so casual. Why aren't you wearing a suit? Josh is wearing *jeans*." He sounds scandalized as he straightens the lapels of his suit jacket.

"They're very nice jeans," Hattie consoles. "A lovely dark indigo. No holes or anything."

"And they fit *so* well." Maisie titters.

Oh my god. This can't be happening. I meet Daniel's gaze, and he grins evilly.

"Do you have condoms?" Carter asks. "Or does Josh use the PrEP too? How does that work, exactly?"

"Yeah, Ewan, how does it work?" Daniel asks innocently.

"I don't have time to go into it, but you should ask Daniel to help you google it." I smirk. "Have lots of fun!"

I'm still chuckling over the look on Dan's face when I get to the house and find Josh waiting out front. I turn off the engine and get out of the car as he comes forward, my nerves returning in a flood.

"Hi. You look great." He does, but he also looks just as nervous as I am, making me feel better. We're in this together.

"…AND then as I walked out, Maisie was asking if PrEP is what you need lube for, because she had a recipe for a 'lovely' lubricant that her 'gentlemen' always thought was the real thing."

Josh is laughing so hard, I think he might choke. Good thing he's already cleared his plate. "Did…," he wheezes, "…did Daniel tell her that men don't have 'the real thing'?"

I shrug. "I didn't stick around, but I hope so. Because that would have led to so many questions."

He sits back in his seat, sighs, and swipes moisture from the corner of his eye. "They were waiting in the hall outside my apartment to 'wish me well,' as Hattie put it. Johnny wanted to know why I wasn't bringing you flowers."

I shake my head. "Don't get me wrong, I love them all, but they're hard work."

Nodding emphatically, he says, "Yeah. I'm pretty sure they're all going to be waiting impatiently for a debrief when we get home. Wanna delay going home?" He chuckles, but it works perfectly with my plan.

"We could take a walk and get some ice cream," I suggest, and the smile that spreads across his face is warm and intimate.

"That sounds perfect."

We settle the bill, only squabbling a little bit over who's paying. I win when I say, "Let me get this one, and you can pay for our next date." He gives in with a grin that matches mine.

It's almost ridiculous, the way we've both reverted to being gushy, moony teenagers. But I can't stop the little thrill that runs through me when we exit the restaurant and I take his hand. I can't remember the last time I held hands with someone, but it's one of those things that's so innocently intimate, and doing it with Josh settles satisfaction over me like a warm blanket. Weird, right? Sex has gotta be more intimate than holding hands, but this feels so much more important… like a declaration. And I'm happy about it.

The ice-cream place is just down the street, so we stroll over and order, then cross to the park in the middle of the town square. The trees are strung with fairy lights, and there are plenty of people taking advantage of the balmy spring evening, but still it's like we're in a fairy tale. If I believed in fairy tales. Which, even with all the stuff I'm tangled up in right now, I don't.

Although I don't exactly *dis*believe.

Josh sighs.

"Okay?" I ask, studying his face. "Are you cold?"

He shakes his head. "No, I'm good. I was just thinking that I've never considered myself to be the romantic type, and yet…" He grimaces. "You'll think I'm an idiot."

"And yet, this is like a fairy tale?" I finish dryly. "I was thinking the same."

His gaze flashes up to meet mine. "So we're both idiots, then."

"Looks like."

He bites his lip. "Is it bad that I'm okay with that?"

I don't even try to hold back my smile, giddiness rising in me. "Let's just go with it."

He rises on tiptoe, his face turned up, and I instinctively lower mine. Our lips meet. It's not like the hot, wet kisses we've exchanged in private, not the light, meaningful-yet-casual ones I've been giving him when others are around. This is… deeper. Our bodies don't touch, except at the mouth, but I can feel the heat of him, so close, and fine tremors vibrate through me. I could happily spend hours just kissing him like this.

Somewhere close by, people erupt into cheers and

laughter, and the spell is broken. I pull back, hoping we're not the focus of their attention—Josh would hate that—but the small group is just as absorbed by their own news as Josh and I were by our kiss.

"Shit," Josh mutters, and I look back to see him swiping ineffectively at the melted ice cream on his hand with the single tiny napkin that was wrapped around the cone. Come to think of it, my hand feels kind of sticky... yep. I don't know how long we were kissing, but it was long enough for our ice cream to give up.

I grimace. "This is not the kind of cream I expected to have all over my hands tonight."

Josh gives a choked gasp, then starts laughing so hard, his face turns red. "Me either," he wheezes.

We dump what's left of our cones in the trash, then go in search of somewhere to wash away the stickiness, our arms brushing together as we walk. The romantic haze might have dissipated, but what's left behind is just as wonderful, if not more so.

I PULL the car into the staff parking at the side of the house and park. Dan and I have our own little portico to park under behind our cottage, but I don't want to make Josh walk across the estate in the dark. Plus, I'm hoping he'll invite me in. The ghosts are much more respectful of his personal space than they (read: Carter) are of ours.

For a moment, we sit in silence, enjoying the quiet hum of the dark and the suspense of these last few minutes of our first official date.

"Are you coming up?" Josh asks quietly at last, stirring in the dimness.

"If you want me to, nothing could stop me." I feel oddly invincible in this space, with just the two of us. His quiet chuckle just reinforces it.

We get out and slip into the house, moving sneakily in an attempt not to alert the ghosts to our presence. If we can just get into Josh's apartment, they won't disturb us… probably.

Too bad they're lying in wait for us in the hallway right outside it. We skid to a stop, and I sigh.

"Busted," Josh mutters. A hysterical giggle bursts from my throat. It does feel kind of like we snuck in after curfew and were caught by our parents.

"Ooooh, Ewan's not going home! We all know what that means," Maisie titters.

So, not quite like being caught by our parents.

"I still have questions about the PrEP," Carter says. "Can I watch?"

"NO!" Josh and I shout it in unison, then glance at each other. I gesture for him to take the lead. He's the ghost expert, after all.

Before he can say anything, Johnny whines, "I ain't gonna watch, but I got questions too."

Josh clears his throat. "If you think I'm going to answer questions about sex, you're so wrong. Go away."

"You heard him," Joe snaps. "Leave them in peace."

Hattie starts shooing the others away over their complaints, until only Joe is left.

"Something you need?" Josh asks warily.

Joe squints. "I was going to warn you not to let this ruin our family, but…" He eyes us both so hard, my palms begin to sweat. "…I don't think I need to."

I'm still blinking in surprise when he walks away.

Josh shakes his head and unlocks the door, and I follow him inside. "Did Joe just give us his blessing?" And why am I so pleased about it?

"Consider our relationship ghost official. Let's seal it with a kiss."

I close the door behind me and lean against it as Josh stalks toward me with a predatory gleam in his eye. I like this side of him—how he takes control and goes after what he wants. I especially like that I see it most when he wants me.

He snakes a hand around my neck, rises on his toes, and yanks my head down. We crash together in a kiss that goes from zero to a hundred in the space of a breath, and I haul him closer, wanting to feel him pressed against every inch of me.

But he wriggles away. "Shirt off," he demands, grabbing my shirt in both hands and tugging. "You should always be shirtless. It's a law. Hiding those muscles is criminal."

Chuckling, I free my shirt from his grip and take it off, enjoying the way he stares with glazed eyes. I flex, unable to help myself, and he moans.

"Oh my god, how am I this lucky?" he mutters. "How do you exist? Nobody's as nice and fun as you and also has a body like that."

"I'm a unicorn. Why are you still fully dressed?"

"Shhh. I just wanna bite you." He eyes my pecs with a hunger that I'm only 99 percent sure is sexual.

"I'm beginning to think putting out on a first date might be a bad idea," I say dryly, crossing my arms over my chest.

He pouts. "Fine, I'll strip. But you need to get the rest of the way naked too."

"Deal." Within a minute, we're both stark naked and surrounded by discarded clothing. This is starting to feel a bit weird, so I grab Josh, haul him into my arms, and kiss him.

Much better.

He grabs my shoulders and boosts himself up so he can wrap his arms and legs around me, and I brace my hands under his perfect ass and spin to press him against the door.

"Yeeeeeeessss," he moans as our cocks rub together. He bites my lip, then licks it. "Make me come like this."

Oh fuck yeah.

Adjusting my grip on him, I line my dick up with his perineum, trapping his between us, and begin a slow thrust-and-grind. The sound that's wrenched from Josh's throat makes me smile against his lips.

He wrenches his mouth away from mine, letting his head fall back against the door, then meets my gaze. "Harder."

It takes only a dozen more thrusts to bring me to the edge. "Are you close?" I gasp, burying my face in his sweaty neck. His response is a visceral groan as his cock spurts between us.

That's all it takes to make me explode.

Chapter Seventeen

JOSH

"I'm so glad you enjoyed your stay," I say politely with a smile I hope doesn't look as fake as it feels. "Keep an eye on the website for that theme weekend you were interested in." The smiling couple thanks me again and leaves, and I slump.

That's it. The inn is empty. We have some tourists in the museum, and there's a school group at the smithy with Ewan, but once they go, the estate will be empty except for staff. It could all be over tonight, if Kieran decides to go ahead.

He comes out of the office. "They gone?"

"Yep."

He nods, the fine lines around his eyes standing out. Kieran's a worrier by nature, it seems, and this whole thing has been incredibly stressful for him. Especially since he's the boss and has to make the decisions. The buck stops with him, unless he brings the owners into it, which the ghosts are dead set against. They weren't impressed with how the owners reacted to the demon being accidentally freed during the renovations.

"I guess I should decide what to do," he sighs.

I want to say yes, because the wait is killing me, but Kieran's become a friend, and friends care about each other's mental health, right? So instead I say, "A few more hours won't hurt. We have everything we need."

He shoots me a grateful smile but shakes his head. "A few more hours won't make a difference. I know what we need to do. It's tonight. Anyone who doesn't want to be there doesn't have to be." He winces. "Except you. Sorry."

I wave away the apology. "I want to get it done." I don't add that while part of it is that I don't like having a demon in the house, it's mostly because I want to see if I can actually do this… banish a demon. I've spent my whole life up until now thinking of my ability as a curse. It's held me back in every part of my life. But since I got here, that's changed dramatically. Not only am I accepted, is my ability accepted, but it's considered a gift. Something useful and helpful. Suddenly, I find myself wanting to use it. To stretch it, experiment, see what I can do.

"Six o'clock?" Kieran suggests. I consider it. By then, the gates will be closed to tourists, and the day staff will be long gone. Without any guests tonight, the kitchen staff will be gone too. It'll just be those of us who live on the estate and whoever chooses to stay—and it should still be light out, which will make me feel a lot better, even if NEDDT didn't mention sunlight or dark making a difference.

But then, I didn't ask. Maybe I should email and ask them.

Pushing the sudden worry aside—surely they would

have said something if it mattered—I tell Kieran, "Six sounds good."

Ewan comes up to the house to have lunch with me. The school group is safely munching on sandwiches on the front lawn, after which they'll go out to the fields with Daniel to talk about corn or whatever. Ewan and I go up to my apartment and make our own sandwiches, eating them curled up together on the couch.

"So, it's tonight, then," he muses, brushing crumbs off his chest. I eye the broad expanse lasciviously and think about offering to do it for him.

"Tonight," I echo absently. Because chest. The old-fashioned shirt stretches across it, open at the neck, showing off plenty of tanned skin and a teasing patch of hair.

"Josh!" He's laughing, exasperated, and I figure it's not the first time he's called my name.

"Yes? Sorry. It's just... you're you." I wave a hand to encompass him, as though that explains my distraction. Which it does. This is the sixth day since our date, and each one has been better than the last, even when we were both buried in work and exhausted. Even when the ghosts and our living friends tried to pry into our lives. We've spent every evening together, mostly at my place, but twice at his, since it's still on the property and within reach of the guests if they need me, and I can't see myself ever wanting to end this. He's kind and funny and hot as fuck, but most of all, I feel so comfortable with him. It's like he *gets* me. I don't need to be on guard or worried, and even when I was nervous about our date because it was our first date, I knew it would be okay. Ewan would make it okay.

I never thought I'd be the kind of person who wanted to be looked after, and I still don't, not really, but I can't deny how good it feels to know that if I do, Ewan would step up to do it.

"I know I'm me." He chuckles, leaning over to kiss me. I'm pretty sure he meant to say more, but we both get distracted, and it's some time before we break apart, lips swollen and eyes dreamy.

Ewan clears his throat. "Uh, what were we talking about?"

I sprawl across his lap, where I somehow ended up, and walk my fingers up his chest to his strong throat. "How hot you are."

He snorts. "No. Oh, now I remember." Capturing my hand with one of his, he grabs my chin with the other and directs me to look at him. "Tonight, if you're at all uneasy, even a tiny bit, promise me you'll back out."

"Ewan—"

"No, hear me out. You can give me a sign and I'll call the whole thing off, if you don't want to be the one who backs out. But I don't want you doing anything you feel uncomfortable with."

I swallow, warm feelings I'm not quite ready to name swelling in my chest. He's so amazing. "Thank you. Seriously, thank you. For caring. For being you. I'm not going to lie, what we need to do does make me nervous. But I think that's good? I mean, shouldn't we be nervous about dealing with a demon? But I want to get this done. I want it out of here, and…" I hesitate, but he's been honest with me, and I want him to know all of me.

"...and I want to see if I can do this. I want to do this. For once, I want to know that I bring value to something."

His eyes blaze. "You *do* bring value," he says fiercely. "You're valuable. I've never met anyone more valuable, more precious than you. You light up the world."

My whole being aches with his words. Does he really feel that way about me? Nobody's ever felt that for me.

I look away.

There's an awkward little silence, and then Ewan sighs.

"That was... intense. I didn't mean to make you uncomfortable."

My gaze snaps up to his. "No. I'm not... I mean, I am, but it's not your fault. I just..." I really don't want to tell him I've never been wanted by anyone before I came here. If he thinks I'm awesome, I don't want to be the one who shows him the truth. At least, not until I've had the chance to maybe prove that I *could* be awesome. "It's not your fault," I repeat, because that's important. "I'm not g-good with compliments." I wrap my arms around his neck and bury my face in his throat, feeling his sigh with my whole body as his arms come around me.

"Just... promise that if you feel unsafe, you'll let me know. Don't take risks."

I nod against his throat. I won't do anything that might lose me this.

"I can't believe we're doing this," Skye says nervously hours later. It's his day off, but when Kieran texted him that we were going ahead, he came in. I guess he's like me: nervous as all fuck, but not willing to miss out.

I mean, we *are* going to banish a demon. How many people can say they've done that?

At least… I hope we're going to banish a demon.

I glance for reassurance at the giant bags of salt and the boxes full of quartz. Even if this fails, the demon's not getting away from us. That's why we decided to do it in the basement: there's a better chance of keeping it contained down there. So now Skye and I are waiting in the storeroom for the others, since Kieran asked that we all go down as a group.

"I can't believe it either," Johnny says, flickering in a way I know means nerves. He's not manifested yet—none of the ghosts are. They're saving every ounce of their strength for when we confront the demon.

"Think of the peace we can have once it's done," Hattie soothes him. "First the dark spirit, then we close the vortex, and we can spend the rest of eternity pranking tourists and watching television. Doesn't that sound lovely?"

"Ooh, I heard there's going to be a new season of *Love Island*," Maisie says. "Just think how lovely it will be to see all those gleaming bodies without worrying about the dark spirit getting loose and devouring us all before the season's over."

I wince and mutter, "There's a comforting thought."

Skye looks around. "Ghosts?" I nod. "What's a comforting thought?"

"You're better off not knowing," I say, shaking my head, and he turns pale.

"We are going to win this, right?"

"The salt and quartz will keep it trapped," I declare

as cheerfully as I can. "If we can't manage it today, we can always try again another time." *Please don't let it come to that.* If I feel this nervous now, imagine how it will be if I've already tried and failed.

Kieran comes in, followed by Ewan and Daniel... and Arissa. I'm kind of surprised. She hated the idea of going into the basement last time, and this time we'll actually be freeing the demon from its tomb. But her face is set in determined lines, even if her smooth brown skin is paler than usual.

"Are we ready?" Daniel asks, confident as always.

"No," Kieran says. "But let's do this anyway." He passes out battery-operated camping lanterns. I saw the boxes when they arrived, and if they're as good as the manufacturer boasted, this many should light up the basement brighter than an operating room. Next, we all get a quartz medallion to hang around our necks, as well as a good-sized chunk to put in a pocket. That's followed by little silk bags filled with rock salt. Kieran's taking no chances.

Finally, he unlocks the basement door and we go down the stairs, though we first have to clear away the salt there so the ghosts can come. I was right about the lanterns—every nook and cranny of the basement is visible. Surprisingly, there are no spiderwebs or spiders.

"It's shockingly clean in here." Arissa echoes my thoughts as she turns in a circle.

"It's the dark spirit," Freddie explains. "The bugs don't like it."

"Of course. Well, I don't think 'demon in the basement' will ever catch on as a form of insect repellant." Her voice only cracks a tiny bit, and I reach out and squeeze her arm.

"Can you imagine advertising that?" Skye jokes nervously. "It'd be the perfect solution to moths and silverfish eating your clothes… as long as you don't mind keeping a trapped demon in with your knitwear."

A weak chuckle runs through the group.

"Okay," Kieran says. "Okay. What now?"

Everyone looks at me. Great.

"Uh… well, let's set up some salt lines. And one of quartz closest to the stairs. The ghosts can be the, uh…" How do I say this without making it seem dramatic? "…the last line of defense." I wince. Yeah, those were probably not the right words. "I mean," I add hurriedly, "since the salt will hamper them just as much as the demon, they need to be outside the salt barriers. With the quartz. So that if the demon gets past us, they can stop it from leaving the basement." That's a bit better, right?

"How would the demon get past us?" Arissa's eyes dart toward the bricked-up tomb in the wall.

"It won't," I say, putting every ounce of assurance I can into my voice, even if I don't feel it. "But just in case we get distracted and it slips past, this way the ghosts can stop it."

"Let's start pouring salt," Kieran suggests. "Arissa, help me?"

She goes without question. I think it helps that he wants to pour the first line over near the stairs, away from the tomb. As soon as she's distracted, I pull the others into a huddle. "Check every inch of this place for something it can use to hurt us. Any garbage, anything that might come loose from the walls." I hesitate, then motion for Joe to join us. He slips around Kieran, scowling at the salt.

"What?" he grumps.

"I'm sorry about the salt, but—"

"Don't be a fool. Use whatever tool you can."

"Thanks. Uh, do you think the demon would be able to pull items from the storeroom and down the stairs to attack us with?"

Joe's jaw drops as Daniel swears.

"I didn't think of that," Ewan admits, glancing up toward the open doorway.

"Me either," Joe says, looking troubled. "It's possible. I can't say for sure."

I nod, my stomach sinking. "Then we have to close the door before we begin. Even if it can somehow open it, at least that would give us warning."

Skye shivers. "I'm having horror movie flashbacks," he mutters. "What kind of idiots close themselves in a basement with a demon when the only door has a bolt on the outside?"

"We're the only ones here," Daniel reminds him but then exchanges a glance with Ewan. "We'll close the door from the storeroom to the hallway and barricade it from the inside. If someone tries to get in, we'll hear them and be able to get up there before they make it to the basement door."

That plan seems holey to me, but I guess it's the best we've got. Ewan and Daniel head up the stairs to build a barricade, and Skye and I begin searching the room for anything that could be thrown at us. There are only a few, and we haul them upstairs and then check the walls, especially the bare rock. If a chunk of that came loose and was hurled at our skulls, it could do serious damage.

The lanterns pose a different problem. We need them to see, but they have enough heft to be dangerous.

In the end, we decide everyone will be responsible for hanging on to their lantern as though it's worth their life not to. Except me. Skye offers to hold mine for me, since I might need both my hands.

Ewan comes back and checks the banister and each of the spindles, making sure they're all secure. I hadn't thought of that and am glad he did. By the time he reaches the bottom of the stairs, Arissa and Kieran have laid out three lines of salt in concentric rings, the first about three feet from the tomb, and the last a few feet from the bottom of the stairs. Each line is also studded with chunks of quartz at random intervals. The ghosts are clustered behind the last line, at the foot of the stairs, with an array of quartz.

Daniel comes to the doorway at the top of the stairs. "Are we ready?"

I look around at everyone's faces, set with determination as well as fear, then nod. "Yeah."

He steps down, then closes the door firmly. The click of the latch seems to echo.

When he joins us at the bottom, I take a deep breath.

"Here's the plan. I don't think I can do this through stone, so we need to unbrick the wall."

"We figured that." For all his worrying ways, Kieran sounds absolutely calm right now.

I nod. "If we're really lucky, it'll be too weakened from captivity and from all the salt and quartz in here to even come out of the hole. We're probably not that lucky, but I'm still hoping to keep it contained to the first circle." If the ghosts were able to herd it here and into its prison using quartz, I doubt it will be able to cross that first salt-and-quartz line. In fact, I'm kind of counting on that. Because if it can cross the first, the second and third will be essentially useless, and it will once again come down to the ghosts—with maybe some living human help—to keep the demon contained.

"I like this plan," Arissa says, trying to sound confident even though her voice is shaking. Kieran puts an arm around her.

"Riss, there's no shame in waiting upstairs," he tells her quietly. "None of us would judge you for it."

She shakes her head. "I would judge me for it. And anyway, if I don't see the demon banished with my own eyes, I'm not sure I'll ever truly believe it's gone. And I don't want to be afraid to go into the storeroom for the rest of my life." Setting her chin, she meets my gaze. "We unbrick the opening. What next?"

Pride soars through me. It's such a privilege to know some people.

"Next, I hold the herbs on the demon and banish it."

From the way they all frown, I know they want more detail. I wish I could give it to them. Even though NEDDT's instructions clicked with something deep inside me, I don't know how to explain it. I just *know* that this will work.

As long as I don't think about it too hard. When I do, I'm riddled with doubt.

"Okay," Kieran says, seemingly more to himself. "Let's do this."

As we approach the wall, I see the first problem. "Wait, stop."

They freeze.

"What is it?" Ewan demands fiercely, gaze darting around the room.

"We can't all do this. The tomb is too small for us to crowd around it like this. If the demon leaps out or something, there's too much chance of someone getting hurt. And I won't have room to maneuver." I'm not sure if I'll need to maneuver, but I don't want to take risks with my friends' safety.

Kieran runs a hand through his hair. "Good point. We need to think tactically. How many of us will it take to open the hole?"

Annnd there's the second problem. How are we going to unbrick the hole with our bare hands? The stones have been cemented in.

I groan. "We're really bad at this. Scooby and Shaggy were smarter than us." I explain what I've just realized.

"Are we sure getting the living involved was the right decision?" I hear Freddie ask.

"They do seem to be…" Carter trails off doubtfully. "But I'm sure they'll rally."

"This is a dilemma," Ewan says thoughtfully, eyeing the tomb. "If we bring tools down to open it up, the demon can use them against us. But how do we open it without tools?" He moves closer, carefully stepping over the salt line and crouching to examine the patch of wall. A moment later he makes a sound that's part shock, part disgust. "Who did this work?" he calls over his shoulder toward the ghosts.

I look back and see them exchanging glances. "We did," Hattie calls back. "We had to do it in a rush while everyone was attending to the injured workmen."

"Why?" Joe barks.

"You've done a great job cementing the stones

together, but you didn't cement or otherwise seal around the edges. It's just wedged in here."

"We were in a rush," Carter defends. "And we didn't wedge it in. We *built* it in. With all the quartz in that, there's no way the dark spirit could push it out."

"I'm sure you're right," Ewan placates. "But my point is, with time having eroded the edges a bit, I can probably get my fingers in around it and pull it free without tools. Maybe."

"Let me do it," I demand. I don't really want Ewan or his fingers that close to the demon.

He shakes his head. "I don't think you could. It's still in there pretty firmly, and it's going to take a lot of muscle." I'd be offended, but only an idiot would compare my muscle to Ewan's. All those things they say about blacksmiths being strong are absolutely true. "Plus, it's better if you're ready and waiting for it."

I want to protest, but he's right.

"New plan," I begin. "Ewan pulls out the… door." I don't know what else to call it. "As soon as it's loose, step back out of the way. And whatever you do, don't let go. Those stones could do a lot of damage." Especially all cemented together into a slab like that.

"Got it," he affirms. Kieran takes his lantern so he'll have both hands free.

I turn to look at the others. "Could you stay behind the next line?" I point to the second salt circle, almost halfway to the stairs. "That will give us all room. You'll also have a clearer view of what's happening. Warn me if the demon somehow finds something to throw at me."

Daniel looks like he wants to protest, but they all agree and step over the salt, spreading out a bit to form a line of defense.

Which means… I guess this is it.

I turn back to the wall. Ewan's still inside the first circle, watching me. I take my position just outside the salt line. Ideally, Ewan will get out before the demon is even aware it's been "freed," and then it will be contained within the circle while we're all outside it.

Gripping the bundle of herbs tightly, I steady my nerves and nod. "Do it."

Ewan puts his fingertips to the edges of the patch and… wriggles them. Or does something. I can't really tell. But I can definitely tell when he starts straining to pull it out, because all his magnificent muscles are suddenly on full display. Thank you, Jesus, for short-sleeved T-shirts.

"Oh my," Skye murmurs behind me.

"God does good work," Arissa agrees.

"Do… you… mind?" Ewan grits out.

"Ignore them," I coo. "You're doing great. Later, I'm gonna rub you down as a reward." *For me.*

Ewan starts to say something else, but it turns into a yell as the stone patch suddenly flies loose, slamming into his chest and sending him scrabbling backward.

"Ewan!" I yell as his head hits the hard floor with a *thunk*, but then the demon bursts free, and I don't have time to think of anything else.

I raise the herbs, but it's already shooting past me, and I realize with horror that Ewan must have accidentally scuffed a hole in the salt line when he got knocked back.

"Ghosts, manifest!" I shriek, suddenly terrified that it'll get to them while they're vulnerable. In the next second, it screams, a sound that fills me with fear like I've never felt before, and turns on me.

The second salt line held it back.

At the back of my mind, I know that's a good thing, but I can't think right now. Waves of hatred and fear are beating at me, pushing, tearing as the demon bears down on me, and I can't—

Behind the demon, Daniel hands his lantern to a shaking Arissa, steps quietly over the second line, and goes to Ewan, pulling the remainder of a bag of salt from one of the deep pockets of his cargo pants.

Strength floods into me.

Hope.

As Daniel pours the salt in a rough line, protecting his friend—my guy—I pull myself together and face down the demon.

It can't hurt me directly, I remind myself. The stone slab is behind salt now, and hopefully Daniel will remember to hold on to it. But I can't focus on that.

The demon is everything the ghosts described. A darkness, a foulness. It has no distinct form, but rather seems to be a collection of shadows, even in the bright light of the lanterns. The air seems thick with the horror of it.

But my mind's eye sees more than just the shadows. The part of my brain that sees ghosts when others can't also perceives the essence of the demon. It's a deep malevolence, a violent urge to feed and keep feeding, no matter what it must do to make it happen. There is no sentience that can be reasoned with, just an instinct to kill and consume.

This thing cannot be allowed to escape.

I raise the herbs and let my ability fully loose for the first time ever. Power I didn't know I had bubbles up inside me, the fingers of it reaching out to the demon, wrapping around its stolen energy, the energy it's been hoarding for fifty years, tightening, squeezing the power loose from the matter that is pure demon.

It shrieks, a sound that is not a sound, that I hear not with my ears but with my soul, and tries to flee, beating against the salt-and-quartz barrier. Skye, eyes blazing with determination, steps forward and thrusts out the chunk of quartz in his fist, and the demon recoils. I keep up the pressure, watching with my *other* senses as the stolen energy slowly drains from it.

I feel the surge of hatred in the second before Daniel yells and risk a quick glance. He's holding on to the stone slab with white-knuckled, bleeding fingers, his face set as he kneels in front of Ewan, the slab seemingly trying to wrench itself free. I guess the salt doesn't completely limit the demon's abilities.

Grimly, I intensify my efforts. It can't be allowed to hurt anyone else.

It lurches back from me, throwing itself at the salt line between me and Daniel and Ewan, and the fear trickles down my spine again. That line isn't as strong as the others—less salt, no quartz, hastily drawn. If any is going to give way, that would be it.

As though my thoughts were a foretelling, I see the dark essence of the demon *blur* over the salt line. Where before it was as though it touched a solid, if transparent, wall, now the wall is giving way.

Ewan stirs. I'm not sure how I know, because I don't dare take my eyes off the demon again, but there's a tickle at the back of my mind that tells me he's awake. My knees want to give way with relief, but this isn't over yet, and he's currently in more danger from the demon than he was before.

The demon is weakening, I can see it, but somehow, even after all this time, it's managed to hold on to more energy than I would have thought possible. Or maybe it's me? Maybe I just don't have the strength and experience to do this?

It blurs against the salt line again, and then, for an instant, part of it slips through. Daniel screams as the slab is ripped from his fingers, and as it hurtles toward me, I brace myself, pouring every ounce of effort into squeezing the demon of energy. I dare not even close my eyes ahead of the impact.

The demon shrieks again, and the slab drops to the floor, tiny shards splintering free.

Ewan slowly staggers to his feet, a chunk of quartz in each hand held before him, warding off the demon, forcing it back. One slow, painful step at a time, he drives it toward me, and finally I'm able to wring the last of its energy from it. I raise the herbs and channel the flow of my power directly into the demon, and with one last soul-shaking screech, it comes apart into billions of subatomic particles.

The darkness is gone.

Adrenaline crashes, and I start to shake.

"Josh—" Ewan gasps, staggering to my side, and I whirl on him.

"What the *fuck* did you think you were doing? You got closer to it on purpose!"

"It was going to kill you," he says hoarsely, his gaze locked on my face. His pupils are blown, and I'm pretty sure he has a concussion. Plus whatever is making him walk funny.

"And what if it had turned and decided to kill you? It could have changed the direction of that slab and bashed your already damaged brains in." I lift shaking hands to cover my face and nearly put my eye out with the herbs I'm still clutching. "You can't die, Ewan. I need you. I lo—" I stop. It's too soon for that.

Isn't it?

Ewan's eyes blaze. "I love you," he proclaims, his voice cracking. "I love you, and I would risk anything to keep you safe."

I drop the battered herbs and hurl myself at him. He makes a pained sound, but when I try to pull back, he closes his arms around me tight.

"Love you, love you, love you," I mutter into his neck, and he squeezes until there's no breath left in me to say it anymore.

"Uh, guys?"

Ewan's arms loosen, and we both turn to face Kieran. He's even paler than usual but seems solid.

"Sorry," I mutter. "Emotional moment."

"No, that's… I get it. But Daniel needs a hospital, and I bet Ewan does too."

"I'm okay," Ewan protests. I elbow him, and he makes a noise that proves he's definitely not okay. I glance over at where Skye and Arissa are helping Daniel up. It looks like his hands have been shredded; even from here, I catch a glimpse of something white that might be bone.

"Let's get out of here," I agree, stepping forward toward the stairs. My knees buckle, and I collapse. "Whoa."

Ewan leaps forward to help me and nearly ends up in a heap beside me.

"Stand still," Kieran orders him sharply before turning his attention to me. "Were you injured?"

Shaking my head, I try to get my feet under me. "No, I... I think I'm just tired. But now that I'm down here, I don't think I can get back up." My limbs are like jelly, and my mind starts to swim.

Thankfully, Kieran is still in possession of all his faculties. I dimly hear him and Arissa clearing away the salt so the ghosts can help them and Skye haul the rest of us up the stairs.

It's so good to have friends.

Epilogue

JOSH

I stare at the blinking cursor and will the words to come. It doesn't work, and I can't say I'm surprised. There's no standard format to thank someone for telling you how to banish a demon. I already looked for an e-card.

Sighing, I put my fingers back on the keyboard and start with a basic greeting.

Hi,

We spoke on the demonsummoning.com site, and you gave me instructions to banish the soul-eater demon in my house. I just wanted to thank you so, so much. It worked, and the demon is gone. I can't tell you how grateful we all are.

The house is still haunted, and I think something else hinky might be going on. Is it still okay if I email you with questions if some come up?

Thanks again,
HauntedByMistakesOfOthers

I read it over, then bite my lip. Whoever this is seriously saved our bacon, and it seems wrong to treat them like a predator. I quickly add *(Josh)*, then hit Send on the email before I can change my mind. It's a pretty common name, so I doubt that will give anything away.

I push back from the computer and stretch my arms over my head. It's been over a week since I banished the demon, and things have been hectic. Kieran insisted that Daniel, Ewan, and I all go to the hospital in the next town to be taken care of. I was fine—just exhausted. As in, that was the literal medical diagnosis. Since I'd fallen asleep in the car on the way over and then again in the ER while I was waiting, I don't think it came as a surprise to anyone. I slept for the better part of the next day, ate enough to sustain a herd of horses, and feel amazing now.

As I suspected, Ewan had a concussion and also sprained his knee. It's only a minor sprain, and even though they said recovery could be two to four weeks, it's already mostly better. He only gets pain if he's been on it all day (cue eye roll, right? My guy can't stand to be laid up). The concussion is more serious, and the doctor thinks he's going to be dealing with the effects of that for another couple of months.

Daniel got the worst of it, though. His doctor keeps saying how lucky he is, because he's going to retain the full use of his hands once they've healed. There might be some minor numbness occasionally, and if he'd been a surgeon or anything like that, his career would be over, but overall the biggest reminder of it will be the scarring. Daniel being Daniel, he laughed that off and asked if the doctor wanted to see the scars on his leg from the time the scythe got away from him. As long as his hands *will* heal and he can go back to farming, he doesn't care about scars.

The ghosts and the senior staff have been taking

turns to look after them both. Daniel just came home two days ago, but obviously he can't use his hands yet, and Ewan's still getting bad headaches. He's been banned from the smithy until the doctor gives the all-clear, so Kieran found someone to fill in, though they can only be here on weekends. The smithy is closed during the week until further notice. He also found a couple of teenagers to look after the farm. Daniel's already declared that he plans to continue giving farming lectures himself, though the teens can do the actual demos until he's got the use of his hands back. He wanted to start working again right away, but Skye and Kieran insisted he have a few more days off. He's still on pretty heavy-duty painkillers.

"Hey."

I turn my head and smile at Ewan where he's lounging in the office doorway. "Hi. How're you feeling?" When I left his place right before lunch, he was sleeping off a headache.

"Better. Kieran wants to see us—in the Garden Suite."

Ah, the vortex. I've been expecting this.

I get up, grab the portable monitor that will let me know if anybody comes to reception—although this late on a Tuesday, it's not likely—and head toward the door. I pause beside him and kiss his cheek, just to see him smile. This whole wanting-him-to-smile thing is new, but I like it. I like how it feels to have Ewan in my life. To go to sleep and wake up in bed with him. To rub his temples when he has a headache. To be held by him. To kiss him. To glance over at him and see him looking at me like I'm the most precious thing in his world.

I like talking to him and knowing I can say anything,

and even if he thinks it's stupid, it won't change how he feels about me. He loves me.

I like being loved.

He grabs my hand, kisses it, then keeps hold as we walk through the house to the elevator. His knee might be nearly better, but I refuse to let him test it with stairs just yet.

The others are waiting in the Garden Suite, which seems lonely without most of its furniture. And crowded, with six living people and six dead ones in it. As I always do, I glance over to the vortex. It's ringed with salt and quartz, which we check every day, but nothing's changed. Part of me had been hoping that when the demon was banished, the vortex would close, but it didn't. Honestly, we don't even know how the vortex was opened. Nothing in Emma's diary even hinted at it, and while NEDDT might know, the ghosts are too nervous to let me ask. I get it, but it leaves us in a weird situation.

"Thanks for coming, everyone," Kieran begins. "I won't keep you too long."

"Feel free to keep us until bedtime," Daniel says. "This is the most exciting thing that's happened to me all week. You know, since *someone* won't let me do anything." He glares at Skye, who throws up his arms in exasperation.

"Do you want to lose the use of your hands? Well? Do you? I'm trying to *help* you, and you're whining like a toddler who doesn't want a nap!"

"Anyway," Kieran interrupts hastily. We've all heard this argument many, *many* times over the past few days. "Now that the demon's gone, we need to decide what to do about the vortex."

As one, we all turn to look at it. Well, I think it's just the ghosts and me actually looking at it. The others are just pointing their eyes in that direction.

"What *can* we do?" Arissa asks. "We don't know what it is or how it works."

Kieran sighs. "Yeah. That's the stumbling block."

"Do we have to do anything right now?" Maisie asks. "I don't mind sharing my room with it, as long as no more dark spirits come through."

"The block is still there," Johnny says helpfully. "Maybe nothing else will come?"

The silence speaks volumes.

"We'll keep the block strong," Joe says at last. "It's easier now that we don't need to expend any energy checking on the dark spirit."

"And we can keep researching," Skye says. "Maybe we'll find something. In the meantime, the block worked for fifty years. That probably won't change?" It sounds like a question, and he glances at me.

I shrug. "We can hope. The demon was pretty well contained, so it might not have been its presence keeping others away. It could have been the block." I honestly have no idea.

Kieran runs his hands through his hair. "Okay. I guess that's really our only option." He squints at the ghosts, then sighs. "I'm going to put a TV in here for you. That way you can hang out and relax while keeping an eye on the vortex."

Johnny cheers and grabs Maisie in a hug. "Yes! Having representation works!"

Um… okay?

"With cable?" Carter demands. "I want porn channels. Gay porn, so I can do research, since I've been *banned* from my own home."

I roll my eyes, and Ewan squeezes my hand. Since I've been staying over at the farm manager's house to be with Ewan and look after Daniel, I had a very firm chat with Carter about boundaries, then threatened to salt him out of the house when he protested. He was so offended by the very idea that he left the house of his own accord and hasn't come back. I've explained several times that he's welcome in the house, just not the bedrooms, but he's too busy enjoying his snit.

"To watch in a shared space?" Freddie gasps, aghast.

"No porn," Kieran says as Daniel snickers. "And just basic cable. But I'll get a smart TV and log you in to all my streaming services."

The ghosts huddle up to confer, and Kieran shakes his head in exasperation.

"Nobody would ever believe this," he mutters.

Smiling, I lean against Ewan. Kieran's right: nobody would ever believe this. I have firsthand experience with that. But here, in this room, on this estate, these people know the truth. They believe. They accept.

"Agreed!" Hattie declares, holding out her hand for Kieran to shake. He does, and Maisie immediately begins nattering about new curtains and a plush sofa.

"Something to make it feel like home," she insists.

Ewan kisses the top of my head.

Home.

Finally, that's where I am.

Thanks for reading *Spirited Situation*! Want the scene

where Josh gets his driver's license? Subscribe to my newsletter: bit.ly/LouisaMBonus

And there's more from Mannix Estate! To see Kieran clashing with a snarky demon expert, check out *Vortex Conundrum.*

Join my Facebook Reader Group to talk spoilers: https://www.facebook.com/groups/RoMManceWithBeccaLou

Can't wait for the next book? Interested in exclusive bonus scenes, serials, early chapters, and artwork? Check out my Patreon: https://www.patreon.com/louisamasters

Also by Louisa Masters

Saddles & Suits
Alistair's Extraordinaries
Grave Situation
Elemental Men: The Complete Series

Style Me
Rebrand
Couture

Elf Magic
Wooing the Wiccan
Enticing the Elf

The Collective
Higher Demon
Demon Hunter

Demons-In-Law
Asher
Micah
Zachary

Franklin U
Mr. Romance
The Holigay Hookup *related novella
Batting Style

Ghostly Guardians
Spirited Situation
Vortex Conundrum
Conduit Crisis
Gateway Catastrophe

Here Be Dragons
Dragon Ever After
The Professor's Dragon
The Dragon Experiment
Conspiracy of Dragons

Hidden Species
Demons Do It Better
One Bite With A Vampire
Hijinks With A Hellhound
Sorcerers Always Satisfy
Hidden Species Box Set

Met His Match
[Charming Him](#)
[Offside Rules](#)
[A Christmas Chance (novella)](#)
[Between the Covers (M/F)](#)

Joy Universe
I've Got This
[Follow My Lead](#)
[In Your Hands](#)

Take Us There

Novellas

Fake It 'Til You Make It (permafree)

One Golden Night

O Hell, All Ye Shoppers

Out of the Office

After the Blaze

Blokes Down Under Novella Collection

About the Author

Louisa Masters started reading romance much earlier than her mother thought she should. As an adult, she feeds her addiction in every spare second. She spent years trying to build a "sensible" career, working in bookstores, recruitment, resource management, administration, and as a travel agent before finally conceding defeat and devoting herself to the world of romance novels.

Louisa has a long list of places first discovered in books that she wants to visit, and every so often she overcomes her loathing of jet lag and takes a trip that charges her imagination. She lives in Melbourne, Australia, where she whines about the weather for most of the year while secretly admitting she'll probably never move.

http://www.louisamasters.com

www.ingramcontent.com/pod-product-compliance
Lightning Source LLC
LaVergne TN
LVHW040614250326
834688LV00035B/561